THE WISDOM OF MADNESS

THE MINISTRY OF CURIOSITIES, BOOK #10

C.J. ARCHER

C.J. ARCHER

MINISTRY
OF
CURIOSITIES
THE SERIES

Thank you to reader Krysta Rangel for naming the puppy mentioned in this book. I hope you all agree with me when I say it's the perfect name.

CHAPTER 1

SETH

Watching Charlie and Lincoln talking quietly together, it was difficult for Seth to remember that he'd once been half in love with her.

Perhaps not love. Not really. At least not the depth of love a husband has for his wife—or ought to—and clearly not the depth of love Lincoln and Charlie had for each another. They thought alike, finished one another's sentences, and knew each other better than they knew themselves.

It was a marvel that anyone could love a cold, calculating man like Lincoln. Even more miraculous was that Lincoln loved her back. They'd all thought him incapable of emotion. Before Charlie came to live with them at Lichfield Towers, Seth, Cook and Gus joked that Lincoln had been created in a mad scientist's laboratory.

How wrong they'd been.

No, Seth had never really been in love with Charlie, but he did adore her. She'd once said their relationship was like a brother and sister, but in his experience, brothers and sisters bickered. He and Charlie rarely argued. Favorite cousins? No, that wasn't right, either. He loved Charlie like a...like a man who'd be there to pick up the pieces when her husband died.

Like a man who knew she wasn't the grand love of his life, his soul mate, but didn't want to see her suffer, either. There. That described them perfectly, and quite poetically too, if he did say so himself.

He propped his booted feet on a footstool, clasped his hands over his stomach, and watched his two good friends share a secret smile. A pang twisted his gut. No one had ever looked at him that way, and sometimes he wondered if anyone ever would.

Thoughts of Alice threatened to rise but he quashed them. There was no point thinking about her. She simply wasn't interested in him, and that was the end of it. If only they didn't keep bumping into each other, Seth was quite sure he'd lose interest. If only she weren't always around. He was a fickle lover, after all; he rarely kept his paramours for more than a few months. Just as soon as Alice moved out of Lichfield, all would be well again. He could find himself a lonely widow or bored governess, someone older but not too old. Someone who appreciated the attentions of a younger man. Not someone like Alice with a biting wit, fierce intelligence and formidable elegance.

Not someone who'd be shocked by his past.

Seth's mother swanned into the drawing room as if she were mistress of the house. It was a testament to Charlie's good nature that she put up with the indomitable Lady Vickers. Seth's mother could be trying, to put it mildly.

She clicked her tongue and shooed his feet off the stool so she could pass.

"You could have gone around, Mother," he said.

"Your boots are filthy. Charlie doesn't want dirt on her velvet stool." She lowered herself onto the sofa and regarded him levelly.

"That's for Charlie to decide, not you."

She sighed. "Seth, why are you being so disagreeable of late?"

"I am not."

"You are. You don't like anything I say or do, not to mention you mope about the house like a listless schoolboy. Indeed, you're worse than when you were a schoolboy home for the holidays. At least then you'd spend all day in the stables or out riding."

"I'd gladly spend all day in the stables now, but apparently it's not a suitable occupation for a gentleman."

"Not the manual labor part, no," she admitted. "However, you can still go riding." She glanced at the clock on the mantel. "You have a few hours before you must dress for dinner. You haven't forgotten you're dining with me at the Beecrofts' tonight, have you?"

He planted his elbows on his knees and buried his fingers in his hair. "Must I go?"

"Yes! Lizzie Beecroft is desperate to see you again, so her mother tells me."

"Lizzie Beecroft can't even look me in the eye. And when she does talk, it's about horses. Nothing but horses."

"You like horses," Charlie piped up from the other side of the room.

"Not as much as Lizzie Beecroft, apparently."

"She knows *you* like them, Seth dear," his mother said. "She's trying to attract your attention by talking about *your* interests. Honestly, I thought you understood women."

"Some women," he muttered, once again pushing thoughts of Alice away. He frowned. "And what makes you think I understand women?" As far as he could remember, he'd rarely mentioned his previous lovers to his mother. She knew about Julia, of course, and a handful of others, but not all. Not nearly all.

His mother avoided his gaze. "I hear things."

What had she heard? How much did she know? Did he want to hear the answers?

"You should go, Seth," Charlie said quickly, no doubt

thinking he needed rescuing. Bless her. "You've been cooped up at Lichfield ever since the wedding and deserve an enjoyable evening out."

That was the problem—it wouldn't be enjoyable. Once upon a time, he would have been delighted to dine with the Beecrofts—or anyone, for that matter—but now he found it a chore. Now he found the girls to be silly or dull, and he simply couldn't be bothered flirting with them. What had happened to him? Why couldn't he do as he used to and enjoy an evening with pretty girls, teasing the ones who were too shy to meet his gaze and flirting with the bolder ones?

Ever since the wedding, a week ago, something in Seth felt different. Perhaps it was seeing Charlie and Lincoln happily settled. Or perhaps it was the quiet lull following the chaos leading up to that day, with Lincoln being arrested, Swinburn trying to destroy the ministry, and the Queen of Hearts's army coming for Alice. While he was glad it was all over, he had to admit that the days since had been slow. Visiting Gus's great aunt and the orphans just wasn't enough. He needed something more, yet he didn't know what. He did know that dining with the Beecrofts wasn't the answer.

He appealed to his mother. "We had dinner with the Beecrofts three nights ago. Must I go again?"

"Yes."

"Why, since I won't be marrying Lizzie Beecroft?"

"You might, if you put some effort into getting to know her. She's quite fetching when she looks up from her lap."

"I require more than a fetching woman for my wife." Even in his lovers, too. Beautiful but dull had never interested him.

His mother wasn't ready to give up the very tasty morsel of a Beecroft bride, however. They weren't a wealthy family but they were established and respectable, something his mother craved and, to be perfectly honest, the Vickers name needed. Seth's father had pushed the boulder down the hill of their disgrace, and Seth only managed to stop it by employing somewhat dubious methods, but pushing it uphill again was proving a task beyond both him and his mother. They needed to attach themselves to a family like the Beecrofts to haul up the final climb. The problem was, he didn't particularly care.

"Lizzie is demure, sensible, and well behaved," Lady Vickers went on.

He couldn't help his smile. "Lucky you never had to marry off a daughter. You're not very good at touting a girl's qualities to a fellow."

"Lizzie would make the perfect wife."

"Not for someone like me. I require someone more like Charlie."

"Is that so?" Lincoln countered, sounding like he wanted to smash Seth's nose.

"Not like Charlie," Seth said before he turned to ice from Lincoln's glare. "Definitely not like her. At all."

"Someone like Alice," Charlie added, her eyes twinkling with mischief. She plucked the sleepy beagle off the carpet near her feet and settled him on her lap. Lincoln's gaze defrosted as he followed her every move.

"Alice is a dear girl," Lady Vickers said, "but she's not for Seth, and he knows it."

"You do recall that she's a princess," Charlie said.

His mother plucked off one of her black gloves. "Not here."

"Would it be different if she weren't exiled?"

"And lose my Seth to another world entirely? I missed him terribly when I went to America. Imagine if we were separated by..." She flapped the glove. "By more than an ocean? It would upset me too much."

Seth opened his mouth to protest but found he didn't have the heart for it. He had no idea what to think regarding Alice anymore. Perhaps his mother was right. Or perhaps she was very wrong. He sighed. Why couldn't he be more like his old self? Enjoying life and the world around him, happy to give and receive affection, and grateful for somewhere comfortable to land when he'd had his fill? Rather like Gordon, the puppy.

Christ, had he really been that immature mere months ago?

"Besides," his mother went on, "the Beecrofts know very little about…events from your past."

Seth felt the heat rise up his neck. It would seem his mother knew more than Seth realized. Alice didn't, thank God.

"The Beecrofts rarely come to London," Lady Vickers said. "Lady Beecroft brought her daughter down only last week after more than two years absence and hasn't yet had time to hear all the gossip. You would be smart to secure the girl before she does hear it."

Seth followed the thought that flittered through his head of his future, faceless wife learning of his past and all the dissolute things he'd done to make ends meet, quite willingly at the time. It wasn't that he regretted the choices he'd made, it was just that he preferred certain people didn't learn about them. Chief among them being the woman who was supposed to admire and respect him, whoever she may be.

He groaned. "Help me out, Charlie."

Charlie's fingers stroked Gordon's long ears. "Leave me out of this."

Seth looked to Lincoln. Lincoln's eyes tightened at the corners. Seth wouldn't get help from that quarter either.

Charlie placed the puppy in Lincoln's lap and offered a hand to Lady Vickers. "Why don't we see to the week's menu together? I could do with your advice."

"You don't need it," Lady Vickers said. "You're perfectly capable of speaking to Cook without me, although I do want to see him about another matter."

Another matter? Oh God, what was she up to? First the footman—*second* footman—and now the cook. Seth's friend, no less. Did she have to flaunt their...whatever it was...in front of her own son?

"I know what you're trying to do, Charlie," his mother said, "but it won't work. I will not be distracted from my task. Seth, promise me you'll come to dinner tonight."

If he made a promise and then broke it, would he go to hell? Surely God would see that it was necessary.

"I have to go out," Seth said, rising. "I remember something important I'm supposed to be doing."

He was rescued from the sharp point of his mother's glare by the entry of Doyle, the butler. "Miss Eva Cornell and David Cornell," he announced.

Seth sat again. *This* he would stay for. It was always fun watching Lincoln struggle in the presence of his half-brother and sister.

Charlie, ever the gracious hostess and sister-in-law, greeted them with smiles and kisses. Even the stern David returned her smile with a genuine one of his own. It faded upon seeing his older half-brother stand to greet them. Not even the puppy in Lincoln's arms could soften David's features.

"Fitzroy," David said.

"Cornell," Lincoln said.

Seth made a point of shaking David's hand and kissing Eva's cheek. He'd stepped in for the kiss and, because of their closeness, he could feel her tense. It was the same reaction she always had upon first seeing him, but he was grateful that it rarely lasted. She just seemed to need a moment to get used to his presence. It was a reaction he often noticed timid people have. Except Eva wasn't timid.

"To what do we owe this pleasure?" he asked, deliberately taking a step back to give her space.

David glanced around the room. "Our mother isn't here?"

"No," Lincoln said.

"We haven't seen Leisl since the wedding," Charlie added. "Why did you think she'd be here?"

"She left us a note telling us to come."

"Me, not *us*," Eva said to her brother. "She addressed the note to me. You're supposed to be working." She asked Lincoln if she could hold the puppy and he handed the beagle over. She clutched him to her chest and snuggled him. Seth had to hand it to the puppy—he was better at getting Eva to relax than he was. "What did you name him?"

"Gordon," Charlie said. "After Gordon Thackeray, a friend who helped us on occasion. He's gone now but not forgotten."

"How lovely." Eva laughed as Gordon licked her chin.

Seth couldn't help smiling at her. Not only did she have a lustrous laugh but he still marveled at how much she looked like Lincoln, with her strong cheekbones, dark hair and eyes. Lincoln never laughed like that, though. Not in Seth's presence.

"If our mother's not here then where is she?" David asked, unmoved by the puppy's floppy ears and big brown eyes.

"Perhaps she decided to do some shopping first," Lady Vickers said.

"She doesn't like to shop."

"Perhaps today is different."

David looked as if he would protest, but Eva got in first. "She has certainly been acting oddly in the last few weeks."

"She has tried to get you to come here several times in recent days," David added. "Do you know why?"

Eva scratched Gordon behind his ears and stroked her cheek against his head. "No."

"Now that you're here, stay for tea." Charlie signaled to Doyle. "Please bring refreshments. Oh, and ask Gus and Alice to join us."

David perched stiffly on the edge of an armchair and Eva sank down beside Lady Vickers on the sofa, still holding Gordon. The wriggling puppy nipped at her fingers and she laughed again. She might seem prim, with her hair tightly pinned back and her high collar buttoned up, but when she laughed, her gypsy heritage shone through. He'd wager she was more carefree than she let on. Seth resolved to always have Gordon around when Eva came to visit; that way her stiffness upon greeting him wouldn't last more than a moment.

"We should get a puppy, David," she said.

"Absolutely not!" David turned to Lincoln. "A search party should be sent out for our mother."

"Where would you like the search to start?" Lincoln's sarcastic edge was a slender thing but sharp. Charlie winced.

"You're the expert at investigation. Start the search where you think it should be started."

"Or we could have tea first and see if she turns up." Eva pressed the puppy into her brother's hands. "Good boy." Seth wasn't entirely sure if it was directed at Gordon or David.

David set Gordon down and the puppy gamboled over to Charlie, where he gave her shoes a thorough sniff before plopping down on the floor near her feet.

Alice entered with Gus. She greeted Eva and David cordially but it lacked the vivacity Seth so admired in her. She hadn't been herself ever since the wedding. Or, rather, since the Queen of Hearts's army had tried to take her back to the Wonderland realm to face charges of treason. Alice had been badly shaken that day—they all had—and she hadn't fully recovered. Knowing that an entire army could reappear to capture her at any moment must weigh on her mind. Seth just wished she'd allow him to shoulder some of the burden of that worry by talking to him. She didn't even confide in Charlie. Seth assumed it was because Alice didn't want to trouble her in what was supposed to be her happiest days, but he also knew Alice's predicament was the reason Lincoln and Charlie hadn't yet gone on their honeymoon.

The mood in the drawing room suddenly changed. It was

so subtle that it took Seth a moment to realize it had happened at all and several more moments of polite conversation to understand where it came from. It certainly wasn't Gus, who'd brought a sense of heightened anticipation with him. The big idiot was…well, a big idiot. He wouldn't know how to spell heightened or anticipation, let alone have the depth of character to be the cause of an intrigue. It was what made him so loveable—not that Seth would ever tell him that.

After a quick study, he realized it wasn't Alice's fault, either. She seemed as outwardly calm and elegant as always, and the only mood she brought with her was one of sadness and worry.

The change came from Eva. Seth felt her gaze flicker over him like a flutter of a bird's wing, but when he looked at her, she'd switched her gaze to Alice.

Doyle brought in the tray of tea things, and Seth's attention followed the butler's movements and then Charlie's as she poured the tea. Seth helped her pass around the cups, but again he felt Eva's gaze fall on him. He suddenly turned, catching her staring, and he was gratified to see her cheeks flush.

"Are you too warm?" he teased as he handed her a cup. "Shall I open a window?"

"It's cool enough in here." Realizing she was admitting to blushing because of him, she changed her tune. "On second thoughts, it is quite warm."

Lady Vickers agreed. "A little air would be pleasant. Gus, dear, would you throw open the windows?"

Gus obliged and jerked his head at Seth. Seth followed, expecting to help his friend with the windows. Instead, Gus whispered, "Don't flirt with her. She's Death's sister, for Christ's sake."

"Lincoln doesn't care."

"Cornell might."

Seth glanced at David, sipping tea with the ladies like a

well brought up middle class gentleman. "You've got the wrong idea, Gus," Seth whispered back. "I'm not interested in Eva."

"Then stop flirting with her, because she thinks you are. You break her heart and you'll have both her brothers wanting to break that ugly nose of yours."

"She's not interested in me either. It was just a little harmless flirting. It doesn't mean anything." Seth threw up the sash so hard it drew everyone's attention. Good, because he suspected Gus had been about to continue. If there was one thing Seth disliked more than a lecture from his mother, it was a lecture from Gus.

"How are your studies going?" Charlie asked Eva.

"Well enough, thank you." Eva sipped her tea and didn't elaborate.

"Don't lectures stop for the summer and the pupils go home?" Lincoln asked.

"You're thinking of university," she said smoothly, her gaze not wavering from his. Seth got the feeling he was watching two fierce warriors face one another across a battlefield, yet he wasn't sure what the battle was about. "A nurse's training continues through the summer. We learn our trade in hospitals, not universities, something which I'm sure you know very well, Lincoln."

David lowered his cup to the saucer and blinked at her. "You've been home more this last week. And the week before that, come to think of it. Why?"

"I had fewer shifts."

Seth watched her closely, searching for any signs of her lie. Lincoln suspected Eva was in fact studying to become a doctor, not a nurse, and Seth had no reason to disbelieve him, although he didn't know why she needed to lie at all. What was so wrong about becoming a doctor? It was a noble profession, and an interesting, progressive field of study.

Yet if Lincoln thought she was lying, she must be. He did,

after all, have an innate ability to sense when some people told falsehoods. Far be it from Seth to question him.

"You have been working hard in the lead up to summer," David conceded. "I suppose it's only fair they give you some time off."

Eva's lips thinned. She sipped again.

Seth could swear Lincoln looked satisfied to have made his sister feel uncomfortable in her lie, but apart from a quirk of his eyebrows, there was no change in him. Charlie rolled her eyes at her husband.

"I'm surprised to find you two home," David said to Lincoln. "I thought you'd be on your honeymoon by now."

"Soon," Charlie said.

A weighty silence cloaked them until Alice finally broke it. "Do urge them to go," she said to Eva and David. "They won't listen to me."

"They won't listen to *us*," Seth countered. "They think they need to be here in case of…a situation."

"In case the army come for me again," Alice added. "Tell them it's not necessary and that I'll be all right. The army may not come. They haven't shown up for an entire week."

"Alice, we've discussed this," Charlie said. "It's not that we won't go, it's just that we won't go *yet*. We need to be here for when they do try to take you again."

"Sorry I brought it up," David muttered.

"I agree with Alice," Eva said. "You should go." She spoke in a rush, as if she wanted to say her piece before anyone else. Or before she changed her mind.

Doyle entered again and announced the arrival of Leisl Cornell before bowing out. Seth and the other men rose to greet her. Lincoln kissed his mother's cheek briskly. Charlie hugged her then poured another cup of tea.

"Where have you been?" David snapped. "You said to meet you here."

"I am here." Leisl frowned at him. "I did not ask you to come, only Eva."

David crossed his long legs and regarded his teacup with more interest than the Spode deserved. "I took the liberty of coming anyway."

"And work?"

"The office is closed today."

"Why?"

He shifted in his seat. "I'm not entirely sure."

Leisl's frown deepened. Perhaps she detected a lie with her seer's senses. While that didn't surprise Seth, his heart skipped a beat when her gaze suddenly pinned him to the chair. She had an unnerving stare, dark and deep as a pit, like her eldest son. Seth felt as if the gypsy knew all his secrets, even those he couldn't bear to speak to anyone about.

"Leisl, will you try to convince Charlie and Lincoln not to delay their honeymoon any further?" Alice pleaded. "They seem to think we need their protection."

"You do," Lincoln said.

"They will go." Leisl sounded as if she were repeating an answer spoken many times. "Do not worry. They will go when they are ready."

"But when will that be?"

"After we can be certain the army won't come for you," Charlie said.

"They may not come."

"They will," Eva and Leisl said at the same time.

Charlie's lips parted. Alice paled and Lady Vickers covered her mouth with her hand. Gus sat forward, alert and ready, but Seth went still. Only his heart picked up its pace as it sank like a stone. He'd hoped the army had given up. It would seem not. The prospect of their return hung over Lichfield like a guillotine.

He tried to catch Alice's attention, to give her a reassuring smile, but she didn't look his way. She accepted Charlie's offered hand and clung tightly to it.

Only Lincoln seemed unsurprised by his mother's and sister's pronouncement. "It's just a matter of when," he said.

"We don't know," Eva added. "I can't quite see…"

"Mother?" David urged. "When?"

"I cannot say," Leisl said.

Seth bit back his retort but Lincoln said it anyway. "Cannot or will not?"

Leisl sipped her tea. Seth shot to his feet but did not march up to her as he wanted. He paced the room and tried to breathe his way through his frustration. It was of no use. This was too important to dismiss so easily.

"You *must* tell us what you've seen," he said, voice raspy.

"Yes!" Eva cried. "Tell us. We have a right to know."

We? Didn't she mean Alice? Or Charlie, Lincoln, and the other residents at Lichfield? How did any of this impact Eva?

"Come now, Mrs. Cornell," Lady Vickers said, her voice trembling. "When will the army come?"

Leisl didn't answer.

"For God's sake!" Seth exploded. "This is—" He broke off as Lincoln ran from the room.

Seth didn't understand, but he trusted Lincoln's instincts better than he trusted his own and raced after him. Gus's pounding footsteps lumbered behind. Several voices followed them from the drawing room but Seth didn't look back. They ran downstairs to the gun room. Lincoln ordered Gus to tell Doyle to keep the servants at the back of the house. As he peeled away, Lincoln and Seth unlocked the cabinets and pulled out the weapons. They quickly and quietly set about loading them and tucking them away. Seth shoved two pistols into his waist band, and held a set of dueling pistols in each hand. Lincoln slung a rifle over his shoulder and picked up another. He handed it to Gus upon his return before placing pistols and knives where he could quickly retrieve them.

They were about to leave when Charlie appeared in the doorway. She was as pale as the corpses she'd resurrected, and her eyes were too big for her face.

"General Ironside is here," she said, her voice remarkably steady. "There are at least a hundred soldiers on the front lawn and another hundred moving into formation out the back."

Hell. They were trapped.

CHAPTER 2

ALICE

The dark stain of fear spread quickly and mercilessly through Alice. Moments ago she'd been sipping tea in the drawing room, and now she was being bundled into the tower room like a prisoner. It might be for her own safety but she still felt like the walls were closing in on her, that the bars on the windows were as much to keep her in as the army out.

They were surrounded. She could hear the general barking orders to his men. The catapult rumbled into place, once again digging up the lawn that had not yet recovered from the last time the army arrived at Lichfield.

Because of me.

"Stay away from the window," Eva warned. "Don't let them see you."

All the women were there in the tower room, like good wives, daughters, sisters and mothers. The men were downstairs, preparing to return fire. Even David, a man Alice hardly knew. A man who shouldn't even be there, according to Leisl and Eva.

Alice regarded Leisl, who sat on the bed while the others paced around her. The gypsy woman was calm. Too calm. She lifted her gaze to meet Alice's and nodded once. That knowing nod said far more than her words in the drawing room.

Alice gripped the bedhead to steady herself, swallowed heavily, and nodded back.

"I'll do it now," Charlie said.

There was no need to explain what "it" was. They'd discussed summoning the dead from Highgate Cemetery at length in the last week. In the event of the army's return, the dead were their best weapon. One army could only be bested by another. An army that couldn't be killed was even better.

A shudder tore through Alice. All those dead bodies coming back to life. Some would be horribly decayed, others no more than bones. It would be hell on Earth. It would be wrong.

The women had moved to the highest part of the house to keep them away from both armies. The tower room wasn't the safest place to be if the catapult were aimed at it but it would take time for the catapult to be pushed into place and yet more time for the bricks to come loose and the tower to fall. That was all they needed—time for Charlie to speak the names and order the spirits into their bodies. And a little more time for the bodies to walk from the cemetery to the house.

Too long.

Charlie flattened the sheet of paper on which she'd listed hundreds of names, gathered during a long afternoon inspecting the headstones in the cemetery. She drew in a breath and blew it out slowly. She did not want to do this.

Nor did Alice. "No, Charlie. Don't."

Charlie's head snapped up. "You are *not* going with them."

"It'll take too long for you to summon enough."

"Then let me get started."

Alice stood, but Charlie lunged and grabbed her arm, holding her back from the door. Lady Vickers caught Alice's other arm. Seth's indomitable, regal mother had never looked so afraid.

"Don't do this," she said to Alice. "I know we've had our differences, but please stay. You'll break Seth's heart."

Alice gave her a sad smile. "I doubt it."

"He'll follow you. He won't let you go."

"Where I'm going, he can't follow."

"He can," Leisl chimed in from where she sat on the bed.

Alice wanted to strangle her. Lady Vickers looked as if she would cry, and a crying Lady Vickers was not a sight Alice wanted to endure. This parting was going to be hard enough without the woman she admired crumbling into a blubbering heap.

She patted Lady Vickers's hand. "Let me go."

"No!" Charlie dug her fingernails into Alice's arm. "Leisl, Eva, why aren't you helping?"

Eva looked away, but Leisl did not. She sat there, unmoving yet looking a little worried. Alice suspected she wasn't worried for her but for her own relationship with Charlie. She didn't want her new daughter-in-law to hate her for not helping keep Alice in the tower room.

Charlie's big eyes swam with tears. Alice peered down into them. "They're not helping because they know I'm going to do this. They've seen it, Charlie. They've seen me leave with the army."

Charlie whipped around to face them. "Leisl?" she whispered harshly.

Leisl nodded. Eva did not.

Outside, far below, someone barked orders. They were relayed through the army's ranks, growing more distant until Alice could no longer hear the voices. She pictured Lincoln, Gus, David and Seth taking up their positions, discussing a plan, readying their weapons.

Seth. If only he had been more himself around her, things might be different. Alice's choice might have been easier. But he wasn't the same with Alice as he was with Charlie, and she couldn't love a man who thought he had to pretend to be someone else to be worthy of her.

Leisl had said he could go. He could follow Alice to Wonderland. Knowing how chivalric Seth could be, he would try. Hopefully Lincoln would be strong enough to keep him back.

Charlie's fingers loosened but did not let go. "If she goes," she said to Leisl, "will she be all right?"

"I cannot see," Leisl said.

"Then what can you see?" Charlie snapped.

"Many things, but they are not for you to know yet. One day, yes. For now, trust Alice. Trust her choice. It is her future, and it is for her alone to decide."

"How is it a choice?" Lady Vickers asked, her voice reedy. "You've seen her future. It's written."

"I see *a* future," Leisl said. "Not the only one for her."

"She still has a choice," Eva assured Lady Vickers and Charlie. "No one's future is set in stone."

Alice didn't quite believe it. There was an inevitability about it all, a sense of rightness, now that she'd made up her mind.

A thunderous crash erupted downstairs. The floor shuddered and the whole house seemed to groan. They had begun to use the battering ram. Soon the catapult would join in the assault.

They'd run out of time.

"I have to go, Charlie," Alice pleaded. "Please, don't stop me."

Charlie hesitated. A tear slipped from her left eye. "Will she come back?"

"I do not know," Leisl said.

"We'll see each other again, Charlie. I promise." Alice drew her friend into a fierce hug. She felt Charlie cry though she made no sound.

The battering ram struck again. Alice picked up her skirts and ran from the room, down the stairs to the entrance hall. Lincoln barred the way, rifle in hand. Behind him, the front door bulged inward, the middle hinge broken in half, the pieces hanging from the screws.

Lincoln's gaze slipped past Alice to Charlie. Then he wordlessly stepped aside.

"What are you doing?" Seth cried, emerging from the library. "Alice, get back upstairs. All of you, go!"

"No, Seth," Alice said. "I will not."

He blocked her path to the front door, his too-handsome face set hard. She marveled at how this man could be as simple and fun-loving as Gordon the puppy one moment and so masculine and commanding the next.

"You're not going with them," he said.

The door shattered, sending splinters of wood and pieces of stone exploding into the entrance hall. Lincoln dove forward, covering Alice and Charlie with his body.

When he moved to help them to stand, Alice saw that the others had flattened themselves to the floor. No one looked injured, thank God.

Soldiers surged through the doorway, brandishing swords. Gus and Seth lifted their guns and aimed.

"Stop!" Alice shouted. "Don't shoot! Put your weapons away." She stepped between her friends and the advancing Wonderland army, her hands in the air. "I'll go with you."

Lincoln could have stopped her. He was close enough, fast enough and strong enough. But he let her go.

"Alice!" Seth barked.

General Ironside's big frame filled the doorway, blocking out the light and casting his face in shadow. He moved into the entrance hall, his gait purposeful and unafraid. His son, Sir Markell Ironside, followed. They were alike in stature, although the older man showed signs of age in his thickening middle and ruddier cheeks. Both sported green eyes that quickly assessed the situation, although Sir Markell's were deeper, like emeralds. Despite the rough-hewn features of the general, it was easy to see other family resemblances in the strong brows, the determined set of the lips, the somewhat arrogant way in which they held themselves.

"Greetings, Your Highness," Sir Markell said, bowing.

"Don't call her that," Seth spat. "She is no longer your princess. You gave her up."

"Now it's time for her to come home."

"To face a trial presided over by a mad queen who wants her dead."

Sir Markell arched a brow. He and Seth were of an age, a similar height, and equally handsome but not in the same way. Not in the least. Where Seth was sunshine, Sir Markell was an ominous cloud.

"You'll come with us willingly, Miss Alice?" the general asked. Miss Alice, not princess or highness.

Alice nodded.

"Good." He thrust his sword back into its sheath to the hilt. "Come." There was no pleasure in his voice, no sense of victory. Neither he nor his son looked as though they'd won.

Alice swallowed. What was she getting herself into? "I wish to say goodbye to my friends, first."

Sir Markell nodded. Unlike his father, he kept his sword in hand and a watchful eye on Seth.

Alice turned to Lady Vickers and hugged her. "Goodbye, Lady V."

"Goodbye, dear girl," Lady Vickers whispered. "Be careful."

Alice didn't know the Cornells quite so well, but she hugged them anyway, even David. She moved on to Lincoln next.

"I would ask you to take care of Charlie," she told him, "but I know I don't need to say it."

His grip tightened around her for the barest moment before he stepped back.

She turned her attentions to Gus. "Make sure he makes a better choice than me," she whispered. "And say goodbye to the orphans and your aunt. I shall miss them."

She thought she heard him choke back a sob but when he stepped away, he didn't lift his face, so she couldn't tell.

Then came Seth's turn. They shared an awkward hug. Alice could think of nothing to say to him and he offered nothing in return. Her throat was too clogged with tears anyway.

She cried when she hugged Charlie, and she felt Charlie's small frame shudder with emotion. Alice had few friends growing up, isolated as she had been by her parents. Charlie was her first true friend. Somehow, through her tears, Alice managed to tell her so.

"And you are mine," Charlie said into Alice's shoulder. "I'm going to miss you."

"And I you. Take care, Charlie. Stay safe. Remember me."

"Of course I will. Do not forget your promise to visit."

"I will, first chance I get." Neither mentioned the unlikelihood of that happening.

Alice stepped toward Sir Markell and lifted her chin. She closed her hands into fists and dug the fingernails into her palms to stop them shaking. She would not let him see her fear. "I am ready."

"No!" Seth grabbed her hand. "Don't do this, Alice. We'll fight them. We'll fight them all. You don't have to go." The anguish twisting his features almost undid her. Did he really love her that much? Or was his chivalric pride dented because he felt he hadn't protected her?

"I want to go, Seth. I am a princess of Wonderland. This is my destiny." They may be only words but they ricocheted through her. This felt right. It *was* her destiny, no matter what

Leisl said about free choice. Alice didn't belong here, she never had. She belonged in Wonderland.

Home.

Sir Markell escorted her outside ahead of the general. The wall of soldiers spread across the lawn watched her, some openly curious and others indifferent. The sun struck their swords, and she raised a hand to shield her eyes from the glare. Several of the soldiers took that as a sign of hostility and shifted their stance. Beside her, she felt sure she heard Sir Markell huff out a humorless laugh, but when she looked at him, his jaw was rigid.

He directed her forward and down the steps. He did not touch her but she felt his presence keenly. He was so tall—so broad and masculine. Even if she wanted to get away from him, she doubted it would be possible. It was definitely impossible to get away from the army. Charlie could not raise enough corpses in time to save her now.

Alice blew out a measured breath, but it did nothing to calm her racing heart. "Is the journey to Wonderland difficult?"

"No," Sir Markell said. "It'll be over in a flash, and you won't feel a thing. Your Highness, when we get there—"

"Sir Markell!" The general strode toward them holding a watch by its chain. "Bring the prisoner to me."

Prisoner. Alice's insides recoiled. "My name is Alice." She thought she saw Sir Markell smile before he looked away.

General Ironside hesitated. "Miss Alice, if you please." He held out his hand and she took it. The soft leather of his glove was warm against her bare hand.

She wished she'd thought about practical matters like gloves, a coat and a good pair of boots instead of her inside shoes. It might be cold in Wonderland, and prisoners were unlikely to be treated to comforts.

The general began to chant some words and Alice felt a pulsing sensation in every fiber of her body. She lifted a hand in farewell to her friends standing on the steps of Lichfield Towers and tried so hard to hold back her tears. But Charlie looked so worried, so forlorn, that Alice couldn't help releasing a sob.

"No!" Seth broke away and ran toward Alice.

Charlie reached for him but he was too fast, and Lincoln's arm, clamped around her waist, too strong. Seth kept running, but he was not alone. Gus lumbered behind, his strides not nearly as graceful but he kept up a fast pace through sheer strength alone.

"Seth!" Gus shouted after him.

"Don't!" Charlie cried out, struggling against Lincoln.

Lady Vickers screamed. She picked up her skirts and rushed forward, but she was too slow and too far away to reach him in time.

Eva wasn't, however. She too broke away. Despite the hindrance of her skirts, she caught up to Gus. While he looked worried, she simply looked determined. David chased after her, shouting at her to stop. She paid him no mind.

The pull of the watch's magic increased. Alice felt pieces of her begin to disintegrate, like dust caught in a breeze. She could still see Seth and the others coming for her and wondered if they saw her whole. They were so close now. Gus reached out a hand to grab Seth but missed and stumbled.

"No further, Seth!" Alice shouted. But she couldn't even hear her own voice. The rush of air was too loud, like a waterfall. It filled her head, yet she continued to scream at Seth to stop.

He did not stop. The edges of her vision blurred and blackened. The world closed around her, and all she could see was a tunnel filled with Seth, and behind him, Gus, Eva then David.

Seth lunged. He knocked Alice, and she careened into Sir Markell who stood behind her. They all went down in a tangle of legs and arms, and she landed heavily, knocking the breath from her lungs. Everything went dark.

Slowly the light returned. It took her a moment to realize she was staring up at a sullen sky, the threat of rain hanging in the air. It had been sunny a moment ago.

"Alice?" Seth's face came into view. He looked worried. "Are you all right?"

"I...I think so." She held out a hand for him to assist her to stand, but Seth didn't take it. Sir Markell stepped in and lifted her. He held her until she felt steady. Alice touched her aching head. She must have hit it on the ground when she landed.

"You fool," Sir Markell snarled. "You damned fool. You don't belong here!"

Seth didn't appear to hear him. He was too busy taking in his surroundings. Behind him, David dusted off his trousers while Gus helped Eva to stand. She quickly glanced around before her gaze settled on Seth, as if she needed to satisfy herself that he was all right.

The twinge of jealousy in Alice's chest quickly faded as she too took in her surroundings. They were all there—her friends, Sir Markell, his father the general, the army and even their catapult and battering ram. They stood in a grassy meadow edged with trees on three sides. To their left, the wooden buildings and thatched roofs of a village belonged to a different time. But it wasn't a different time; it was a different *place*.

Behind the village, a road coiled up a hill like a snake and disappeared behind high stone walls. Castle turrets and towers erected from the same dark gray stone rose above the walls like stern governesses overseeing their charges in the village far below.

The thread of a distant memory tugged at Alice, but when she reached for it, she couldn't grasp it. The thread disappeared before she could make sense of it.

She didn't need to remember to know where she was. "Wonderland," she whispered.

"Welcome home, Your Highness." Sir Markell's whisper brushed her ear and stirred something within her, something as small and fragile as a butterfly's wings.

She looked sharply at him. He winked.

"Sir Markell!" the general barked. "What are you saying to the prisoner?"

"Alice," Alice reminded him without taking her gaze off Sir Markell. She wanted him to wink or smile again, something that marked him as a friend, not an enemy.

"Get away from her." It wasn't the general who snapped at Sir Markell and pulled him back but Seth. He was all heaving chest and clenched fists, not a shred of fear in his eyes as he stared down the man who had an army at his back.

Sir Markell crossed his arms.

"You shouldn't have come, Seth," Alice said. "Now you're stuck here too. And them."

Poor David had gone rather green, so different to his sister. Her curious, clever gaze darted about. Gus stood behind Seth, backing him as he always did. They might bicker but they loved each other like brothers. It was no surprise that Gus had followed Seth through the portal.

"Don't worry about us," Seth said to her. "*We're* not under arrest."

Thank God.

But Alice's relief was shattered when the general shouted, "Seize them!"

CHAPTER 3

EVA

Eva clasped David's hand. She felt him tremble and wished he hadn't come. He wasn't made for this. He wasn't like Seth and Gus, with their fighter training, brawny physiques and experience with the otherworldly. David was made for desk work, not brawling. Their mother had been determined that her children wouldn't grow up too Romany, afraid as she was of the discrimination that clung to their culture, but in doing so, she had perhaps raised them to be too English.

Eva hardly dared breathe as several soldiers broke ranks to detain them. Despite knowing things the others didn't, Eva was afraid. She had not foreseen this. She had not foreseen anything at all of Wonderland and their time in it, but she had seen *beyond*. She had trusted her mother's instincts too. *She* had foreseen some of this. When it became clear to Eva why Leisl had left her the message to go to Lichfield, she had accepted her fate.

What scared her was David's part to play. Their mother had not mentioned him being here. He wasn't supposed to be there.

"No!" Alice cried. "They're innocent! It's me you want. Let them go."

"They are not under arrest," the general said. "But they must come with us until we know what to do with them."

"And who decides that?"

"The queen."

"So no one can visit Wonderland without the queen's permission?" Alice scoffed. "That's ridiculous."

"She has you there, Father," Sir Markell said lightly.

The general shot his son a flinty glare. "I am your general. You will address me as such, Sir Markell." To Alice, he said, "These are exceptional circumstances. Your friends will try to rescue you and so must be kept under guard. They will not be harmed and will be returned to your realm, if that's what the queen wishes."

What he did not say, but what Eva feared, was that the queen might want them dead.

Seth and Gus struggled until one of the soldiers punched Gus in the jaw. "We'll go quietly," Seth assured them, hands in the air in surrender. He slowly lowered them again and sought out his friend's shoulder.

He looked as Lincoln often looked—serious, in command, as taut as a drawn bow. He'd never looked more dangerous or more appealing.

Eva licked dry lips.

The general directed half of the army to lead off. They formed themselves into two columns and marched toward the village. The second half fell into step behind the prisoners. Eva was under no illusions—they were prisoners in this strange land, no matter what the general claimed.

Alice fell back from Sir Markell and into step alongside Seth. "You shouldn't have followed me," she said. "They are all here because of you."

"I can't let you face this alone." Seth glanced over his

shoulder at Gus, Eva and David. "*They* shouldn't have followed *me*."

"Where you go, I go," Gus said.

Seth's features softened a little, making him seem more like himself. Would he ever return to being the happy-go-lucky boy-man she knew? Eva suspected it would depend very much on what happened here in Wonderland. She wished she knew what to do, what to say. She liked that old, familiar Seth. Liked him very much.

Seth scowled at her over his shoulder. "Why did you come, Eva?"

He made her feel like a naughty child who'd been caught in a room she shouldn't be in. He'd never been anything other than charming to her. The change unnerved her, made her feel more off-balance than being in a strange land did. "I'll be needed."

His brow plunged but it was Alice who spoke. "You shouldn't have come. None of you should have. This is my destiny, not yours."

"Don't tell me where my destiny lies," Eva spat.

Alice bristled and Eva regretted her harsh tone. This wasn't Alice's fault, and Eva needed to remember that she didn't know what Eva knew. As far as Alice was concerned, Eva ought to be home in England, training to become a nurse. She didn't know that Eva's life was based on a lie or that their fates came to a crossroads in Wonderland.

"She's right," David said. "You shouldn't have come, Eva."

Eva sighed. She didn't want to fight with him too.

The village was like something out of a storybook. The buildings were made from a mixture of dark stone and wood with pitched slate roofs. None were higher than two levels, and all were crammed close together on streets as narrow as some of London's alleys. The streets themselves were little more than cleared strips of compacted dirt with trenches dug on either side to act as gutters. There were no pavements to speak of, and thanks to recent rain, the soldiers' boots flicked up mud as they marched. Eva's skirts quickly became caked in filth. Thank goodness she'd worn boots, not soft indoor shoes like Alice. The satin wasn't made for these conditions. Her feet must be squelching.

Word quickly spread among the residents. All along the street, windows and doors opened and curious faces peered out to watch them pass. They murmured to one another and whispered behind their hands, but there was no hostility in their eyes. It was difficult to gauge the general mood, however. Whenever Eva thought she detected hope in one set of eyes, she'd see sorrow in the neighbor, or fear, even wariness. More than one young man admired Alice, the beautiful, fair former princess of this land. Did they remember her? Did they want her back? Or were they glad to see her being led to prison?

Eva's questions were answered, in part, when one elderly man bowed as Alice passed. "Have faith," he said quietly. "All is not lost."

Alice paused and gaped at him.

A soldier broke ranks and lifted his sword to strike the man.

"Halt!" The general pushed forward. "Leave him be."

"But, sir—"

"I said leave him!"

The soldier fell back into formation.

"Think you can protect her, Loren?" the old man said. The two men must have known one another well to be on a first name basis. "Think the queen'll treat her fairly?"

Ironside ignored him.

The walk through the village was excruciatingly slow. Eva felt like a sideshow act at the fair—ogled, assessed, gossiped about. Ironic, considering her mother had been a fairground fortune teller. It was how she'd met Lincoln's father—the Prince of Wales—and Eva's own father. She'd told both their fortunes and seen her future twined with theirs. Eva often wondered which event begot the other—did the events become true because her mother saw them and acted, or did her mother see them because they were inevitable?

How much was fate really a choice? Her mother always said it was, but Eva couldn't be entirely sure. All she knew was that she had to come on this journey. She *had* to. If she hadn't…it didn't bear thinking about.

The hidden vials sewn into the hem of her skirts bumped against her ankles. They were small, and safely protected by layers of gauze, yet she still felt they were as conspicuous as Alice's beauty.

The walk became a steady climb as they approached the hill on which the castle stood. Guards standing to attention saluted as the procession passed through an iron gate. The road forked and many of the soldiers peeled off to the right to follow the branch that seemed to traverse the base of the hill, while the rest of the soldiers, the general, Sir Markell and the prisoners all forged onward and up.

Dirt gave way to cobblestones, shielded on the steep side by a thick wall that reached to Eva's chest. The village below spread out like a blanket. It was bigger than she'd originally thought, sprawling along the valley before coming to an abrupt end on the banks of a wide river. Several small boats were docked there but no ships. It was nothing like the chaotic, industrious Thames.

They passed through another gate, and then another, both topped with guardhouses and manned by soldiers. They stepped into a courtyard surrounded by a high, thick wall on one side and the castle wall on the other. There were two exits, not including the way they'd come, and Eva could see another courtyard up ahead through an archway. People stopped what they were doing, except for a groom leading two horses away. He disappeared around the corner of the castle, his wide-eyed stare glued to Alice.

Alice, however, wouldn't have noticed. She'd tipped her head back to look up at the castle. The bare stone walls were punctured by the occasional small window or arrow slit, and were topped with crenellated towers that punched heavenward. This was no Buckingham Palace, built to show off the monarch's wealth. It was a working castle, fortified to withstand sieges.

A man dressed in a black tunic, belted at the waist, emerged from the castle's arched door. He walked briskly toward them and asked to speak with General Ironside.

"What is it?" the general barked.

The man spoke quietly then stepped back. He waited.

The general frowned at him. "Even the— Even Miss Alice?"

"Yes, sir."

The general hesitated. It was the first sign of uncertainty Eva had seen from him. "I'd like to speak with someone of authority. Where is Lord Indrid?"

"Indisposed, sir."

"Convenient," Sir Markell muttered.

"My instructions come from the queen herself," the man said. "She awaits your report in the war room. The soldiers can see to the prisoners."

"They're not prisoners," the general told him. "They are our guests. Miss Alice, as a member of the royal family, should also be treated with respect and not thrown in the dungeons. I demand to speak to Lord Indrid."

Dungeons!

"So you *are* going to jail us," Seth said. "I might have known we couldn't trust you, Ironside."

The general put up a hand for calm, but it was his son who spoke. "Allow me to speak with the queen before you decide where they should go." He stepped forward but the man blocked his way.

"It has already been decided, Sir Markell. They are to go to the dungeons until Miss Alice's trial."

"We ain't going nowhere," Gus said, crossing his arms.

Seth stood by his friend, arms crossed too.

Eva curled her fingers around David's hand. He patted her shoulder but it did nothing to soothe her nerves.

"You have to." The general signaled to his soldiers. "Go quietly or my men will not be gentle."

Gus dropped into a squat, a knife in his hand. Seth removed a pistol from the waistband of his trousers.

"Don't shoot!" Alice cried.

"Alice—"

"No, Seth. This is my world, my home, and I will not have you shooting innocent people."

"They're not innocent," Seth said. "They're going to take us to the dungeons."

"They're just following orders. Besides, you don't have enough bullets. You'll be overpowered and then we really won't get out of here alive. Put your weapons down and let's go quietly. We'll sort this out in a non-violent manner." She glared at him until he lowered his pistol to the cobbles.

Gus did the same with the knife. The general signaled his men to check their pockets for weapons. More knives and guns joined the first. The soldiers checked David then approached Eva.

"I say!" David protested. "You can't manhandle my sister like that."

"Leave the ladies alone," Seth growled. "Or I'll rip your throat out, Ironside."

"We're not armed," Alice quickly assured the general. "I give you my word."

The general signaled for them to be taken away. "Go quietly and no harm will come to you. I promise."

"Thank you, General. I'm very grateful."

Eva blew out a breath. Her vials were safe. For now.

"We'll see that you're released soon," Sir Markell said. His uncertain glance toward the castle didn't instill Eva with much confidence.

They followed the small cohort of soldiers along the path the groom and horses had used before entering the castle through a yawning door barred by an iron grate. The guard on duty used a heavy key to unlock both door and grate. Unlike the soldiers dressed in crimson, he wore all white.

Inside, they were met by another guard and another locked, barred door. The air felt cooler, damper, and it was certainly darker. It grew blacker still on the other side of the second door. The only light came from the flaming torches positioned at intervals along the corridor.

"Christ," Gus muttered as they descended a narrow staircase in single file. "I can't see where I'm going."

Eva half expected Seth to tease him, but no one spoke. It wasn't a moment for teasing.

The base of the stairs was barred by yet another locked door. Once through it, the stench of stale air and human filth was overpowering. Eva and Alice covered their noses and mouths with their hands.

They headed along the corridor, passing cells. Eva thought them unoccupied at first, but once her eyes adjusted, she could see well enough through the bars. What she saw shocked her.

A fox stood up as they passed, balanced on hind legs. It clutched the bars in its paws and thrust its nose between them. "Your Highness," it said in a sonorous, male voice.

The party stopped and stared until the guards urged them on.

"Bloody hell," David murmured. "What *is* this place?"

"Wonderland," said an imprisoned donkey.

Charlie had told Eva about the white rabbit who'd visited Alice in her dreams, but she'd not truly believed it until now.

David swore in Romany under his breath. He never

swore, and never spoke their mother's native tongue. Perhaps Eva should have mentioned the stories of the white rabbit to him. Then again, he wouldn't have believed her.

The leading soldier stopped at an empty cell. "Women in there, men there." He pointed to the opposite cell.

"We stay together," Gus said.

David clasped Eva's hand. "I won't be separated from my sister."

"Women in there, men here." The solider unlocked the nearest cell. "Get in."

"Together," Seth growled.

"For now," Alice said to the soldier. "Please."

He heaved a sigh. "Just get in."

They all dutifully filed into the cell and the soldier locked the grill. David clutched the bars and watched him walk back along the corridor. Eva slumped against the back wall and tried to breathe through her mouth. The stink invaded anyway.

"Eva, Alice, sit on the bed and rest." Seth eyed the bare wooden bench dubiously. "If that's what that is."

"At least there's nowhere for lice to hide," Gus said.

Alice wrinkled her nose. "I think I'll stand for now."

David wheeled around and stabbed a finger at her. "This is all your fault. None of us would be here if you hadn't surrendered."

"David," Eva snapped. "That's not helpful."

"If I hadn't surrendered, you might all be dead," Alice said. "And I did not ask you to follow me. I wish you hadn't."

Seth grasped Alice's shoulders and dipped his head to meet her gaze. "I couldn't allow you to come alone. Besides, I've always wanted to travel to interesting places." He shot her one of his famous smiles, dimples and all. It gladdened Eva to see it, even though she knew it was false.

"This castle reminds me of a famous play I once saw," Gus

said. "It had a mad king, though, not a queen. Lots of blood, fighting, and something about getting a spot out."

"Shakespeare," Seth said.

"No, that ain't it."

"It's Macbeth."

Gus clicked his fingers and pointed at Seth. "That sounds like it."

"Macbeth but with animals," Eva said, welcoming any conversation that would stop her brother from becoming too morose.

Alice peered out between the bars. "Are they animals or humans?"

Seth joined her at the bars. "We should have made the white rabbit talk when we had the chance."

"I wouldn't have told you anything," said a raspy voice from a cell across from theirs. A rabbit dressed in a waistcoat moved into the patch of wan light cast by a nearby torch. Some of his whiskers were bent and his fur was mostly brown from dirt and grime instead of pristine white. He was fully clothed. "It was forbidden."

"You!" Gus pointed a finger at the rabbit. "I hurt my shoulder trying to catch you, you slippery cur."

"Not a cur, a rabbit." The rabbit sounded weary. "Take a good look. Stare all you want and laugh. I'm beyond caring."

"Did they jail you because you failed to bring me back?" Alice asked.

"I hate you people," was his only answer.

Alice visibly baulked.

"You hate your princess?" Seth said.

"Haven't you heard? She's no longer a princess." The rabbit plopped down on the cell floor and scratched his head between his long ears. "The queen cast her out of the family and stripped her of her royal title. She's just plain old Alice, now."

"There's nothing plain about her. Take a look."

"Seth," Alice said, sounding as weary as the rabbit. "Don't."

"It's true," he muttered.

Her eyes suddenly flashed. "I'm so much more. Why can't you see it?"

Seth stumbled back a step. He blinked rapidly at her. "Of course you are. That's not what I meant."

But they all knew it was precisely what he meant. Like most people, he couldn't see past her beautiful face, her desirable figure. It was why most women envied her, and why many men fancied themselves in love with her. Eva hated to admit it, but she was one of those women. She must change that. She hadn't been fair to Alice.

It seemed Seth was coming to the same realization. He retreated to the back of the cell where he slid to the floor and sat with his knees drawn up. On a whim, Eva joined him.

"Don't feel bad," she said.

"I should have understood."

"Because people fall in love with your beautiful face?"

One corner of his mouth quirked. "I prefer handsome to beautiful."

"It must happen all the time."

"Not so much, of late."

Perhaps he simply hadn't noticed because women certainly stared when he walked into a room. Eva could personally vouch for it.

"It just never occurred to me that I saw Alice as simply a pretty face," he went on.

"Are you sure you do? I mean, just because she thinks so doesn't mean it's true. And just because you think her pretty doesn't mean you don't also see her other qualities."

He stared at Alice's back. She was still speaking with the rabbit through thc cell bars, flanked by David on one side and Gus on the other. If she knew she'd hurt Seth's feelings, she didn't show it.

"If you truly love her, persist," Eva said.

Seth stretched out his long legs and crossed them at the ankles. "That's the thing. How do I know if I am in love with her? Shouldn't there be some sort of sign?"

"I suspect it's more of a feeling that you can't live without one another, or wouldn't want to." She watched him carefully but he said nothing, simply continued to stare at Alice. "My mother once said that you'll know love when you're prepared to give up everything to be with that person, even when everyone is warning you not to. She was referring to her and my father, of course."

"She gave up a lot to be with him."

"Her family and friends, her culture. Although I'm not certain she didn't want to give those things up anyway. She has often told me the Romany life wasn't really for her."

"My mother gave up a lot too for her second husband—her friends, status, good name and reputation. I've been unfair to her. I've reacted like a child, but I'm an adult now, and I do understand why she did what she did. I should have told her."

She nudged his shoulder. "See, you're not just a pretty face. You can philosophize too."

"That's not all I can do. I can ride a horse like an American cowboy, recite poetry in Latin, and tie a cravat in no less than nine different knots."

She laughed. "Goodness, you are positively a genius!"

"Shhh. Don't tell anyone. I quite like having a reputation as a twit."

"Seth," she said, quite seriously, "no one thinks you stupid, least of all the friends who know you well."

"You count yourself among them?"

She felt her face heat and was glad for the dim light. "Yes."

He kissed the top of her head. "Good. You've brightened an otherwise bloody awful day." He rose and put out his hand.

She took it and together they joined the others at the cell bars.

"Listen to this," Gus said. "The rabbit says the queen turns anyone who fails to do her bidding into an animal."

"My name is Sir Uther," the rabbit said with pomposity. "I was one of her advisors until..." He spread out his arms and performed a little bow.

"Some get second chances to redeem themselves," Alice went on. "Like Sir Uther. But if they fail again, they are sent down here to spend the rest of their days locked away in a cell, never to return to their human form. Others are tried and executed immediately. It's barbaric."

"How does she change you?" Eva asked.

"Magic," the rabbit said. "She found a spell book, long thought lost, and used it on me, them...Miss Alice's parents."

Alice gasped. "Did she turn them into animals?"

"Geese. Then she had them hunted and killed. They saved you first, Miss Alice, by sending you through the portal."

Alice's knuckles went white as she gripped the bars. "Did you know them?"

"No."

"You said the queen turns anyone who fails her into an animal," Seth said. "That means you failed her, Uther."

"*Sir* Uther. And yes, I did, stupidly."

"How?"

"None of your business."

"He passed information to the renegades," came a voice from another cell.

"Shut up, Ass."

A donkey brayed.

"Who or what are renegades?" Alice asked.

"Your supporters," Sir Uther said.

Alice pressed against the bars. "You...you wish me to retake the throne?" she whispered.

"I wish I wasn't in here, that's what I wish." The rabbit

retreated into the shadows at the rear of his cell. "I wish I hadn't believed them."

"The renegades?"

The rabbit said nothing.

"Sir Uther!" Alice cried. "Tell me about the renegades. Are there many? Are they strong? What do they want?"

The white rabbit hissed. "I'd keep my mouth shut if I were you, Miss Alice. These walls have ears. It won't go well for you if you stir up talk of treason. "

"Would the queen turn us into animals too?" David asked.

"You, perhaps, but she'd just execute Miss Alice."

Eva's stomach dropped.

"She's too dangerous to have walking around Wonderland alive. The renegades have lived in hope for years that she was alive, and when they see that she is, they'll gather their forces and make a plan to overthrow the Queen of Hearts. Keeping the rightful heir to the throne alive is an enormous risk."

Eva touched Alice's arm as a show of support. A slight tremble rippled through Alice but her voice was steady when she spoke. "Thank you for your honesty, Sir Uther. I appreciate it, and I appreciate what you did to help the renegades. What has happened to you is awful, and you don't deserve this."

"Like I said, I wish I'd done things differently," the rabbit muttered.

"Spineless, that's what you are, Uther," said the voice from the neighboring cell. "You were twitchy and scared then, and you're twitchy and scared now. No wonder she chose a rabbit form for you."

The rabbit didn't respond. His cell had gone completely quiet. Eva felt the silence settle around them, thick and stifling. It was broken by the sound of boots on the stone floor. Several pairs, if Eva wasn't mistaken. She tensed.

"The queen commands your presence," the leading soldier announced.

"She's not going alone," Seth told him. "Where she goes, I go too."

"Don't fret, pretty boy. You're all going." He unlocked the door and directed them out.

Sir Uther rushed forward. His ears flopped and his paws tightened around the bars. "Good luck," he whispered. "May the gods and goddesses protect you."

Several armed soldiers escorted the party along the corridor, back the way they'd come.

"Good luck," the donkey said as they passed his cell. It was difficult to tell, but Eva could swear he looked worried.

Alice, however, didn't look concerned to be led away to an uncertain fate. She looked inspired.

CHAPTER 4

SETH

Seth had expected someone taller and more beautiful, like Alice. The Queen of Hearts was neither tall nor beautiful. She was stocky, and there were so many wrinkles on her brow and around her mouth that she looked as if she'd sucked on lemons every day of her life. It was how Charlie described Queen Victoria. She would have found the similarity amusing.

The prisoners had been brought up from the dungeon to what Seth assumed was an audience chamber, used for receiving subjects who were supposed to bow and scrape to the queen. It was cavernous but mostly empty of furniture except for a large carved wooden throne on a dais and a red carpet leading up to it. Men and women dressed in fine outfits of a medieval style and dripping in jewels, stood on either side of the carpet and watched as the soldiers ushered Alice forward. Seth spotted General Ironside and Sir Markell at the front, flanked by another six soldiers. More armed men stood against the walls, but they were dressed all in white, like the dungeon guards, not the red of the soldiers or black like the general and Sir Markell.

The queen lifted her hand and the soldier halted Alice.

The queen rose and stepped off the dais. Her footsteps thudded with her every step as she proceeded toward Alice along the carpet.

"So this is her," she said in a booming voice that echoed off the beams.

"Yes, Your Majesty," Sir Markell said.

"How do you know?"

Despite the challenge in her voice, the queen's advisor didn't miss a beat. "Her story fits with what we know of her."

"And she looks remarkably like her mother," the general added. "Even you must concede that."

The queen's eyes flashed, and Seth thought she'd order him from the room or chastise him, but she merely turned to Alice. "Do you know why you are here?"

Alice straightened, looking regal despite her muddy shoes. Seth had always thought she had a dignified air about her, but it seemed amplified in this room. "I am the rightful heir to the throne and you fear me taking it from you."

Hell.

"Why did she say that?" Gus muttered. "She's in enough trouble."

The queen's nostrils flared. Seth quickly calculated how many guards and soldiers he had to fight to reach Alice before the queen struck her. There were too many, the distance too far. Not even Lincoln would make it.

"You are mistaken," was all the queen said. "You are *not* the rightful heir. I am. My brother, your father, was younger than me. He shouldn't have inherited from our father. *I* should have."

"Then why didn't you?" Alice asked.

"My father deemed my brother more fit to rule and named him as heir." The queen leaned in. "But he was wrong. I am better than your father ever was. He was weak. I am strong."

Fabric rustled, feet shuffled, but when Seth studied the

small gathering, he couldn't determine which of them felt discomforted by the queen's pronouncements.

"I see," Alice said. "Thank you for the history lesson. So what happens now? Am I to be executed for being your rival?"

"Of course not. I am not a monster. You are to face trial first." The queen flapped her hand at a black robed man standing by the throne. "Proceed, Lord Indrid."

"Here?" Alice asked. "Now?"

"Why not?" the queen said. "You are here, as am I, and several witnesses. Lord Indrid will oversee the trial."

"What about a judge?"

"*I* decide your fate."

"Shouldn't there be a verdict before you decide her fate?" Eva snapped.

The queen ignored her.

"This is a farce," Seth said. "Let us go. We don't belong here. Alice doesn't want your damned crown. She'll return home with us and you can go on reigning here until someone overthrows you."

The queen arched one thin brow. "Is that your husband?"

"No," Alice said. "I am not married."

"Very wise. Husbands tend to think what is yours is theirs, even though I have changed the law to state otherwise."

"Well?" Seth went on. "Will you let her go?"

The queen returned to her throne and fidgeted with a large heart shaped ruby ring on her finger. "He acts like a husband."

"Let's get this over with then," Alice said with a tilt of her chin.

What was she doing? Why wasn't she putting up a fight? "Alice, don't." If Seth's warning reached her, she showed no sign.

The withered Lord Indrid shuffled forward. "Her Majesty the Queen of Hearts, Ruler of Wonderland, charges Miss Alice of...England with treason after she left Wonderland without permission from her queen."

"She was a child!" Seth shouted. He tried to move forward but the soldiers on either side of him pinned him between them. "She didn't have any say over what happened to her. If you want to charge someone, charge those who sent her there."

"I already have," the queen said. "Then I executed them."

Seth's mouth went dry.

Alice half turned and gave her head a slight shake.

"Her highness has a right to legal representation," Sir Markell announced.

The air seemed to be sucked from the room. Dozens of heads swiveled in Sir Markell's direction. Sir Markell didn't appear to notice.

"Markell," the general hissed. "What are you doing?"

"The honorable thing," Sir Markell said. "She is still a princess of Wonderland and deserves to be referred to as highness."

"You dare to call the usurper by the title that was stripped from her?" the queen spat. "The title that *I* stripped from her?"

"According to the royal charter, that's not lawful. She is a princess for life. It's only her lands and possessions that are forfeited upon being found guilty of treason. Speaking of treason," he went on, as if the entire audience hadn't just gasped at his audacity, and as if the queen wasn't casting him murderous glares, "it's not entirely clear whether she is guilty of departing Wonderland at the age of three. After all, she had no say in it. It could be argued that she was kidnapped. A proper unbiased trial is required to—"

"Her departure was illegal because I say so! She has committed treason because I say she has!" The queen's face had gone as red as her dress. "General! Cut out your brat's tongue. It offends me."

Sir Markell swallowed. He lifted his gaze to his father. The general met it and gave the barest of nods before squaring his shoulders. "I cannot. He's right. Furthermore, Her Highness the Princess Alice is the true heir—"

"Enough!" The queen stamped her fist on the throne arm, over and over as the audience gasped. "Guards! Seize him!"

The men dressed in white stepped away from the walls and advanced, swords drawn. The general was unarmed, as were the rest of his soldiers.

For what seemed like a long moment, the audience of nobles simply stood, unmoving, as if they were watching a play on the stage. Then a woman screamed and chaos erupted.

The audience ran for the doors, pushing one another out of the way, calling one another names.

In contrast, the queen's guards advanced in silent, deadly unison.

"Men!" the general ordered. "Formation!"

The soldiers moved into the middle of the room and stood in a circle with their general, their backs to one another. They hunched into fighting stances and withdrew knives from their boots. Not unarmed, then; the general was no fool.

Seth pulled out the knife he'd stashed in his boot back at Lichfield and saw that Gus did the same. The blade felt good in his hand, its weight balanced, the metal cool and hard. If he timed his first move right, he could dodge the nearest guard's sword and strike low and fast. But they were outnumbered, and Seth couldn't be certain if the soldiers could hold their own against the guards.

"Back," Seth ordered Eva, Alice and David. "Get behind me and Gus."

But Sir Markell already had Alice's hand. "Come with me, Your Highness. I know a way out."

"My friends too," Alice said, taking Eva's hand. "All of them."

Sir Markell pressed his lips together, and Seth thought he'd refuse. "I'll try, but I can only defend you."

"We'll take care of Eva and David," Gus said.

"Alice too," Seth said. "I'll protect her, Ironside."

She moved to join him but Sir Markell put his arm around her. "She stays with me. The guards are highly trained."

"You think us incapable?"

Sir Markell simply grunted and drew a knife from his boot. As he straightened, the guards attacked.

Seth dove and rolled, thrusting up with his knife as the nearest guard's sword sliced down. The stab, although not deep, unbalanced the guard and his blade missed its target. Seth pushed to his knees and jabbed his knife into the guard's side, finishing him. He snatched up the sword and jumped to his feet, just in time to deflect a second guard's strike.

Seth dispatched him, only to find two more replaced him. Out of the corner of his eye, Seth saw Gus take on another two. He'd also grabbed a fallen guard's sword, but he didn't have fencing training like Seth, and he wielded it more like a barbarian with a club. Seth needed to help him but he couldn't get away from his attackers.

An unlikely ally arrived in the form of the soldier who'd marched them up from the dungeons. He bled from a cut on his cheek, but he was armed with a sword now and used it with finesse.

There was no more time for admiration, however. There were more guards than soldiers but the general had taught his men well and they held their own. Sir Markell had joined Gus and they fought as a team. The women and David stood to one side, out of the way. The queen was nowhere to be seen. Perhaps she'd fled. Her guards couldn't save her now. The tide had turned, and the numbers were even.

Then the doors flung open wide and more of the white-clad guards surged in. Distracted, Seth didn't see the blade until it was too late to do anything other than flinch.

Another sword intercepted it inches from Seth's face and the general dispatched the guard with a killing blow to the throat. Blood sprayed across Seth's face and gushed onto the guard's white tunic.

The general didn't seem to notice that he was covered in blood. "Go!" he shouted. "Get away! Markell, protect the princess."

Sir Markell dispatched a guard and eyed off the advancing replacements. "What about you, Father?"

"I'll stay. I trained most of these guards. Perhaps some will listen to me." He readied himself for the onslaught. There were only four soldiers left, including the general, and more than twenty guards. They didn't stand a chance. "Go now before it's too late."

Sir Markell looked pained. "I'm sorry, Father."

"Don't be. I should have done something years ago, but..." His fingers flexed around the sword. "But I was afraid for what they'd do to you and your mother. I'm proud of you for doing what I could not. Now go!"

Sir Markell clasped his father's shoulder before joining Eva, Alice and David. He ushered them to the back of the room. Sir Markell touched a panel and a hidden door opened. He pushed David in and the rest followed.

Seth caught a glimpse of the narrow corridor ahead before the door behind them closed, cutting off the light. Eva's hand reached back and caught his. He squeezed gently to reassure her.

"Put your left hand on the wall to guide you," Sir Markell ordered. "This corridor bends and forks but we always want to keep left."

"How far?" Alice asked.

"As far as it goes."

The sounds of fighting grew fainter. Somehow the general and his soldiers had managed to keep the guards away from the hidden corridor, but it wouldn't be for long.

Seth's eyes grew accustomed to the dark enough that he could make out Eva's shape but no one ahead of her. Their footsteps and breathing were the only sounds. No one spoke.

And then he heard it. Voices from behind, the pounding of boots. The guards were coming.

Seth, Gus and Sir Markell would have to hold them off while the others went on ahead. Hopefully there would be no guards to meet them at the end of the tunnel.

Yet Seth held out little hope. If Sir Markell knew where the tunnel led then surely the queen and her guards knew. There could be more waiting for them. They had no choice now but to continue.

Seth wasn't sure when he noticed the darkness recede. It happened gradually. He could make out the figures up ahead; the dark green of Eva's dress, the bouncing tendrils of her black hair.

Then he saw why it had grown lighter. The corridor came to an end at a set of narrow stone steps. The steps led up to a door that had been thrown open. David, first in line, hesitated.

"Go!" Sir Markell shouted.

When David didn't move, Alice pushed past him. He followed. Eva's fingers tightened around Seth's. He found it oddly comforting. If whatever was on the other side killed them, at least they wouldn't die alone.

The first thing Seth saw as he exited the tunnel was four dead bodies clad in the white uniform of the queen's guards. "Who—"

Hands grasped his shoulders, pulled him forward. He stumbled into Eva and she put her arms around him to steady them both.

"Sorry," Seth said, absently.

Six men surrounded them. They wore no uniform, just the same dun colored tunics the villagers wore. Blood stained their swords red.

They silently helped Gus and Sir Markell from the tunnel then pointed along a steep path that led down the hill. One of them clasped Sir Markell's arm in greeting.

"How many?" the man asked.

"I don't know," Sir Markell said. "But they're not far behind."

"You go. Get the princess to safety." His glaze flittered to Alice, who stared wide-eyed back him. It was the only sign that she was afraid.

Sir Markell hesitated.

"They can only exit one at a time," his friend said. "Go."

Sir Markell clapped him on the shoulder and moved up alongside Alice. "This way," he said. "Once we reach the forest, we'll be safe."

"What forest?" Gus asked.

Sir Markell didn't answer. He took the lead, checked to see that everyone followed, and descended the hill.

Seth glanced back toward the castle's outer wall looming over them, blocking out the sky. Gus shoved him, and Seth fell into step behind Eva.

The path wasn't well trod. Bushes grabbed at his sleeves and scratched the backs of his hands, and his boots slid on loose rocks. Eva lost her footing and Seth grabbed her around the waist to stop her falling.

"Careful," he said.

She peered up at him. Her dark eyes swam. "Thank you."

They made it to the base of the hill where the village swallowed them. They traversed down crooked lanes and wove between the stalls in the market, taking first one direction then changing. Despite their caution, people stared. Seth heard them utter Sir Markell's name followed by "Princess Alice" in hushed tones. Seth didn't know if they would protect their exiled princess or give her up. He didn't dare wait to find out.

Someone must have given them away, because two guards

caught up to them at the edge of the village. The fools shouted for them to halt, alerting the party to their presence. Gus and Seth fell back and dispatched a man each. Sir Markell hadn't waited. Only Eva slowed. She drew in a deep breath when Seth and Gus rejoined them.

Residences gave way to warehouses, a weighing house, shipping offices and even a temple. A giant white marble statue of a semi-naked man holding an octopus in one hand and a boat in the other overlooked the wharf. The octopus was twice the size of the ship and its tentacles reached the statue's knees.

"Impressive," Gus muttered, staring up at it.

"Admire later," Seth told him. "Looks like our ship's about to set sail."

Gus followed his gaze. "You call that a ship? Doesn't look like it'll stay upright in a stiff breeze."

"Fortunately there's no wind today," Eva said. "Come on. Or would you rather add more blood to what you're already wearing?"

They piled onto the boat and two dockworkers pushed them away from the wharf. Without a breeze, the sail hung as limp as an empty sack. Sir Markell and two of the crew took up the oars. Seth and Gus joined them but they needed another. Everyone looked to David.

"I can't row," he said.

"Nor can I," Gus said. "But a man's got to do it."

"I'll do it wrong."

Alice hitched up her skirts and went to sit down at an oar.

"No, Your Highness!" Sir Markell sounded offended. He glared so hard at David it was no wonder he gave in and took the vacant seat across from Seth.

He grabbed the oar in both hands from underneath.

"Not like that, like this," Seth said, showing him the proper grip. "Lean forward when the man in front of you does, oar square in the water, then push back when he pushes back. That's it. Oar out now, skim it flat across the surface as you lean forward again. Now back, oar square in the water. Keep in time."

After a few more directions, David found his rhythm and Seth stopped talking. He liked rowing. He'd been a member of the university eight until he'd been kicked off the team for turning up drunk to training.

They rowed in silence until the village disappeared on the horizon and farmland gave way to trees. The thicker the woods became, the more Sir Markell and the crew relaxed.

"Are you all right, Your Highness?" he asked.

"Fine, thank you," Alice said. "We owe you our lives, Sir Markell."

"It was my honor to rescue you."

"You had some help," Seth reminded him.

"And I'm all right too," Gus chimed in. "In case you were wondering."

Sir Markell scowled at them over his shoulder. "Your companions are disrespectful."

"Her companions are right here," Seth said. He bit back further comments. Sir Markell had most likely just lost his father. It was no wonder the charms he'd displayed in London were no longer in evidence.

"Please address me as Alice, Sir Markell," Alice said.

"I can't."

"Try."

He nodded.

"Is it much farther?" David whined.

"Around the bend," Sir Markell said.

"Will we be able to rest?" Alice asked, shifting her weight from one foot to another. She had not sat even though there was space at the front of the boat.

Sir Markell nodded. "We'll camp for the night."

Seth had to admit he was relieved. It had been a long day. He found his mind wandering as the rhythm of the oars soothed him. He looked around but there was nothing to see except trees, water, and a cloudy sky. It looked very much like the English countryside. For a moment, he thought perhaps it was all a trick, and Sir Markell would laugh at them for being taken in.

But the blood on Seth's skin and clothes, and the sting of his cuts, were very real.

"Charlie would like all these trees," Gus said.

Seth smiled. The orchard was her favorite place on the Lichfield estate. She would indeed like to climb one of these giants.

They rounded the bend and headed toward an inlet arced by a sandy beach. It wasn't the first beach they'd come across but it was the widest. They beached the boat and were about to alight when a dozen men and women emerged from the forest like wood sprites.

Seth picked up the sword but Sir Markell put out his hand. "It's all right," he said. "They're with me."

"They expected us?" Alice asked.

Sir Markell jumped out of the boat and held out his hand to assist Alice. "Your rescue has been planned for a long time."

Alice sucked in a breath and watched as the newcomers went to work alongside the crew, pulling down the sail. Sir Markell spoke quietly to a man with a crooked back and white beard and signaled for Alice and the others to enter the forest with him.

"What about the boat?" Seth asked. "If the guards realize we escaped on the river they'll spot it easily."

"That's why my men are dismantling it and hiding the parts in the forest," Sir Markell said. "When they're finished, there'll be no evidence visible from the river."

"You've thought of everything," Alice said, picking up her skirts. "Thank you. All of you," she said to those working on the boat.

Some of the men nodded and the women performed an awkward curtsy before returning to their task.

"It's our pleasure, Your—Alice." Sir Markell bowed but not before Seth saw the color rise to his cheeks.

Alice must have noticed it too, because she smiled. Not a regal smile or a friendly one, but the small, secret smile of a woman pleased to make a man blush.

Seth turned away, unsure what to think anymore. He was grateful not to be chased by guards, and that they appeared to be safe, but ever since being thrown in the dungeon, he'd felt like everything was spiraling out of control. No, it had begun before that, when they were back in Lichfield and he'd made the decision to follow Alice through the portal.

Uncertainty wasn't something he was used to. Even in his darkest hours, when he sold himself at private auctions, he'd only ever made decisions with a clear head and careful thought, always working toward the final goal of clearing his father's debts. He'd made those decisions knowing the consequences and was prepared to face them.

Not this time. He'd barreled through that portal on a whim, on a feeling that it was something he must do, but not knowing why. Then to be held prisoner, with the prospect of Alice's execution... He felt as though he'd failed. Thank God she wasn't friendless in this realm. Without Sir Markell's planning, and the general's sacrifice, they'd be dead. Seth found he couldn't even blame the Ironsides for taking them to Wonderland in the first place. They were only following their mad queen's orders. As the general had told his son in the audience chamber, he'd feared for his wife and son's lives. Seth couldn't hate him for that.

No path had been cut through the forest so they pushed aside low hanging branches and stepped over fallen logs. The dense layer of leaves deadened their footsteps, and the thick canopy overhead blocked out much of the afternoon light. Seth had never smelled air so fresh. He breathed deeply, over and over. Perhaps if he breathed deeply and often enough, London's soot would blow out of his system altogether.

The forest suddenly cleared and a beam of sunlight pierced a camp ringed by tents. Two men who'd been tending to a pot on the fire straightened. Seth realized they were actually women dressed in short tunics over a pair of hose like the men. The elderly fellow who'd greeted them at the riverbank beckoned them to join him as he sat on a log.

"Are these the renegades?" Alice asked.

"Some of them," Sir Markell said.

"How did you get them to help you?" Seth asked.

"They were willing. Every one of them believes Alice is the rightful princess, not the witch who sits on the throne."

"Alice?" the man echoed. "Not Your Highness?"

Sir Markell blushed again.

One of the women stepped forward. "Even if Her Highness wasn't the rightful ruler, we'd still want to overthrow the queen."

"She's a mad bitch," the other woman spat. "Especially since getting her hands on that spell book."

"It sounds like a spell book from our realm." Alice looked to Seth and Gus. "Remember the one at Freak House?"

"This must be a different one," Seth said. "Langley wouldn't lose it or send it here for safekeeping."

"Aye." Gus sat on one of the logs and rubbed his knee. "He's no fool."

"You must tell me all about the spell book," Alice said. "We need to know what we're up against."

"Of course," Sir Markell said. "Do you want to freshen up first? There's suitable clothing in that tent."

"Enough for the others?" she asked.

"Just you. I didn't realize we'd have anyone else."

"Don't worry about us," Eva assured her. "We at least have serviceable boots. Your feet must ache like the devil, Alice."

Alice lifted her skirts and inspected her shoes. The toes

were badly scuffed and Seth expected the soles to be in a very poor state after navigating the hill path.

"If you don't mind, I think I will change," she said.

The women and elderly man bowed. She smiled shyly back then slipped into the tent.

"Come, sit," the white-haired man said to Seth and the others. "You're very welcome here. My name is Lord Blaine."

"You don't look like a lord," Gus said, accepting a tin cup. He sniffed the contents and sipped. "Tastes good. Come try it, Seth. He's a lord too," he said to Lord Blaine.

"Is that so?" Sir Markell said. "Then it's no wonder Alice chose you as her protector in England."

Seth managed to not roll his eyes, but only just. "First of all, she didn't choose me. She came to live with us because she's friends with… Never mind. It's a long story. Second of all, I'm not her protector, I'm her friend."

"The grand house where we met belongs to you?" Sir Markell asked.

"No."

"Is your estate nearby?"

"No." Seth shot Gus a sharp look to keep him quiet.

Gus was too busy refilling his cup from the pot over the fire to notice.

Sir Markell handed Seth a cup. "You seemed very protective of Alice, yet you are not her protector or her husband. So what are you to her?"

"In our country, a gentleman protects a lady no matter whose wife they are or where they're from."

"How chivalric."

Seth gave him a flat smile over the rim of his cup. "Nor do we go about kidnapping innocent ladies and ripping them away from the only home they know."

Sir Markell's nostrils flared. He looked like a bull. A handsome one, Seth conceded, but a bull nevertheless. "Alice belongs here," Sir Markell said. "She'll be our queen within days, if all goes to plan."

"If," Seth growled. "What makes you think she even wants to be queen? Just because she's the rightful ruler doesn't mean she'd like to take on the role. Perhaps she wants to go back with us, now that she's seen the place."

Sir Markell stiffened. "Are you disparaging our realm?"

"Do stop," David said on a groan. "Alice belongs here. We don't. So how can we get home?"

"An object becomes a portal between worlds when a particular spell is imbued into it," Lord Blaine said. "We have found a watch to be the most functional."

David removed his jacket and unbuttoned his watch chain from his waistcoat. He held out his watch to Lord Blaine. "Go ahead. Speak the spell so we can go home."

Lord Blaine and Sir Markell exchanged glances. "We can't," Lord Blaine said. "We don't know it. It's in the queen's spell book, back at the castle."

David looked as if he would cry, and Seth couldn't blame him. They'd been almost killed trying to escape the palace, and now they had to return in order to go home? Seth dragged his hand through his hair.

"Damn," he muttered.

"You could stay here," one of the women said, smiling at him. "It's very pleasant, and once Princess Alice takes the throne, everything will settle down again. You'll find the people are *very* nice."

She was flirting with him. Seth knew the telltale signs, the little smile, the bright eyes, and the flush in her cheeks. Usually he would flirt back in the hope she'd be willing to tumble in the bushes with him later. But he found he didn't have the heart for it. He simply nodded and muttered something he hoped was kind but not encouraging.

"Thank you," Eva, sitting on his other side, whispered.

She was thanking him for not flirting?

"For helping David in the boat," she added when he simply stared at her.

"Oh. Yes. Of course. I know what it's like to step into a boat for the first time when everyone else knows what to do."

"It was kind of you, but his masculine pride won't let him thank you so I wanted to on his behalf."

"You're very different to your brother. More like your half-sibling, really."

"I am? In what way?"

"Many ways. Your strength of character reminds me of Lincoln, and you have his cheekbones. But you're much prettier." He reached up to remove a twig stuck in her hair but it was tangled and he needed two hands. Not only that, but he found that removing it caused more of her hair to come loose. "Sorry. I made a hash of that, but I got it." He showed her the twig.

She laughed softly. He smiled back, gladder than he could ever say to see her laugh at a time like this. There'd been very little to be glad about today.

"I think that twig was holding my hair in place," she said as another tendril came loose and flopped in front of her face. She worked the pins from her hair until it all tumbled out. It fell to the middle of her back in thick, black waves that gleamed despite the poor light.

Why had he never realized how beautiful she was?

"You fight well," Sir Markell said. "Both of you."

"We know," Gus said. "Been trained by the best."

"A general?"

"Lincoln Fitzroy. He's a..." Gus appealed to Seth. "What would you call him?"

Seth could think of so many names—a killer, a madman, a villain, the stuff of nightmares, an unlikely friend, the best ally. "A man who'll stop at nothing to avenge the deaths of his brother and sister if they meet an untimely end," he said.

Sir Markell seemed impressed. David looked somewhat shocked. Eva looked like she was trying not to laugh.

"Nicely done," she whispered. "I think he believes you."

"You don't think Lincoln would come for you?"

"I think he'd come for you and Gus. You mean more to him than we do."

"You're his family."

"No, Seth, *you* are his family."

He blinked owlishly at her.

Seth was dimly aware of the tent flap opening and Alice stepping out. It was Gus's "Blimey!" and David's gasp that forced him to look away from Eva.

His jaw dropped. Sir Markell had said there was suitable clothing for Eva to change into, but *that* clothing was *not* appropriate. Indeed, it was scandalous. Seth liked it.

CHAPTER 5

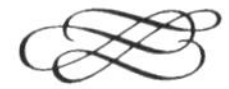

ALICE

Alice liked her new outfit of a dun colored tunic over a pair of black tight-fitting hose. Paired with sturdy boots, it was perfect for traveling through the forest. The ensemble was much lighter than her dress and petticoat, too, and far less restrictive. She'd wavered on whether to dispense with her corset but decided to remove it in favor of the softer bodice that laced up the front. It would take some getting used to, however, and she might even change her mind and put the stiff corset back on tomorrow.

She could see from Seth's reaction that he liked it too, probably because the hose accentuated the curve of her calves and revealed her knees. Sir Markell took in her new appearance with brisk precision before he quickly looked away. Alice thought she saw heat in his gaze, but she couldn't be sure.

She didn't quite know what to make him. Ever since their return to Wonderland, he'd been aloof, where he'd been charming in England and a little roguish. The poor man had just lost his father, though, and betrayed his queen. He'd gone from valued advisor to traitor in the space of minutes, and he was now running for his life. There was the added burden of protecting her, too. It was no wonder he wasn't himself.

She sat on the log beside him, her legs together and to the side, as she would sit when wearing a dress. It looked somewhat odd so she stretched her legs out in front, like the men. Better.

"Sir Markell, you were going to tell us about the spell book," she said.

"There's little to tell. Nobody knows who wrote it or when, but it contains pages of spells written in an elegant hand."

"Are some of the letters colored?" Seth asked.

"The first letter on each page is brightly colored, and some are gilded."

"Are there pictures, symbols?"

"Sometimes. Why?"

"It could be a medieval manuscript, similar to the one found at Freak House," he said to Alice.

"What is medieval and freak?" Sir Markell asked.

"Look around you," Gus muttered.

Alice shot him a warning glare. "There is a similar book in our—their—world with spells. Perhaps the same people wrote it. They died hundreds of years ago and the book was lost, except for a single page with spells on it that transport people between realms. It's kept safe by acquaintances of ours."

"Our book is not safe," Lord Blaine said. "Not while the queen possesses it."

"What I don't understand," Gus said, "is why the transporting spell at Freak House only works at the portal on their estate, when your transporting spell works with watches."

"Our book contains a spell that, when spoken into an object, turns it into a portal. Then a separate spell is required to activate it."

"And yet another turns people into animals?" Seth asked.

Sir Markell and Lord Blaine nodded. "It's her way of

warning them," Lord Blaine said. "If someone fails her once, she turns them into a creature, but not fully. They can still function as a human and perform their usual duties for her. If they fail again, she puts them on trial."

"Trials which she orchestrates," Sir Markell said. "If she wants someone found guilty, they'll be found guilty."

"And executed." Lord Blaine shook his head. "We've lost good men that way."

Alice thought about the white rabbit—Sir Uther—afraid of failure, and the donkey in the dungeon who'd taken Alice's side. "We must save as many as we can before they face trial."

"The only way to do that is to take the castle and overthrow the queen," Sir Markell said.

"And the spell book?" David asked. "Where is that precisely?"

"Only the queen knows."

"And Lord Indrid," Lord Blaine bit off.

"Her most trusted advisor," Sir Markell clarified.

"And a traitor to his kingdom, a greedy sycophant, a slimy —" Lord Blaine cleared his throat. "Fellow."

"It's all right," Alice said. "You can call him a turd in my presence if that's what he is."

"Now that you have Alice, how difficult will it be to rally the renegades?" David asked. "Is there enough of you? When can you overthrow the queen?"

"Not today," Sir Markell said with a flicker of humor in his eyes. "And the revolution isn't scheduled for tomorrow, either."

"But we have to go home! Our mother is all alone."

"Lincoln will take care of her," Eva assured him. "But I agree, we do need to get home. I have studies to attend to, and my brother can't afford to be absent from his work for too long."

David buried his head in his hands and groaned.

The men and women who'd seen to the boat returned,

their footfalls almost silent. They helped themselves to the broth in the pot and sat on the log or the forest floor. They took great interest in Alice, and she suddenly wished she still wore her dress. She felt conspicuous in the tunic and hose, not to mention indecent without her corset.

"How many renegades are there?" she asked.

"Hard to say," Sir Markell said. "We act in cells, with very little information passing between us. That way, if one cell is discovered, they can't reveal too much about the others."

"My guess is hundreds are active," Lord Blaine said. "Thousands more across the realm support us in minor ways, such as hiding us or offering shelter as we pass through. The queen is loathed, but she's also feared, and fear stops many people from doing what they know to be right."

Sir Markell swallowed heavily. He must feel awful about his father.

"Now that you have returned safely to us, Highness, many more will join our cause," Lord Blaine went on.

Alice's heart swelled. Then it dove. So many people had been working toward bringing her back to Wonderland, so many lives had been lost to the cause...how could she ever make it right? How could she, an ordinary girl from Dorset, rule a country? She knew nothing about politics, or economics, or law. She knew nothing about this realm. She didn't even know what gods they worshipped.

"Alice might not want to stay here," Seth said.

Some of the renegades looked as if they wanted to throw their cups at him or draw their swords. But Alice could only give him a fond smile. He knew her well enough to guess that she was struggling with the notion of becoming a queen.

"We are aware of that," Lord Blaine snapped.

"We'll help you, Alice," Sir Markell said gently. "We'll teach you about our ways and advise you until you're able to make decisions alone."

"Thank you," she said. "I appreciate it. I really do. But Seth's right. I…I need time to think this through."

"You don't want to be queen?" Lord Blaine blurted out.

"She has time," Sir Markell told him. "Without the spell book, she can't go home, anyway."

Lord Blaine looked relieved. No doubt he had a vision of all his hard work coming undone, and all because the young princess was home sick.

They talked some more about the country and its people as the sun went down. Clouds and the trees blocked out the moon, and the only light came from the fires. The men and women cooked over one, working quietly together. Alice was hungry. Hungry and tired. It had been a long day.

Even so, she didn't retire when the others did. She sat alongside Sir Markell and stared into the dying embers, aware that she was being watched by Seth. She wondered what he'd do if she decided to stay in Wonderland. She wondered what she wanted him to do.

She'd worry about that later. They had to overthrow the queen before Alice even considered her future.

"I wanted to express how sorry I am about your father, Sir Markell," she said. "He seemed like a fine man, and I could see that he respected and loved you very much."

He shifted his weight, crossed his ankles then uncrossed them. "Please call me Markell."

She said nothing, hoping to draw more out of him. The tactic worked.

"He never told me he was proud of me until today. He was an absent father, in all interpretations of that word." He drew a deep breath. "I think he knew I would betray the queen. I think he knew I would try to squirrel you away and expected to come to my assistance in the audience chamber."

"That's why he hid a knife in his boot." Alice touched his arm. "He fought bravely."

Markell's chest rose and fell. He touched his nose, his

brow, his ear, constantly fidgeting. Alice knew the signs of someone trying to hold back their emotions.

"I didn't want him to die," he said, voice gravely.

"Of course not."

"I knew deep down he didn't like the Queen of Hearts. I expected him to join us after today and help me put you on the throne."

"I'm sure he would have."

He looked at her. "You don't understand. I was counting on his men following him."

Alice's breath hitched. "A military coup."

"Having the army on side would be enough. She has her own personal guards, who are the best of the best, but the army outnumbers them ten to one. And as my father said today, some of those guards might choose to follow him rather than risk their lives for her. He's much loved by his men. *Was* much loved."

"And she is widely hated."

"But now… Now she'll install one of her favorites to lead the army, someone who'll be rewarded handsomely for their loyalty."

"And we have only a few hundred active renegades." She looked at the handful of tents rimming the clearing. This was the entire number of Markell's cell, and they had little hope of gathering the rest together to form any kind of army. "It's not enough is it?"

"It has to be."

She wanted to ask him what he'd do if she decided not to remain, but she didn't have the heart to disappoint him. He'd endured enough for one day.

"You've been remarkably calm," he said, seeming to shake off his melancholy. "Every time we've come for you, you've been composed. The only time you looked worried was when you were afraid for your friends."

"Composed on the outside, perhaps. I admit to feeling

immeasurably relieved when I saw your wink. I knew then that you had something planned and wouldn't hurt me."

"All that from a wink. If I'd known it held such power, I'd have winked more often." He winked again and she laughed.

"Even before it, I suspected I had nothing to fear from you," she said.

"Why?" he asked on a rush of breath.

She found herself caught by his emerald-green gaze as it focused completely on her. All humor had fled and he was back to being serious, thoughtful, intense. She felt as if she were drowning in his eyes and struggled to breathe. Tearing her gaze away saved her, but it wasn't easy. "I don't really know," was all she said.

"Tell me about your family in England. What are they like?"

"The couple who adopted me were kind when I was a child. But after my brother died…they changed. That's when I started having nightmares about the Queen of Hearts coming for me. Those nightmares became real, and they were afraid. They thought the devil possessed me. The last time I saw them, we did not part on good terms."

"So you won't want to go back for them?"

She narrowed her eyes. "Are you creating a tally of things that would keep me here versus things I'll want to return for?"

Markell grinned, and the breath left Alice's chest. His smile turned his face from run-of-the-mill handsome to dazzling. "So far the pro-Wonderland tally is winning," he said.

"Is that so? What is in the pro-Wonderland column?"

He winked. "That's a secret, but I can tell you he's handsome, clever and can sew a split seam faster than any seamstress."

"Please introduce me to this remarkable man. I cannot wait to meet him." She laughed. God, it felt good to laugh.

Markell reminded her of Seth, in a way. Or rather, the way Seth was with other women—charming, confident, and above all, himself. Seth had never quite relaxed enough around Alice. That's where he and Markell differed.

Out of the corner of her eye, she saw the tent flap move. How much had Seth seen and heard? And how did it make him feel to see Markell flirt with her?

"In all seriousness," Markell said quietly, "I know you have very good friends in England. That small woman, for one."

"Charlie is my dearest friend, but she is only one person."

He glanced at Seth's tent but said nothing.

Alice yawned. "Markell, tell me about my parents."

"I know very little about them. I was young when they died and had met them only rarely. They say you look a lot like your mother, but I'm afraid I can't remember her features well. She was liked by those who knew her. Your father was respected as a king, but his reign was plagued by his mad sister's desire for the crown."

It was difficult to reconcile these people as her parents. She'd wondered for so long about them, but now it felt like she was hearing about two strangers. It wasn't right. She ought to *feel* something for them.

"It must have hurt them deeply to send me away," she said, almost to herself.

"By all accounts, it did. Your baby brother, too, after he was born."

"Myron," she whispered, tears pooling in her eyes. "He died so young."

"I know." He went to place his hand over hers but hesitated.

So she clasped his instead. His fingers curled around hers, the gesture comforting and, in some way, a link to the past and the people she only remembered in her dreams.

* * *

THEY AWOKE with the birds at dawn, and after a quick breakfast of leftovers, they packed up their tents. Lord Blaine asked Alice not to help when she set to work, but she assured him she was capable. She *wanted* to help. Waiting would not only bore her to death, it would be somewhat embarrassing. They were doing this for her. The least she could do was contribute.

"You had a long discussion with Ironside last night," Seth said as he helped her roll up the tent.

"We have a lot to discuss. We hardly scratched the surface of things I need to know."

He stopped rolling and sat back on his haunches. "You've already decided to stay?"

"Not yet. It would be foolish to make up my mind after being here less than twenty-four hours. But I can't dismiss it so quickly, either."

"You would abandon Charlie?"

"Charlie doesn't need me. She has Lincoln. I would miss her, though."

He resumed rolling. "What about the rest of us? Would you miss us too?"

"Of course. But I suspect none of you need me either."

"What makes you say that?" He didn't look at her. Because he couldn't? Or wouldn't?

"I just know."

"Lucky you," he muttered.

They finished rolling the tent and tied it together with the strips of leather. Seth took the bulky tent while Alice reached for the pack containing her dress, corset and petticoat. She went to join the others dousing the fire but Seth caught her arm.

"We may not need you," he said quietly, "but we do want you. Err, I mean, we want you around, as a friend. Or…or something more. If that's…on offer."

"Is that what you want, Seth? Something more than friendship between us?"

"I...I suppose."

"Supposing isn't enough. Just because everyone expects us to fall in love doesn't mean we should."

"So...you're not in love with me?"

She thought about it so long that Seth began to look worried. He couldn't stand still, shuffling his feet, looking at her then away, adjusting the weight of the tent in his arms. He was so like Markell when he was nervous, it was somewhat alarming. "I could love the man I sometimes saw in you."

His brows crashed together. "I don't understand."

"You never showed that man to me, Seth. He was always there with others—Charlie, Lincoln, Gus—but never in my presence. The only man I ever saw was a stiff, formal, dry gentleman."

"You find me dull," he said flatly.

"I didn't say that."

"Stiff, formal and dry imply excitement in your vocabulary?"

"You're not being fair," she said hotly.

"And you are?"

She huffed out a breath. "Seth, I don't want to discuss this with you right now. I have a lot on my plate, and my nerves are on edge. I don't want to say something I regret. Let's say I like you very much at this point, but I don't know if it's love."

"Fine. That's exactly how I feel too."

She watched him stride off to join Gus, unsure if he was being honest with her or simply unwilling to admit he had feelings for her. Charlie would say that Seth wasn't like most men and wasn't proud, but Charlie knew a lot more about Seth than Alice did. Although Alice knew Seth had once been a pugilist, she suspected there was much more to his past, and Charlie was privileged to that information. Alice doubted she ever would be.

That was entirely the problem.

* * *

"WHAT DID you two talk about earlier?" Eva asked Alice with a nod at Seth up ahead. They walked side by side on the forest path, following Markell and his small crew of renegades. Markell had told them it would take all day to reach their next stop, a sympathizer's house where they would be kept safe while they plotted their revolution.

"Love and friendship," Alice said, not wanting to divulge too much.

Eva looked disappointed with the answer. "I hope he doesn't sulk all day."

"Gus is trying to cheer him up." As Alice spoke, Gus shoved Seth hard in the arm. Seth lost his balance but managed to stop himself falling.

"Or perhaps he's trying to kill him," Eva said.

"Or knock some sense into him."

Eva looked at Alice. "Do you think he needs sense knocked into him?" she asked.

Alice lifted one shoulder, adjusting the weight of her pack. Despite containing very little, it was beginning to feel heavy. Not that she would tell anyone. Lord Blaine would insist someone else carry it, and Alice couldn't have that. If she was to rule these people, she needed to show strength. "He's a man. Of course he needs sense knocked into him."

Eva laughed. Seth glanced over his shoulder and Alice saw a ghost of a smile touch his lips. Good. He wasn't feeling too miserable then. It lightened her own mood a little.

"If I decide to stay here," Alice said carefully, "will you be a good friend to Charlie for me? She has Lincoln, but she needs female companionship. Someone other than Harriet Gillingham."

"You don't like Lady Gillingham?" Eva asked.

"She's an odd character, to put it mildly."

Eva laughed again. "Very well. I'll be a good friend to

Charlie. I already like her. She's very kind and sweet, and she manages Lincoln extremely well. I rather think she's a saint."

Alice grinned. "Imagine what it was like when those two first met. It would have been a clash of wills."

"She's fierce and courageous."

Alice sighed. "I wish I had half her courage."

Eva glanced at her. "Are you scared?"

"Very."

"No one would know. You hide it well."

"I'm not the only one. You don't seem all that afraid and yet you're in a far-off land too, with the threat of imprisonment and death hanging over your head—as well as your brother's. If you're at all afraid, you're a better actress than I am."

Eva didn't speak, and Alice thought she'd offended her, though she didn't know how. She'd thought their conversation over when Eva finally spoke.

"I'll let you in on a secret," she said. "I know I survive this place. I have seen my future, and it's after this."

"You mean you knew you'd come here?"

"My mother did. I only saw what comes later."

"That's why she left you that note to come to Lichfield! She knew you'd follow us through the portal and wind up here." Alice didn't think it was a very maternal thing, to send your child to another realm, but she didn't say so. Eva seemed unconcerned. Indeed, she seemed to accept her fate. "I thought the events you see in your visions aren't necessarily inevitable? I thought they were one possibility and that we have the power to change them. Is that not true?"

"It's true. As my mother would say, the future is not yet written."

"Have you ever known your mother's visions not to come to pass?"

"No."

Eva's gaze connected with Alice's. Alice felt a chill run

down her spine. Imagine knowing the future. Imagine knowing who around you lived and died. She knew Eva's visions weren't as powerful as her mother's, but clearly her mother confided in her daughter.

"What about the rest of us?" Alice asked. "Did she see our fates too? Or did you?"

Eva focused ahead. "Only one."

"Your brother," Alice said, nodding. It made sense that Leisl would know the fates of her two children. She had to admit to a measure of relief. She didn't want to know if her life was to be cut short here in Wonderland.

A soft thud was all the warning Alice got. The next thing she knew, a gloved hand covered her mouth and cold metal pressed to her throat.

"Alice!" Eva screamed.

Figures dressed in white dropped from the trees on both sides of the path, blades drawn. Seth, Gus and Markell whipped around, swords ready, and engaged. The other renegades pulled out knives and crossbows, but at least two weren't fast enough. They fell to the ground and bled into the soil.

Eva and David huddled together, surrounded by fighting. David held a sword but he didn't look as if he knew what to do with it. Eva wasn't armed. Nor was Alice. That was a mistake, Alice realized as she was dragged away, the blade at her throat. A very big mistake.

CHAPTER 6

EVA

Eva wouldn't die here. She knew that from her vision. It didn't mean she wasn't scared witless. She couldn't be as certain about her friends' lives as she was about her own. And then there was David.

His back pressed against hers. "We have to get out of here," he said, voice trembling. "Run into the bushes—"

"We can't leave the others!"

Since David and Eva didn't engage, none of the guards targeted them. So far, Seth, Gus, Markell and the renegades kept the attackers occupied, but Alice was being dragged off. Her feet scrabbled on the ground, trying to gain purchase, and her hands pulled on the guard's arm, wrapped around her waist. Her huge eyes darted toward Seth and Markell.

Both men slashed at their opponents with deadly precision. The guards fell one by one, yet another always took their place. They wouldn't get to Alice in time.

"She needs help!" Eva quickly checked the nearby guards to make sure they weren't bothering with her then ran after Alice.

"Eva! What are you doing?" he cried.

Eva pushed through the bushes, shoving low hanging

branches aside. Her skirt tangled around her legs and snagged on twigs. Damned thing. Not to mention the restriction of her tightly laced corset made it hard to breathe. Alice had left a trail to follow in the dirt with her heels but no sounds came from up ahead. Behind Eva, the clang of clashing metal and the grunts continued. She glanced back but David hadn't followed her.

She ran as fast as the terrain and her clothing allowed. The sounds of fighting retreated and she focused her seer's senses forward. There. The rustle of leaves, a muffled cry, and an awareness of Alice. They weren't far away.

She slowed her pace and tried to avoid anything that would alert the guard to her presence. She crept on her toes, dodging twigs and carefully parting branches. Up ahead, a flash of metal and a harsh guttural growl.

"Stay still!" the guard growled.

Eva watched through the leaves as the guard dragged Alice across a small clearing. He no longer held a knife to her throat but he'd pinned her arms to her sides and his other hand covered her mouth. She wriggled and tried to stomp on his feet. Their pace slowed as she made it increasingly difficult for the guard.

Eva tried to reach her seer's sense back toward the main fight but failed. However, nor could she hear anyone following. She watched as Alice's kidnapper dragged her into the forest.

Eva couldn't defeat him, and as soon as she revealed herself, he might hurt Alice or even kill her. The queen had been going to execute her anyway, after putting her through a trial, so there'd be no real need to keep her alive.

That settled it. Eva had to act.

Instead of following them, she veered off. Despite her skirts, she maintained a good pace, faster than Alice and the guard. She picked up a thick stick along the way and, using a combination of her seer's sense and her own estimations, cut off their path.

With his back to the way he was heading, the guard didn't see her. She smashed the stick into the back of his head as hard as she could.

He crumpled to the ground without a sound. Blood dampened the hair at the nape of his neck.

Eva's heart dropped. She was supposed to save lives and help the injured.

"Eva! Thank God." Alice clutched her tightly. "Thank you." She followed Eva's gaze. "Is he…?"

Eva crouched and checked the pulse at the guard's throat. She felt a strong beat. Her eyes fluttered closed and she cast up a prayer. "He should live."

"Then let's go before he wakes up."

Eva accepted Alice's hand and allowed herself to be led back through the forest, following the track gouged out of the earth by Alice's heels. Her head felt full of wool and she tripped over her own feet twice.

What was wrong with her? She hadn't killed the guard and she'd saved Alice. She ought to be pleased. She *was* pleased to have saved her friend.

She cast a long look over her shoulder and tripped again. Alice stopped and clasped Eva's shoulders. "I know this has upset you," she said. "But it was him or me, and I'm glad you were here to save me. Very glad." She took Eva's hand again. "Now, come on."

Leaves rustled and twigs snapped. Someone up ahead didn't care about staying silent as they thrashed through the forest, heading toward Eva and Alice. Fear snapped Eva out of her stupor. She darted behind a large tree and Alice took a position behind another.

"Alice! Eva!" The voice belonged to Gus.

Eva almost wept in relief. "Here," she said, emerging at the same time as Alice.

Gus's scarred face split with his grin. "Found them!" he shouted then pulled Alice into a hug.

Seth joined them from one direction and Markell from another. Eva watched Seth closely as his gaze took in Alice's appearance. She expected him to embrace Alice, as Gus had done, but he merely adjusted his grip on his sword and turned to Eva.

"You're all right?" he asked.

She nodded then found herself enclosed in Gus's arms. "Bloody hell, you gave us a scare," he mumbled into her hair. "Both of you."

"Are you harmed?" Markell asked Alice as his gaze tracked a similar path as Seth's, only it lingered on Alice and didn't switch to Eva.

"We're both fine, thank you," Alice said, smiling.

"Why did you charge off like that?" David asked Eva. He'd joined them, along with the rest of the renegades, who all looked relieved to see Alice unharmed. "You could have been killed."

"I could have been killed where I stood," she shot back. "And Alice was in trouble."

"I would have gone after her if I'd seen which direction she went in. But I had my back turned."

Eva sighed. She didn't blame David for staying put. He wasn't trained in swordsmanship like Seth and Gus, nor was he a seer like Eva. Nor could she reassure him and tell him his fate wasn't to die here in Wonderland.

"It's all right, David," she said gently. "I knew I'd be fine, that's why I went."

His brows angled into a severe frown. "You can't know for sure. Mother is always telling you that visions aren't set in stone."

She cocked her head to the side and raised her brows. "Name a single vision of mine or hers that hasn't come true."

"Eva," he warned. "Promise me you'll be more careful in

the future. I'd like both of us to get out of this hell in one piece."

Eva sighed and turned away, only to see several pairs of eyes on her. Did she have dirt smudged on her nose? She wiped it just to make sure.

Alice looped her arm around Eva's. "I was just telling them how marvelous you were, Eva. I didn't see or hear you approach."

"I used my seer's senses to guide me," Eva said.

Several gasps echoed around the clearing.

"Seer?" Lord Blaine said. "You know the future?"

"Not really."

"Some of it?"

"No," David snapped. "She doesn't see anything."

"But she just said—"

"It doesn't matter what she said. I'm telling you that she can't see anything."

Lord Blaine's back stiffened and his whiskers twitched. "Do not speak to me in such a manner."

"Why not? You might be an important man to those people, but you're not to us. To us, you're just a heathen from a Godforsaken country—"

"David!" Eva cried. "Stop at once."

"We have gods," Lord Blaine sneered. "And they have not forsaken us. They have delivered our rightful queen to us, and they will help us put her on the throne."

David opened his mouth but Eva growled, "Don't," and he closed it again.

She pulled him away, out of earshot. Then she rounded on him. "Do not insult these people."

"Why not? What does it matter? Are we even sure they're human?"

She stared at him, unsure what to think anymore. David had never been the easiest person to get along with, but he'd never been outwardly rude to strangers. "Have you gone mad? Of course they're human."

"How do you even know?" He kicked a clump of dirt and leaves. "They're the reason we're in this predicament. If they hadn't come for Alice, we'd be at home, safe. Instead, we're hiding in forests and living in tents, scared for our lives."

"We are in a predicament, that's true, but turning on the people who can save us is not going to help." She was so cross she could hear the hiss in her voice and feel the pent up anger heating her blood.

The others filed off through the forest, back the way they'd come. Seth, the last to go, jerked his head at Eva to urge her to keep up. She nodded and attempted a smile. His lips flattened.

"This is absurd," David whispered.

"Which part?" Seth asked.

"This entire situation. These people are absurd. Look at them, in their ridiculous clothes, fawning over Alice."

"She is their long lost princess," Seth said, as if David was the absurd one. "Of course they're going to treat her with deference."

David snorted. "I would have thought you'd be jealous of all the attention she's receiving, especially from the so-called advisor."

"Do be quiet, David," Eva said with a sigh. "Leave Seth alone. He at least fought bravely today, yet has he pointed out that you didn't help? No, he has not. So I suggest you keep your cruel remarks to yourself."

"I wasn't being cruel," David muttered under his breath. "I was just saying that Markell and Alice seem to be getting on very well together." His chin jutted in the direction of the couple ahead of them. Markell lifted a low hanging branch out of the way and smiled at Alice as she passed him.

Eva glanced sideways at Seth. He watched the couple from beneath heavily lidded eyes.

"I'd be careful what you say if I were you," Seth said darkly.

David flinched, and Eva had to admit the tone made her feel somewhat nauseated, but for a different reason than her brother. He seemed to think Seth was threatening him. Yet it was the way Seth looked at Alice and Markell that worried Eva.

They rejoined their original path where they'd been intercepted by the guards. Several lay dead, their blood seeping into their pristine white uniforms and the leaf matter. Eva could tell by looking at them that there were no survivors. She picked her way past the bodies and drew in a deep breath of fresh air once they were behind her. She hadn't realized she'd stopped breathing until her chest tightened.

Seth touched her arm. "Are you all right?"

She nodded. "I see dead bodies all the time, but not usually by my own hand or that of my friends."

"I don't like this either." He studied his bloodied sword blade then stopped to wipe it on the ground. "I'm not used to it."

"You're not? But I thought your line of work necessitated it."

"Not at all. Lincoln isn't a killer, no matter what people think."

"I...I don't know what to think anymore."

"That's not to say I haven't killed before today, but I assure you it's only ever been in self-defense." He glanced back at David, who'd melted away to the rear of the convoy. "Don't be hard on him. Not every man is comfortable with weapons, and not every man wants to fight. Besides," he winked, "he didn't faint, or cry, or wet himself. That qualifies as a brave first encounter with a cohort of highly trained swordsmen."

She smiled. "Did you faint, or cry, or wet yourself the first time you were in a fight?"

"All three. Of course, I was only five and the fighters were the imaginary vagabonds I'd created to keep myself amused."

"That poor little boy. Now I feel sorry for you and your lonely upbringing."

"Don't be too sympathetic. I had far more than most children, until…well, until it was gone."

Charlie had told her how Seth's father squandered the family fortune. He lost everything, and then his mother left too when she remarried, only returning from America after her second husband died. It couldn't have been easy for him to have money, status, and the respect of his peers, and then lose it all. Charlie said he'd paid off his family debts using every means at his disposal, but she hadn't elaborated on what those means were. Indeed, Charlie wouldn't look Eva in the eye when Eva asked.

"I know that look," he said quietly. "I know Charlie told you some things about my past."

"No! No she didn't. I mean, a little but not much. Hardly anything really."

His laugh was self-conscious. "Well that wasn't awkward."

She bit the inside of her lip. She'd dredged up unhappy memories for him, and for that, she wished she could undo the conversation. "Charlie didn't speak out of turn. She admires you. She's very fond of you."

"And I'm fond of her. She's going to be my second wife, if I outlive Lincoln."

She burst out laughing, attracting Alice's attention. She frowned and only looked forward again when Markell spoke to her.

"Charlie doesn't know it yet," Seth said. "Don't tell her. I want it to be a surprise."

"I think you should be more worried about Lincoln finding out."

"I did say *after* he's gone. Besides, he should be grateful that I'll take care of her. Although the man has the devil's luck. He'll probably outlive us all."

"You have a macabre way of thinking."

"It comes with being friends with a necromancer."

Eva laughed again, feeling somewhat giddy and bold. Very bold. "You said *second* wife," she hedged. "What of your first?"

"Naturally she'll be the love of my life but Charlie will understand completely, since she has a deeply profound love for Lincoln."

Eva's breath left her body and the giddiness worsened. She couldn't quite think.

"Eva? You've gone pale." He put his hand to her lower back. "Are you all right? Are you sure you weren't injured back there?"

"I…I'm fine."

"I'll get some water." He moved off, pushing past Alice to reach the women near the front. He returned with a leather flask.

She drank and handed it back. Their fingers brushed and a wash of tingles rushed up her arm, across her scalp. He did not react at all, except for a benign smile that he could have tossed out to anyone.

"Better?" he asked.

She nodded.

He waited then said, "You seem to have lost your tongue, so I'll have to carry the conversation to pass the time. I've got a good topic. What do you think of trousers for women?" He nodded at Alice in front of them, still talking in quiet earnest with Markell. While her derriere was hidden by the tunic, the shape of her thighs was unmistakable. Clearly Seth had noticed.

Eva swallowed and looked away, unable to meet his gaze. Or, rather, not wanting to see in which direction his gaze lingered.

"I think trousers for women are a good idea. I know, I know," he went on, "the notion will never catch on in England, and I'd be resoundingly chastised for endorsing it. Why do women have to wear dresses anyway? Why can't they wear trousers? It could open up a whole host of new opportunities. They could ride astride, for one thing. I've known many women who could ride exceptionally well side saddle but not fast enough because they weren't allowed to wear trousers and ride astride like the men. Women could work outside more often without worrying about a strong wind revealing too much ankle. Who knows, perhaps they could then work on building sites or as gardeners."

He had very liberal ideas for a gentleman. In Eva's opinion, men from the upper classes were usually the ones who thought women incapable of doing men's work. Perhaps that was because their women—genteel ladies—never had to work at all. Seth's circumstances were different, however. He'd been brought low, and that could explain his egalitarian ideals.

"I mean, you only have to look at Alice to see how freeing wearing trousers is for her." He openly stared at Alice with her tall, elegant figure and blonde hair that now fell down her back in pretty waves. She was striking in her tunic and hose, even more so than usual. "I see I haven't shocked you into speaking yet," he went on, his lips quirked up at the corners.

Eva decided it was time to talk to someone else. Someone not in love with Alice Everheart.

She slowed her pace to fall back in line with David and Gus, but Seth slowed too. He frowned at her, all seriousness.

"You're upset with me," he said. "And I don't think it's because I'm an advocate for women wearing trousers."

She almost choked. How could he be so perceptive? "I'm not upset with you."

"You are, and I think I know why."

He couldn't possibly know. *She* was the seer, not him. "Is that right? Go on then, tell me."

"You're upset that I'm admiring Alice."

He was far too perceptive for his own good—or for hers. Her face heated so much it felt as if it would pop right off with the pressure. "Don't be absurd. I am not upset with you, Seth, nor would I be because of Alice. I like her. She's a wonderful person and very beautiful, so it's natural for a man like you to admire her. I'd be surprised if you didn't, considering you are, er..."

"I'm what?"

"An admirer of hers," she blurted out.

He frowned. "Why do you say that?" he said carefully.

"I can tell these things."

"Because you're a seer?"

Because I'm a woman who admires you, she wanted to admit but did not. Dared not. She didn't want to get her heart broken.

Indeed, she wasn't even sure when her heart had become so fragile where Seth was concerned. She'd been fighting a bundle of mixed feelings for him for so long that she'd almost convinced herself that she despised him.

But she certainly didn't. She could never despise him.

And she could never be anything like the woman he wanted. Her vision must be wrong.

Eva blinked rapidly down at her feet.

"Eva," he soothed. "I know you know something, so please tell me what it is."

She shook her head. "Leave me be."

They walked on a few paces, and she wondered how she could fall back and not have him follow her again.

"It's not healthy to keep secrets," he quipped. How nice that her discomfort and embarrassment was a source of amusement for him.

"Is that so?" she said through a tight smile. "Then you ought to be a very sick man by now."

He stopped dead. She kept walking even though her legs suddenly felt too weak to hold her. How could she be so cruel?

"What does that mean?" he asked, catching up.

"I…I don't know. I'm sorry, Seth. Forget I said anything."

"I'm not sure I can."

She expected him to drop back and join the others, but he kept pace with her. Why couldn't he leave her alone to wallow in self-pity? Why did he have to be so…nice?

The silence stretched so thin, it was inevitable it would break. She wasn't surprised that he was the one to break it. He didn't have the bottle for the silent treatment.

"Say something, Eva. I don't want things to be awkward between us. It's not like we can avoid one another here."

"There's nothing to say. I shouldn't have spoken out of turn, and I'm sorry. The end." She quickened her pace.

He had no trouble keeping up, with those long legs of his. "Not the end. We both have secrets we'd rather didn't become public."

She couldn't look at him. Didn't dare.

"You say you don't know what mine are," he went on.

"I don't. Charlie, Lincoln and Gus wouldn't betray your confidence, and I can't see your past. I am just aware that you keep secrets."

"As do you. But I know yours."

She jerked around to face him, her heart in her throat. He smiled back at her. Smiled!

"Don't fret, Eva. I don't care that you're really studying to be a doctor, not a nurse. I think it's marvelous, in fact. I know it's easy for me to say this, but you shouldn't worry about what other people think, even when those other people are your mother and brother."

She swallowed. A thousand words tumbled through her

brain but in the end, she almost laughed. He thought *that* was her worst secret? Thank God he hadn't guessed the other. It would be more humiliation than she could bear at this point. He might like her enough to be friends with her, but knowing their marriage was an inevitability could destroy that.

Eva certainly didn't want to ruin the connection between them. Not now that her feelings for him had begun to bloom.

CHAPTER 7

ALICE

Alice was so relieved to rest her sore feet that she didn't care that her host and his sister were rude. The renegade party arrived at the home of Lord Quellery after dark and unannounced, so perhaps their rudeness could be forgiven. Markell had asked for a bath to be drawn for Alice, but the sour turn of Lady Oxana's mouth put a dampener on that lovely notion.

"It's quite all right," Alice told their hostess as they sat in a large parlor with their host, Lord Quellery, as well as Lord Blaine, Markell, Seth, Eva, Gus and David. "I only need a basin and some water. Eva too, and the others in our party, if they wish."

Even this request had Lady Oxana rolling her eyes. "All of them? Surely your servants won't mind staying as they are. They'll be housed in the stables, after all, and there's no need for them to smell sweet in there."

Alice was so taken aback, she couldn't think of a retort fast enough. Markell and Seth, however, knew precisely how to handle her.

"The princess appreciates you accommodating us at such short notice," Markell said smoothly. "We've placed a great burden on you and my good Lord Quellery, and we don't wish to add to it."

A sound between a grunt and a groan rose from deep within Lord Quellery's massive frame. "Nicely put, Ironside," he said in a booming voice that set his jowls wobbling as if they had a life of their own. "You're more of a diplomat than your father. You're like your mother, may the goddesses keep her soul in peace."

Markell smiled evenly. "However, we have traveled a great distance under trying circumstances and are in sore need of refreshments and rest. We are grateful for whatever hospitality you can provide, but Her Highness must be treated with the respect she deserves."

"Of course, of course," Lord Quellery grumbled. He lifted a stubby finger and his manservant bowed out to see to the arrangements. Alice wasn't sure if she was getting a bath or not.

Seth cleared his throat and addressed Lady Oxana. "Gus and I are happy smelling of horse and forest."

"Speak for yourself," Gus declared.

"The only problem is, I'm worried it would offend such grand personages as yourselves." He offered Lady Oxana a small bow and one of his winning smiles.

Lady Oxana didn't stand a chance. Alice could see the moment her frostiness melted away. Her features lost some of their sharpness and the lines around her mouth ironed out. "And you are?"

"Seth is known as Lord Vickers in our realm," Alice said before he could answer.

"Among other things," Gus muttered.

"His family is very important," Alice added, trying to ignore Gus.

Lady Oxana's eyes flared. She gave Seth an inspection so thorough that Alice felt her own face heat. She didn't know how he managed not to blush. When Lord Quellery spoke to his sister, and she turned her attention to him, Seth shot a glare at Alice. She gave him an apologetic shrug. She hadn't expected the prickly Lady Oxana to fall for his charms so easily.

Markell had warned Alice on the way to Quellery Castle that his lordship and his sister were pompous prigs. They were both in their forties and had never married. They'd lived in the ancient fortified castle their entire lives and were Wonderland's wealthiest family after the queen. They even had their own private army.

The army was the reason Markell had brought them to Quellery Castle. He knew Lord Quellery disliked the Queen of Hearts and her high land taxes enough to want her overthrown. Markell didn't think they particularly cared who overthrew her, but since Alice's heritage made her the best candidate and the public's favorite, they'd give her their army. The three-hundred strong force weren't as well trained as the guards or the queen's army, or as numerous, but with the right strategy, Markell thought they could prevail.

They just needed Quellery's agreement.

Alice hated scraping to these kind of people, but she would have to get used to it if she was to become queen. She'd thought long and hard about her future on the journey and had made up her mind. Then she changed it. And changed it again.

So many people had lost their lives to put her on the throne that she had to end their hopes now if she wanted to prevent more. But that would jeopardize them anyway, putting them at the queen's mercy, a commodity she didn't have.

Markell had been terribly kind and not rushed Alice. He'd assured her that he would support any decision she made and adjust his plans accordingly. She believed him. The man could be very persuasive.

Lord Quellery rocked himself out of his chair and

approached Alice with a rolling gait as if his legs pained him. He attempted a bow but it was more of a nod. "You're very welcome here, Your Highness. Rest assured, you'll want for nothing during your stay." Lady Oxana's nostrils flared. "You must be tired," he went on. "Allow my sister to show you to your room." He put out his hand and Alice took it. Her fingers seemed so long against his stubby ones.

"Clothing will be brought in." Lady Oxana led Alice and Eva away while the men followed a manservant. Alice could hear their footsteps on the stone floor long after they were gone.

The castle was like something out of a museum with its narrow winding staircase and large tapestries attempting to soften stone walls. Despite the warmth of the day, it was chilly but no fires were lit. Alice shivered.

"You're cold," Lady Oxana noted as she led them through a small parlor and an even smaller room furnished with a single uncomfortable looking chair by the window.

"A little," Alice said.

"I'm afraid my brother doesn't allow fires to be lit in the summertime unless it's required for cooking. I suggest you seek out the kitchen if you want to warm up."

"Is it possible to borrow a shawl?"

Lady Oxana didn't answer immediately. She pushed open a thick door and folded her arms. "Your room, highness. You're next door," she said to Eva.

"Next door?" Eva echoed. "Oh. I assumed we'd be sharing."

"Why would you assume that? She's a princess. You're... what did you say your title is?"

"It's Miss Eva Cornell."

Lady Oxana's eyes tightened. "A maid?"

"My friend," Alice said, trying to keep the tartness from her voice. "The bed in here looks big enough. We'll share."

"But you're the princess."

"Even so, I'd like to be near my friend."

"I'd prefer it too," Eva said.

"If you wish," Lady Oxana said. "Clean water, clothes, and supper will be brought up to you. We've already dined but the cook will manage something."

"We are sorry to put you to such an inconvenience," Alice said. "If Sir Markell had been able to get word to you of our pending arrival, I'm sure he would have."

Lady Oxana's mouth stretched into a smile. She backed out of the room but stopped. She nibbled her lower lip, looking every bit like a nervous subject in front of her princess. Alice steeled herself for the request, expecting Oxana to ask her for a favor after she became queen. She wasn't prepared for the question that came.

"Is Lord Vickers your intended?"

"No," Alice said on a laugh.

"So he's free?"

Alice looked to Eva. Eva busied herself with unbuttoning her cuffs. "As far as I know," Alice said.

The predatory smile that crept across Lady Oxana's face gave Alice pause. Perhaps she should have given a different answer. Then again, Seth could handle the likes of this woman. He had, after all, been with Lady Harcourt.

"She's as stiff as a board," Alice said, once they were alone.

"And as tart as a lemon." Eva pinched her lips together in a very accurate impersonation.

Alice collapsed on the bed, laughing. Eva plopped down alongside her and they both stared up at the canopy. It was carved with chubby faces baring jagged teeth and forked tongues.

"How are we supposed to sleep with those looking down on us?" Eva asked.

"Thank goodness you agreed to stay with me in here. Those are enough to give me nightmares, and we all know how they end."

Eva laughed and rolled onto her side, facing Alice. "Do you think they'd give me an outfit like yours?"

"You can ask." Alice sat up and removed her tunic. She wore only a shirt with the bodice over the top, as well as the hose. She undid the bodice's laces. "This is so much lighter and freer than a corset, and it's no trouble to get on and off by myself."

Eva rolled back and sighed. "Perhaps I shouldn't ask for one. It'll only make me yearn for it again when I have to go back to England and my regular clothes. Speaking of going back, what are you going to do? Have you decided to stay?"

Alice flopped back down again and blew out a breath. "I don't know. I'm torn. There's nothing for me there and so much for me here, but…this doesn't feel like home."

"It will, in time."

"And the situation here is perilous."

"Once the queen is overthrown, all will calm down and you'll have Markell to guide you. You'd make a wonderful ruler, Alice. I mean that. You're always thinking of others, and you have a sort of queenly bearing about you that people naturally look up to."

Alice was taken aback. "Thank you. But…you sound like you want me to stay."

"I want you to make up your own mind."

Alice nudged Eva's elbow. "Does this have anything to do with Seth being free?"

"No!" Eva spat out the word with such velocity that Alice suspected it had everything to do with Seth.

"You make an excellent couple," Alice said.

Eva scooted off the bed and peered out the window. "I don't want to talk to you about Seth."

"Because you think I still like him?" Alice asked gently.

"Because I think he still likes you." Eva folded her arms and rubbed them.

"There's nothing between Seth and I, and there never will be. I know my heart on that score, at least."

"I don't want to be his second choice."

Alice touched Eva's shoulder. "I think you overstate my importance to him."

A knock on the door announced the arrival of maids carrying basins, jugs of water, towels, clean clothes, and a tray of food. Alice forgot about Seth and ate. She was starving. Eva chose to freshen up first then changed into a gown similar to the one Lady Oxana wore. It was all one piece to the floor in forest green with long bell shaped sleeves. A belt in the same fabric with a large circular metal buckle cinched the waist.

"That's very fetching on you," Alice said. "The color reminds me of Markell's eyes." It was out of her mouth before she realized what she was saying. Hopefully Eva wouldn't think it odd.

Eva didn't think it odd. She thought it highly amusing, going by her grin. "So his eyes are green, are they?"

"Of course, and don't tell me you hadn't noticed." Alice busied herself with undressing so she didn't have to meet Eva's knowing gaze.

"I hadn't noticed, as it happens." Eva sat down at the small table by the window to eat her supper, humming to herself. "I'll tell you what I have noticed about your advisor, Your Highness."

"Do stop calling me that. I always feel as though you're teasing me."

Eva put up her hand. "Very well, *Alice*, stop changing the subject."

Alice pretended to ignore her. She really didn't want to hear what Eva had to say, and perhaps ignoring her would make her stop. She was wrong.

"I've noticed how he looks at you." Eva popped a cherry

into her mouth, her eyes sparkling in the candlelight. "Go on, ask me how he looks at you."

"No."

"You want to know." Eva spat out the pip. "Or perhaps you've already seen?"

Alice had seen. Seen and liked it. But... "It's no different to how other men look at me."

That shut Eva up. She ate another cherry in thoughtful silence.

Alice washed then put on the dress. Once the belt was in place, it cinched her waist nicely.

"Does it matter how he looks at you if there is true feeling behind it?" Eva finally asked.

"Of course it matters. I want to be admired for more than my face."

"I think he does. He thought you held your nerve when you were dragged off by that guard."

"He thought *you* even more remarkable for rescuing me. I'm afraid I'm simply the person who can get him what he wants, and what he wants is the queen gone. It helps that my face is pretty to rally the troops, but that's all."

Eva sighed. "You're far too hard on him, Alice, and on men in general. Sometimes they just want to admire you but not... kiss you. And some men are capable of seeing beyond a woman's appearance."

"Like Markell?" Alice shook her head. "He hardly knows me."

"Then don't dismiss him before giving him a chance."

"I'm not."

"Are you sure? That's not how it seems to me."

Alice stared at her. Is that what Eva really thought of her? That she dismissed all men as admirers of beauty but not of substance? It made her sound as if she didn't respect men when that wasn't the case at all. She truly believed Markell had only his realm's interests at heart. He was certainly a man of great substance himself, and pride and honor.

Whether he liked Alice for being herself, however, was not at all clear.

"I'm going for a walk," Alice announced. "I'm too restless to sleep."

"Are you sure that's wise? Lady Oxana looked as if she would flay us alive if she caught us outside these walls."

"I'm not afraid of her. She reminds me of Mrs. Denk, the headmistress at the School for Wayward Girls. She used to terrify me back then, but I suspect she wouldn't now."

It had been Charlie who'd shown her that Mrs. Denk wasn't deserving of her fear. Indeed, Charlie's influence in drawing out Alice's courage couldn't be overstated. It had happened so slowly while staying at Lichfield that Alice hadn't really noticed it until now. She used to do everything Mrs. Denk demanded, for fear of reprisal, and now here she was, prepared to defy Lady Oxana. Perhaps her courage had blossomed after finding out she was a princess. With that knowledge came a certain power.

"Don't wait up." Alice took a candle and the empty tray and headed back the way they'd come, hoping to find a maid to ask for directions to the kitchen. Perhaps there she could warm her fingers by the fire.

The soft leather shoes that had come with the dress made little sound on the stones. The castle wasn't silent, however. Male voices drifted to her but she couldn't make out the words, and somewhere someone sneezed. A door creaked and footsteps echoed.

The moonlight piercing through the windows bolstered the light from her candle so she had no trouble seeing where she was going. She found the winding staircase and descended to the ground floor where she assumed the kitchen would be situated. She was about to make her way to the back of the castle when she heard Markell's voice.

She approached the closed door and was about to open it when she heard Lord Quellery. "She's beautiful and elegant and all that, but she's also young. Is she up to it?"

Alice almost barged in to assure him she was capable as long as she had good advisors around her until she was ready to rule alone, but she held back. She wanted to hear what Markell said.

"She is," he said, "or I wouldn't have brought her to Wonderland. She's clever, a quick learner, and kind."

Alice's heart swelled.

Lord Quellery snorted. "Kindness isn't a requirement for a monarch. It's more of a hindrance, in fact."

"I beg to differ."

"You can beg all you want, Ironside. She might even like that."

"Don't, Quellery," Markell snarled. "Show some respect to your future queen."

Another snort. "I'll say what I bloody well want. I seem to recall you need my help."

Silence.

"So the next question is," Quellery went on, "who will be the lucky man to marry her and become king?"

"That's up to her, naturally."

"Don't be absurd. She should marry from the ruling classes. We can't let any old knave fondle the royal jewels."

Something slammed, perhaps a fist on a table. "Enough, Quellery!"

Quellery chuckled.

"She'll need time to settle into the role first and worry about marriage later," Markell said, calmer. "But it will still be her choice. It's in the royal charter that royal blood can choose their own consort."

"Yes, yes, we all know what the charter states, but you're not such a fool to think the monarch can marry just anyone. She'll need to choose wisely. The man needs to be a good leader, well respected, rich, with lands. Oh, and above all, he should come with an army to put her on the throne in the first place."

Alice's stomach lurched, threatening to toss up her supper. She almost barged in to tell him she could never marry him, but Markell was speaking again and she very much wanted to hear what he had to say. She had to strain to catch the words.

"Is the loan of your forces conditional on her marrying you?" Markell's voice was hard and unemotional, the consummate political negotiator. If he felt anything for her on a personal level, there was no sign of it in his voice.

"Yes."

Alice slumped and placed her forehead against the cool stone wall.

"She belongs to no man, as far as I know," Markell said. "But she's not the sort of woman who'll marry without love. Of that, I'm quite sure. I'll put your proposal forward and—"

"Don't be a brat. We both know you're her advisor, Ironside. So advise. Do your duty to your realm and its people and tell her she *must* marry me. If she does not, you will not have my army, the queen will remain where she is, and the princess's pretty head will do no one any good on the end of a spike where it shall rot in the sun along with the heads of her friends and yourself. Do I make myself clear?"

"Very."

Wood scraped against stone as a chair moved. Alice doused the candle's flame and sank into the shadows. Markell emerged and shut the door. He marched off. When it became obvious that Lord Quellery wasn't following, Alice caught up to him.

"Markell," she whispered, "slow down."

He stopped altogether. It was too dark to see his eyes but she felt his anger as clearly as she could feel the cool air from the drafts on her skin. "Alice," was all he said. He seemed dazed, unfocused, his thoughts elsewhere. Perhaps they were still in that room.

She knew something that would draw his attention. She sucked in a deep breath. "I listened in to your conversation with Quellery."

His gaze snapped to hers. "How much did you hear?"

"The last few minutes."

"I see. Come. We need to talk."

She followed him up the stairs, but instead of entering a bedchamber, he knocked on a door. Lord Blaine invited them in.

"Not here," Markell said. "We need to talk somewhere we can't be overheard."

Lord Blaine gathered up a cloak and handed it to Alice without a word. She set down the tray and candle on a table in the corridor then followed Markell and Lord Blaine down the stairs and outside. More than one servant saw them leave but Markell claimed it didn't matter.

"Quellery knows we're going to discuss this," he said. "He'll be disappointed he won't know what's said, but he knows there's nothing he can do about it."

"Discuss what?" Lord Blaine asked.

Markell didn't answer him until they were well away from the house in a part of the garden that sported no walls, hedges or bushes large enough to hide eavesdroppers. But when they stopped, he didn't explain. All he said was, "There has to be another way."

"Can you think of one?" Alice asked.

Markell paced briskly along the gravel path between the roses, hands on hips. "Not yet."

"What is it? What's happened?" Lord Blaine demanded.

When Markell continued his pacing without answering, Alice told him. "Lord Quellery will only give us his private army if I agree to marry him."

Lord Blaine swore under his breath. "He *promised* me the army."

"And he's giving it to you," Alice said. "On one condition."

"There has to be another way," Markell said again.

"We could buy the army off him," Lord Blaine said. "They're mercenaries. They'll go where the money is."

"How will we pay them?"

"I have lands. I can sell some." He cleared his throat. "You have lands of your own now, too, with your father's passing."

"My lands will have been confiscated by now, yours too probably. The queen will have guessed that you're with us." Markell dragged his hand through his hair, making it stand on end. "Damn it."

It was the most harried Alice had ever seen him. He'd been so confident and competent up until now, so sure of everything. She didn't like seeing him brought low.

He began pacing again, but this time she caught his arm. She forced him to face her. "All will be well, Markell. We just need to think." She wasn't sure why she said it; she just knew she wanted to reassure him, wanted to see that confidence again.

He managed a smile. "I'm the one who's supposed to be reassuring you."

She smiled back and reluctantly let him go, but not before their fingers brushed and something passed between them. Something that set Alice's pulse racing. The moon emerged from behind the clouds and she saw the spark in Markell's eyes and the wonder. It thrilled her and terrified her too.

"I should have known not to trust him," Lord Blaine said, oblivious to the emotions surging through Alice.

She couldn't quite believe that he didn't notice. She felt exposed, raw, as if she were running along Oxford Street in just her petticoat. She couldn't tell if Markell felt that way too. The moon had gone behind the clouds again and the shadows cast his handsome features in darkness once more.

"Markell? Are you listening?" Lord Blaine was saying.

Markell cleared his throat. "Yes."

"Did you see Quellery's face when you informed him about your father's death?"

"He gave nothing away."

"Precisely. No surprise at all. He knew about it. That's what I think, anyway."

"News must have already reached here," Markell said.

"Then why not tell us he already knew?" Lord Blaine had a point.

"You think he's playing both sides?" Markell asked. "Waiting to see which prevails so he can use that to his own advantage?"

"It wouldn't surprise me." It was Lord Blaine's turn to pace along the path now. "Quellery is greedy, and the queen's taxes are high. Make no mistake, that's the only reason he wants her to lose. While the taxes remain, he won't support her."

"She won't lower the taxes now," Markell said. "She needs the money. She has bled the treasury dry to pay for her luxuries, not to mention the recruitment. She's bolstering the army's numbers," he told Alice.

Alice watched Lord Blaine pacing, a hollowness opening up inside her. "We need his army."

"Yes," Lord Blaine said when Markell didn't answer. He stopped pacing and rounded on her. "Could you marry him, Your Highness?"

"No!" Markell snapped.

Lord Blaine and Alice stared at him. "I see," Lord Blaine said carefully.

Markell passed a hand over his eyes. "I'll think of something else."

But Alice knew they could not defeat the queen without an army, and they could not raise their own army without money. Lord Quellery had the power to save them or send them to their deaths.

"I'll leave you two alone," Lord Blaine said.

Alice watched him go, glad he'd given her this moment alone with Markell yet dreading it too.

"Don't even consider it." Markell's voice was honey and spice, silken and nuanced. "I'll send you back to England before I'll let you marry Quellery."

She lifted her gaze to his and waited. He did not move toward her, did not kiss her like she thought he might—like she hoped. He looked away and swallowed.

"That's all well and good," she managed to say, "but I can't go back without the spell to activate a portal, and the queen has the spell book. Even if we don't want to fight her, we have to go to her castle to retrieve it."

The task was impossible without an army.

CHAPTER 8

SETH

Seth stared down at the figures of Alice, Markell and Blaine striding across the garden. "I wonder what they're up to."

Gus joined him at the window. "Wonderland business."

"They should include us in their talks."

"Why?" Gus flopped down on the bed he'd claimed the moment they set foot in the bedchamber, high up on the castle's second floor. Seth didn't bother tossing for it. For one thing, they didn't have a coin to toss, and for another, he didn't care where he slept. The truckle would do him well enough.

Seth turned away from the window. "Because…because… Blaine and Markell don't have Alice's best interests at heart, only Wonderland's."

"Blaine, maybe, but not Markell. Have you seen the way he looks at her? I reckon he'd follow her back to England if she wanted to go home."

Seth had to agree. Markell wouldn't force Alice to rule if it wasn't what she wanted. He was almost sure of it.

Gus clasped his hands behind his head. "That bother you?"

"Not as much as it once would have." Seth picked up the tankard the maid had brought up earlier only to find it empty. Probably just as well. The brew here was strong and he preferred to keep his wits about him when his life was at stake. Getting drunk these days was reserved for special occasions, like Charlie's wedding, and drowning his misery after seeing his mother wink at Cook.

"So you ain't in love with Alice no more?" Gus asked.

"I doubt I ever was. Love doesn't just come and go, Gus. True love lasts forever."

Gus snorted. "You sound like a poet."

Seth sat and stretched out his legs. "Perhaps I should write a poetry book. I know a publisher who'd print it. It could sell a fortune based on my reputation alone."

Gus sat up. "You could make it known that you wrote about your past lovers. They'll all buy it to see if they recognize themselves in it. You'd make a bleeding fortune, Seth."

Seth laughed. The idea was equal parts appalling and appealing.

"You'd have to leave Lady Harcourt out of it." Gus pulled a face. "That wouldn't be love poetry anyway, more like a tragedy."

Seth groaned. "You had to bring her up." Of all the women he'd been with, he regretted that affair the most. She had been a selfish creature who wanted to be the most exquisite woman at any party, and when she no longer was, she'd turned nasty.

"'A wasp by any other name would...still sting?'" Gus offered.

"Your poetry is as beautiful as your face." Seth smiled and Gus threw a pillow at him.

Seth caught it and threw it back, glad to see his friend smiling too.

"Do you think she loved Buchanan?" Gus asked.

Seth shook his head. "She wasn't capable of love. He,

however, was completely under her spell. I wonder how it would have worked out if they hadn't died."

"The world's a better place without them. It gives you a position on the ministry committee and all."

"Not that I can do much stuck here." Seth stood to look out the window again and saw only two figures remaining in the shadows by the roses. From their height, he knew they were Markell and Alice. Blaine was nowhere to be seen.

Luckily Markell kept his hands to himself. Seth wasn't sure what he'd do if Markell tried to take advantage of Alice. On the one hand, he ought to defend her honor and dignity. On the other, she would probably welcome a kiss from the advisor.

"What do you think everyone's doing at home right now?" Gus mused from the bed.

Seth thought they'd probably be worrying about their friends in Wonderland but he didn't say. "I know what Charlie and Lincoln will be doing. As to the rest, my mother and Cook are probably flirting." Seth screwed up his nose and forced that image aside. "And Leisl will be peering into her crystal ball."

"Do you think they miss us?"

"Of course. Who wouldn't miss us? We're the life of the party."

Gus chuckled. "I wish there was a way to get word to them that we're alive."

"Leisl might be able to see something. Her children are here, after all."

Gus rolled to his side, crooked his elbow, and propped his head up. "What do you think about Eva?"

Seth leaned back against the window frame and crossed his arms. "Why?"

"No need to glare at me like that." Gus rolled onto his back again.

"I wasn't glaring."

"You were."

"Why would I glare?"

"Because she's a woman and you haven't bedded her yet."

Is that what Gus thought of him? As a scoundrel who had to have every woman who crossed his path? Is that what everyone thought of him?

Gus sighed. "Sorry. I didn't mean it. You've changed, Seth. You ain't like that no more. I blame Lady H for putting you off bedding as many women as you can."

Seth tried to think of a clever retort but nothing came to mind.

"Charlie changed you too," Gus added.

"I have not bedded Charlie, and do not start that rumor back at Lichfield unless you want to see my face ruined by one jealous husband."

"I didn't mean that. I meant she looks up to you and that made you clean up your act. You didn't want to disappoint her."

Seth rolled his eyes. "So you're a philosopher now."

"Always have been but you never listened. Let me tell you something else I philosophied about."

"Philosophized."

"You need a woman again. It's been a while."

A light tap on the door interrupted Seth's laughter. "Don't lose that thought," he said, rising to answer it. "I want you to define need."

Lady Oxana stood with her hand resting on the door-frame, her gown unlaced to reveal her cleavage, and her hair unbound. Heat banked in her eyes as she slowly raked her gaze over Seth. He wished he'd kept his shirt on.

"Lady Oxana," he said. "Is there something we can do for you?" He winced. That sounded like an invitation.

"There certainly is." Her fingers skimmed over the swell of her breasts.

He tracked their progress, somewhat stunned at her brazenness.

"Do you like what you see?" she murmured.

She wasn't a voluptuous woman but she had a sensual figure. He'd remarked to Gus earlier that Lord Quellery and his sister looked nothing alike. She was slender where he was fat, her skin tight where his was loose. But that had never been something Seth cared about. Indeed, he never cared what his women looked like. He'd slept with all shapes and sizes, not preferring one over the other. He did have one important rule—that he liked them. That was why he stopped waiting for Julia to resume their affair. Her façade had slipped to the point where he saw the rotten foundations behind it

Of course, that rule only mattered when he had a choice in his partner. In that strange time of his life when he would auction himself in the very private clubs and salons, he'd broken his rule on several occasions. Not that every winning bidder had been *un*likeable, but he'd done things he hadn't enjoyed on occasion. That had, after all, been why the bids went so high.

But those days were over. And this woman wasn't bidding.

She planted both hands on his chest, curling her fingers inward, pricking him with her nails. Then she pushed him back into the room. "Do you want to touch me?"

Gus cleared his throat. "Want me to go, Seth?"

"Yes," Lady Oxana said.

"Stay," Seth commanded.

"You want him to watch?" Oxana's mouth curled at the edges. Her smile was as sharp as her fingernails. "Is that how it is in your world? Very well, let him stay. I don't mind, as long as he doesn't come near me." She cupped Seth between his legs. He backed away. He'd met brazen women before, but they'd all bought the wares before touching it.

"Come now," she cooed, "you don't seem like the shy type. Come here and let's play. We don't have much time."

"I think not," he said. "Please leave."

"No."

He was so taken aback, he didn't know what to say.

"You're beautiful." She stroked a fingernail down his cheek. Seth swayed out of her reach but she simply stepped forward and clasped his arms. "So strong." She squeezed.

He backed away again and appealed to Gus for help. Gus merely shrugged.

Lady Oxana followed him until he smacked into the wall. She pressed herself against him, trapping him. The light from the candles flickered in her eyes, making it look as if she was on fire.

"I want you." Her tongue darted across her lower lip and her breathing came in ragged gasps. "And I *will* have you."

He shoved her away. "I don't want to offend, Lady Oxana, so please don't continue."

Her gown slipped off one shoulder, revealing more of her breast, but she did not rearrange herself. Indeed, she pushed her chest out ever so slightly. He focused on her mouth.

She smiled. "I *will* have you."

"I'm afraid not."

"Think again. You see..." She stroked his chest from his collar bone to the band of his trousers. He did not back down, would not show weakness. Somehow he managed to suppress the shiver that threatened to give him away. "I want you, Seth, and you *need* me."

Need. Seth was getting annoyed with everyone thinking he *needed* to always have a woman waiting for him. He could cope very well without one, particularly this one. She made Julia look like a mouse. "You're mistaken," he said.

"I think not." Her smile was slick. "Your friend the princess needs my brother's army, and my brother adores me. He gives me whatever I want. If you deny me tonight then I will tell him that you offended me. He'll be furious and will withhold the army until you agree to spend the night with me." Her fingers walked up his chest to his chin. She tapped it. "So you'll do whatever I want you to do."

The floor shifted beneath Seth's feet and he reached behind him to grab hold of the window frame. It was happening again. He thought he'd escaped that life forever, left it behind when Lincoln employed him. But Lincoln couldn't save him now.

"You're mad," he said. "You'd jeopardize the plans of revolution to lie with a man who doesn't want you?"

"You'll want me. Just wait and see."

He swallowed. "I don't believe your brother would ruin everything. Not for this."

"Shall we put it to the test now?" She grabbed his hand.

He snatched it away.

Her lips hardened and her smile withered. "It'll be worse for you the longer you resist. I'll make sure of that. I'll speak to my brother tonight. I'm sure he'll want to hear how the princess's friend upset his dear sister." She turned to go. "I will have you, Seth."

"You can't," Gus blurted out. Seth wasn't sure when his friend had got off the bed. He stood by the door, not blocking it, but looking very much like a dog guarding his territory.

"Why not?" Lady Oxana asked mildly.

"Because he's married."

Seth's brows shot up. A pulse jumped in Lady Oxana's throat as she turned to Seth. He shrugged one shoulder. He wasn't sure Gus's trick would put her off, but Seth was more than willing to try. He needed to get out of the damned corner she'd backed him into.

"In our world, if a man lies with another woman when he's already married, the law'll cut his bollocks off." Gus indicated his nether regions.

"So?" Lady Oxana sniffed. "Who will tell his wife? Surely not you, his friend."

"She'll just know," Gus said with a glance toward the door.

Lady Oxana followed his gaze. "It's that dark haired girl, isn't it? Eva. Why didn't you say?" she asked Seth. "And why aren't you two in the same room?"

"We thought it best if she stays with Alice," Seth said, without thinking it through. "For protection."

"You think someone would harm the princess? Here?"

"One can never be too careful. Anyway, Eva's a very capable bodyguard. She's excellent with knives. If the law back home didn't cut off my plums for sleeping with another woman, she certainly would. Since I rather like my parts where they are, and I adore my wife, then I'm afraid I'll have to decline your offer." He strode past her and opened the door. He stepped into the corridor to encourage her to follow. "Good night, Lady Oxana."

She did indeed follow him into the corridor, but didn't leave. She stood toe to toe with him, the sickly floral scent she used sticking in his throat. It was hard to breathe. "You'd better not be lying, Seth. If I find you are, not only will my brother be furious, but you and pretty little Eva will see how I treat those who lie to me."

She marched off, her gown snapping at her heels with each stride. Seth blew out a breath and was about to head inside when he caught sight of a movement in the opposite direction to the way Lady Oxana had gone. Eva stood there, her eyes wide. She wore a green dress that hugged her figure from shoulder to hip then fell loosely to the floor. He liked the way it revealed her feminine shape. Her usual attire smoothed out her curves, but this outfit enhanced them. It was very fetching on her.

"Eva," he said as she turned to go. "Wait."

She fixed her gaze on his cheek. It was hard and unwavering as if she was trying not to look elsewhere. Like his bare chest? He smiled and crossed his arms in a pose he knew showed off his muscles. Her cheeks flushed. He should lower his arms but decided against it for now. He rather liked how she seemed all hot and bothered by him.

"Yes?" she said breathily.

"I..." What had he been going to say? "I like that dress."

"Oh. Thank you. What did Lady Oxana want?"

So she had seen. The question was, how much? He opened his mouth to lie, to tell her she wanted nothing from him, that she was just seeing if they were settled. But he found he didn't want to. What did it matter if Eva knew the truth?

"She wanted a liaison with me. I told her no."

Her lips parted in a silent gasp. Was she surprised at Lady Oxana's brazenness, or that Seth revealed it? "Why did you refuse?"

He hadn't expected that question. "She's of no interest to me." He searched her face, looking for any of the anger lingering from their discussion on the road to Quellery Castle. He still wasn't sure what it had been about, or why she was upset with him. He just knew he hadn't liked it. He'd spent the rest of the journey thinking of ways to get her to laugh again but he'd given up. She wouldn't even look at him.

Now here she was, outside his room. Had she come looking for him?

"Did you want to speak to me about something?" he asked.

Her gaze lowered then snapped quickly back up to his face. He bit the inside of his cheek to stop himself smiling. "Alice went out and hasn't returned," she said.

"She's outside with Markell."

"Alone?"

He nodded. "You think we should worry about them being alone together?"

"Don't you?"

He shook his head. "I trust Markell." He did, he realized. The man seemed very upstanding, and Seth was an excellent judge of character.

"Oh," was all Eva said.

"Good, you found her," whispered Gus from behind him. Seth hadn't heard his friend approach. "Come with us, Eva. We have to talk."

Gus led Eva back to their room while Seth walked behind, admiring the way the fabric of her dress swayed with her hips. Gus shut the door and directed Eva to sit.

She frowned. "You both look odd. What's wrong?"

"Lady Oxana was just here," Gus said. "She wanted Seth to..." He whistled. "You know."

"Seth just told me. I saw her walk away, so it seems she's given up."

"It wasn't easy," Gus went on. "She was determined."

"How did you convince her?"

"We lied," Seth said. "And I'm sorry to say we dragged you into the lie." He held up his hands in surrender. "I'm not proud of it, but it was all we could think of at the time." She was looking at him with a very odd expression he couldn't quite decipher. "I could have agreed to her plan, but I didn't want to," he said in case that's what she was thinking. He supposed it's what most women would think. "I don't like to be manipulated by people like her. I've allowed it in the past but...no more."

"Allowed it?" she echoed. She really did have the biggest eyes.

He might as well tell her some of it, at least in part. He could trust her not to spread gossip or think less of him. She wasn't that kind of person. "Before I met Lincoln, I used to auction myself to raise money."

Her mouth formed an O. "And women like Lady Oxana bid on you so they could...have you to themselves?"

He hitched up his trouser legs and sat on the other chair. "Lady Oxana and her ilk think they can click their fingers and whatever they want will fall into their lap. Back when I was desperate for money, I played along. But not anymore." He watched her closely. She still didn't blush or look away. She wasn't embarrassed.

"I'm sorry," she said simply.

"Don't be. It wasn't a terrible experience. Sometimes it was rather fun." He flashed her a grin and a bubble of laughter escaped her lips. "Most of the winning bidders didn't quite know what to do with me. Few were like the Lady Oxanas of this world. I learned how to handle them easily enough, but I also learned to play along. And that's all it was, just play."

"Why are you telling me this?"

Because he wanted her to know his secrets, although he couldn't really say why. He still held something back, however. There were certain things he needed to be sure she could hear without recoiling in shock. He didn't want her to think badly of him, yet he didn't regret telling her this much.

"We're telling you because you need to know why we lied to Lady Oxana," Gus answered for him. "You need to know why Seth didn't want to be with her, or you might not agree to be part of the lie."

"I understand," she said, looking at Seth. "Thank you for telling me. Now." She turned to Gus. "What is my role in this lie of yours?"

"You're my wife." Seth reached for her hand and kissed the back of it. "We're madly in love and you'll gouge out the eyes of any woman who so much as looks at me. So? What do you think?"

"I...I'm not sure."

"Please say you'll agree to be my wife," he said, laughing at the way it sounded. They were going to have a lark playing their respective roles.

He just had to convince Eva. She looked rather scandalized by the suggestion. He was about to reassure her that he wouldn't kiss her or touch her unless she kissed or touched first when she spoke.

"Yes," she whispered. "Yes, I will marry you."

CHAPTER 9

EVA

Eva considered herself to be open-minded. Her combined British and Romany upbringing had exposed her to all sorts of strange situations, and as a medical student, she'd seen and heard far more than most young ladies. Yet hearing Seth ask her to marry him, even in jest, turned her insides to jelly. Learning that he'd auctioned himself off to women of Lady Oxana's ilk hadn't shocked her as much as her own reaction to his false proposal. Perhaps it was because he'd laughed about it, as if marrying her was so unlikely as to be absurd.

He wouldn't be laughing if he'd just proposed to Alice. He'd be waiting with baited breath for her to say yes, no matter the circumstances.

"Right," Gus said, clapping his hands together. "You two have to act all lovey in public from now on. It don't need to be too much, just a smile or sweet look. Make sure Lord Quellery thinks you're in love. That way he won't force his sister on you, Seth, unless he's more of a prick than we think."

"Eva?" Seth asked. "What's wrong?"

"Nothing," she said, a little too brightly.

"You don't have to agree if you don't want to. I can tell Lady Oxana I made it up."

"Don't do that. If you truly don't want her advances—"

"I don't."

"Then we'll go through with it."

"I'd do the same for you, if the positions were reversed. If there's any man, either here or back home, who won't leave you alone, tell me and I'll be the most loving husband you could ever hope for." He patted her hand. "As long as you don't make me give up drinking. You're not one of *those* wives who wants a teetotaler for a husband, are you?"

She laughed, despite herself. "As long as you promise not to come home too drunk, traipse mud through the house, or bring home your rowdy friends, we'll get along fine."

"Gus, you're no longer my friend."

Gus rolled his eyes. "I don't get no rowdier than you after a few drinks. You should tell him not to start fights in taverns, Eva. He's got a habit of that."

"Gus!" Seth cried.

"What? It's not like you're marrying her for real. It's just a lark."

Eva's good mood deflated. "I think I should return to my room. Alice ought to be back soon."

Seth peered out the window. "They're no longer in the garden."

Gus rose to answer a knock at the door. "You two look sweet on one another in case it's Lady Oxana," he said.

Seth placed his hand on Eva's shoulder then must have thought the gesture wasn't intimate enough and stroked her hair instead. "Has anyone ever told you your hair is beautiful?" he asked softly. "It seems to swallow the light."

Eva's heart tripped.

Alice and Markell strode into the room and took in Seth's position beside Eva. Alice's brows rose, and a fleeting smile touched Markell's lips.

"Sorry," Alice said. "Are we interrupting something?"

Seth removed his hand. "We're glad you're here. We have something to tell you."

"And we have something to tell you too. You say your piece first."

"Lady Oxana came here," Gus said, taking up a position by Seth near the window. "She wanted Seth." His words were matter of fact, as if he witnessed this sort of thing all the time. How often had Seth been propositioned by ladies of means?

"But I did not want her," Seth added. "You're shocked, Alice."

Alice touched her throat, her chin, her throat again then self-consciously dropped her hand away. "Are you sure that's what she wanted? Perhaps you misinterpreted."

"There was no mistaking her intentions," Seth said, lowering his gaze and voice. "She was very clear."

"She sure bloody was," Gus added.

Alice's gaze darted around the room as if she didn't know where to focus. Seth looked even more embarrassed. Eva couldn't bear seeing him like that.

"The problem is," she said, "Lady Oxana threatened to tell her brother. She claimed he would withhold his troops until his sister got what she wanted."

"She's mad," Markell scoffed. "You believed her?"

"She was convincing," Gus said. "And how are we to know he wouldn't?"

"So they came up with a solution," Eva said. "Seth and I will pretend to be married."

Alice's gaze finally snapped to Seth's. "You think that will put her off?"

"We hope so," Eva said.

"Can you think of a better plan?" Gus asked.

Alice shook her head. "I think it's an excellent idea. You'll have to be convincing for it to work. Can you do that, Eva?"

"I'm quite a good actress when I put my mind to it," Eva said.

"What about you, Vickers?" Markell asked.

Seth grunted a laugh. "I can manage."

"Seth should be on the stage," Gus told them. "Don't worry about him being caught out."

"So what's your news?" Seth asked Markell. "What were you discussing outside in the garden?"

Markell's face darkened. He and Alice exchanged a worried glance. "Quellery will only give us his army on one condition." Another worried look passed between them. "That he marries Alice."

Seth pushed off from the wall. "No! That is not an option. Don't agree to it, Alice."

"I haven't," she said, sounding put out that he would think such a thing. Or perhaps because she didn't like him telling her what to do.

"Will you consider it?" Gus asked.

"She won't," Markell said. "As you say, Vickers, it's not an option. There has to be another way."

But no one could think of anything. The longer the silence stretched, the more restless Alice became. She couldn't sit still, and her brow became more and more furrowed.

"It's hopeless," she finally blurted out. "I have to do it."

"No!" they all cried.

Eva took Alice's hand. "You are not marrying that revolting man, no matter what's at stake."

Alice blinked back tears. "Then tell me how to refuse him without jeopardizing everything."

Eva couldn't answer that. Nor could anyone else.

"We'll think of something," Seth assured her. "But Eva's right. You're not marrying him."

"We could tell him you're already married," Gus suggested. "Like Seth told Lady Oxana he's married to Eva."

"That would be an excellent solution," Markell said darkly,

"if I'd thought of it at the time. But I didn't and if I say something now, he'll know it's a lie." He swore under his breath. "I'm sorry, Alice. I failed you."

"You most certainly have not." She grasped his hand between both of hers. "I wouldn't expect you to think of such a scheme. Your mind isn't as devious as Seth's or Gus's. It's your unfailing honesty and goodness that I like so much, Markell," Alice went on. "Don't wish to be otherwise."

Seth leaned back slowly, watching the exchange. Did he hear Alice's unspoken words too? It wasn't obvious from his expression.

Gus didn't look the least upset that Alice implied he was dishonest. "If Quellery's going to withhold his army if you don't marry him, Alice, there ain't no need for Eva and Seth to pretend to be married. Lady Oxana's got no leverage."

"Let's play it safe anyway," Alice said.

"Agreed," Markell chimed in. "They should continue with the ruse, just in case."

"Eva?" Seth asked. "Are you still happy to be my wife?" He shot her a winning smile that took her completely by surprise, and stole her breath too.

She nodded.

"I haven't given up on Quellery altogether yet," Markell said. "There's still a chance his desire to get rid of the Queen of Hearts overrides his desire to marry Alice."

Eva doubted it. Even if Quellery wanted to continue with the revolution, he had a stronger position than Alice. They needed him and his army. He'd be a fool not to use it to bargain with them. Marriage to the future queen was a valuable prize.

"I'll go speak with Blaine now," Markell said. "Alice, you should get some sleep." He bowed. "Goodnight."

He left, and Eva walked out with Alice. "You shouldn't be so unfair on Seth," Eva said once they were back in their own room.

Alice removed her dress over her head. "How am I unfair to him?"

"He adores you," Eva said, kicking off her shoes.

"No, he doesn't. He thinks well of me. They're not the same thing."

"And you just told him you think him dishonest."

Alice blinked at her. "Did I? When?"

"When you told Markell you like his honesty and you considered Gus and Seth to have devious minds. It was in the implication, not the words themselves."

"Oh. You're right. How awful of me." Alice placed the dress over the back of a chair and climbed onto the bed. She drew her knees up under the covers and hugged them. "I'll apologize to Seth and Gus in the morning. Seth does keep secrets, though."

"That's his right."

"Yes, but…having secrets doesn't endear him to me."

"Perhaps he would tell you his secrets if he knew you wouldn't be embarrassed by them."

Alice rested her chin on her knees and sighed. "I can't promise that, can I?"

And that, Eva realized, was the entire problem with Seth and Alice as a couple. The secrets Seth had confided to Eva tonight would shock the straight-laced Alice. If she knew them, she probably couldn't look at him again without blushing. A couple that didn't share all their secrets was doomed, in Eva's opinion, but so was a couple that couldn't bear to look one another in the eye.

Eva sat back against the pillows and wondered if either Alice or Seth had come to the same conclusion. She eyed the back of Alice's head and tried to think of a way to ask casually, so as not to show too much interest.

"How am I supposed to be a good queen if I don't even realize I've offended a friend?" Alice muttered. "What if I say something to an important lord or lady and it can be construed the wrong way?" She groaned. "I'll be a hopeless ruler. This whole idea of me being a queen is hopeless. Why did I even come here?"

"Because the general would have destroyed Lichfield if you didn't." Eva scooted forward and circled Alice in her arms. "You'll make a great queen. In time, you'll learn how to phrase things so that no one can take offence. I'm sure Markell will be happy to teach you all the important queenly traits you'll need, privately of course."

Alice smirked. "He really is an excellent teacher. It's no wonder he became one of the queen's advisors at such a young age. I honestly can't think of anyone I'd rather have by my side through this."

Offering good advice was one thing. Getting them out of this predicament was entirely another. "Would you consider abandoning plans to become queen and just going home?" Eva asked.

Alice took a long time to answer. "We have to get the spell book regardless of whether I become queen or not. I'll decide once we have it in our hands."

If they ever got it in their hands.

* * *

EVA DRESSED in her old gown and boots. She fingered the fabric at the hem and was relieved to feel the small bulges. The vials were still safe. She hoped she wouldn't need them, but it was a comfort to know they were there.

A maid delivered a breakfast of hard bread and black sausages with a jug of strong ale. "I think they're trying to starve us into agreeing to Quellery's proposal," Alice said, pushing the plate away. She'd put on the tunic and hose again, seeming to prefer it over the new dress too.

"I'm going to speak to David," Eva said. "He needs to be kept informed."

"Don't be long. I think it wise we all stay together today as much as possible."

The ominous note in her voice gave Eva pause. Alice was scared. They both were. They'd spoken at length the night before about how to refuse Lord Quellery's proposal of marriage diplomatically. Alice had to do it in such a way that would make it seem he was getting out of a bad arrangement. Eva wasn't sure it would work. He didn't look like a man who cared for diplomacy.

She asked a maid for directions to David's room and found that it was between Gus and Seth's, and Markell's. "Sleep well?" he asked, yawning.

"Not particularly." She pushed past him into the bedchamber. It was a cozy room, big enough for only one narrow bed and the washstand. "There's something you need to know." He stared at her, the door still open. She shut it for him. "Come and sit down."

She wasn't sure which piece of news would upset him more so decided that the life threating one should be told first. "Alice is going to speak to Lord Quellery today to try convince him she'd make a poor choice in a wife," she finished.

He barked a laugh. "Don't be ridiculous. How can a future queen be a bad choice for a power-hungry pig?"

"Shhh." Even though the door was closed, she didn't trust the castle's inhabitants. She wouldn't put it past Lord Quellery and Lady Oxana to be listening at doors. "That's not all. Seth and I have to pretend we're married."

"Married! Why?"

"Lady Oxana keeps making advances toward him so he told her he was already taken."

David shot to his feet. "You will *not* be sleeping in his bed. I won't allow it."

"We won't share a room. Not that you have any say in it," she said hotly. "I'm merely telling you as a courtesy."

That shut him up for all of five seconds. She should have known this would be harder for him to swallow than the prospect of the revolution failing.

"I am you brother, Eva, and the head of the household."

"Tosh. Mother is the head of the household. You do as she says and you know it."

"Not true," he muttered.

She went to leave, but he caught her arm.

"If he kisses you, I'll have to call him out," he said.

"Dueling pistols at dawn? Don't be ridiculous, David."

"Don't be so headstrong, Eva. That's always been your problem." He poked his finger at her, stabbing the air near her nose. "You always think you can do as you please." Stab. "Well you can't." Stab. "Certain things are undignified for a young unwed woman."

"Such as kissing handsome men?"

"And becoming a doctor."

She reeled back, stung. "You know?" she whispered.

"Of course I do. So does Mother. We're not stupid, Eva. We both hoped you would come to your senses on your own, but it seems you're more headstrong than we both realized."

This was why she'd kept it a secret from them. *This* was why she'd refused to share her dreams. She shoved him in the chest with both hands. "You are not the master of me!"

"You just said that Mother is." He sneered. "And she agrees with me. Being a doctor is a job for men."

"Not anymore. The London School of Medicine For Women has been training women to become doctors for some time now. If it's good enough—"

"I don't care," he growled through gritted teeth. "Do you hear me, Eva? It's undignified. You know that people like us have to be more careful than most."

"Because we're Romany?"

"Half-Romany. Leave men's jobs for the men, Eva. Let the girls who aren't fighting other prejudices fight the gender battle. *You* need to be more subtle and less of an agitator. Be a nurse, not a doctor."

He strode to the window where he crossed his arms. Eva stared at his rigid back. Who was this person? Her brother had never spoken so cruelly to her. They bickered, but never had he ground her beneath his heel like this. Never had he shown such bitterness.

"I know you're feeling the pressure being here, David," she said with dark calmness that she dredged up from deep within. "We all are. But that's no excuse. If you speak to me that way again, I will never forgive you."

He half turned his head, his face in profile, every muscle taut. "You will behave yourself here, Eva. I don't care if it's another realm, the rules of propriety still apply."

"Seth is a gentleman," she said evenly. "He would never take advantage of me."

He stalked back to her, a tower of simmering anger, of hard angles and bleak shadows. "And you, Eva? Are you a good English gentlewoman? Or are you just like our mother?"

She slapped his cheek. "I wish you'd never followed me here!"

"I did it to protect you."

She marched out of the room, her body trembling, her blood pumping. Everything swirled around her, faded in and out, and she stopped to catch her breath and her balance.

A door up ahead opened and Lord Blaine emerged. Markell stepped into view and spoke quietly to him. Lord Blaine nodded, and patted the pocket of his tunic. Markell's smile was grim as he clasped the older man's arm. It looked like a farewell.

She had stopped in the shadows near the stairs so Lord Blaine didn't see her until he was almost upon her. She greeted him softly and he smiled. It quickly faded.

"Are you unwell, Miss Eva? You look feverish."

She touched the back of her hand to her cheek. "A walk

and fresh air will do me good. Thank you for your concern." She considered asking him if everything was all right but decided against it. Everything wasn't all right. They were on the brink of seeing their hard work ruined because of Quellery's greed.

She watched him head down the stairs and out of sight then glanced at David's door. She would not go back and try to calm him down. He would have to apologize first.

Eva was about to return to her own room when Lady Oxana came up the stairs. The amethyst pendant nestled in the V of her bosom glinted in the sunlight filtering through the window, and the gold rings on her fingers flashed.

"You there," she said to Eva. "What's your name?"

She knew perfectly well but Eva told her anyway.

"What are you doing here? Your room is not on this floor."

"Visiting my husband," Eva said smoothly. "Is that not allowed?"

Lady Oxana's lips pinched so hard they disappeared altogether. "Petulance may be permissible in your realm, but in Wonderland we're taught to show our betters some respect."

"As are we." Eva spun on her heel and left Oxana to contemplate that little gem. She strode to Seth's door and knocked.

He answered it. Shirtless. He leaned an arm against the doorframe and a lazy grin curved his lips. "Good morning, Eva. To what do I owe—"

She flattened her palm against his chest. She only meant to give him a sign that he should be careful in his choice of words with Lady Oxana nearby, but somehow she managed to make contact. He was warm, as if he'd just crawled out of bed. His muscles flexed and twitched beneath her hand. Was he affected by her touch?

He placed his own hand over hers, trapping it. His smile turned mischievous. "Did you sleep well, my dear?" His voice was as smooth as his skin.

Eva felt Lady Oxana's presence behind her. "Well enough, Husband. You?"

Seth made a show of yawning. "Gus snores."

"I do not," Gus called out from within the room.

"And I missed you." Seth brought Eva's hand to his lips and stared into her eyes.

She stared back, still trapped. "I missed you too," she murmured.

He touched her cheek, skimming his knuckles down to her jaw, and his smile turned sad, wistful.

Eva's heart flipped over. Oh, he was good. He was very, very good.

She tugged her hand free to break the contact. It was too risky being so close to him. He might see too much in her eyes. She stared at his ear instead.

Lady Oxana cleared her throat. "Are you styled Lady Vickers?" She believed them. Eva almost laughed from relief.

"She is," Seth answered when Eva didn't respond.

"Why didn't you tell me when you arrived?"

"We didn't want to overwhelm you. Our arrival was unexpected and it must have been difficult enough getting the rooms ready in time. Since Eva wanted to accompany Alice, we thought it wouldn't matter if you didn't know. We're sorry if it upsets you. We should have mentioned it."

Lady Oxana sniffed. "Pretty words, sir. I just hope there is some substance to them as well."

David's door opened and he scowled upon seeing Eva so close to Seth. "Eva, what are you doing?" he snapped.

Seth didn't seem to move yet he was suddenly a few inches further away from Eva.

Lady Oxana noticed. She folded her arms and cocked her head to the side, challenging. "Is there a problem?" she asked David.

"My sister is—"

"Your sister missed her husband last night," Eva said,

tilting her chin up. Seth looked back at her with a slightly bemused expression. She looped her hands around his neck and ruffled the back of his hair. Then she stood on her toes and kissed him.

It was gentle and sweet and everything she expected it to be for a first kiss between a fake husband and wife in front of witnesses. She liked it, but it certainly wasn't enough. Perhaps she ought to deepen it.

"I do hope you spoke the truth," came Lady Oxana's voice, as brittle as dry leaves. "I rather like your head, Seth, and your body. It'll be a shame to see them parted."

Seth drew away and it took Eva a moment to realize Gus was behind him, clearing his throat.

"What?" Seth growled.

Gus jerked his head for Seth to join him inside. Seth let Eva's hands go and tossed her a smile and a wink before following Gus.

"That was uncalled for." David's voice was harsh in Eva's ear.

Lady Oxana was gone. The only sign that she'd been there was the lingering scent of her floral perfume and her threat.

"It was necessary," Eva said. "We had to convince her."

"That's the only reason I didn't say anything. I don't want her going to Quellery. It's bad enough that Alice is about to turn down his proposal, we don't want to make things more tense."

Eva tuned him out. She watched Seth and Gus, both staring out the window. Her seer's senses picked up their anxiety.

"What is it?" she asked, joining them.

"Take a look," Seth said darkly. "They're surrounding the castle."

Outside, hundreds of men dressed in dark green spread out along the banks of the castle moat. The drawbridge was down, but they did not cross. They simply stood there, weapons sheathed. Waiting for orders, Eva realized.

"Who are they?" David asked.

Gus pointed to one of the soldiers at the front holding a green banner with a black crow's wing. "That's Quellery's crest. It's his army."

Seth swore. "We need to find Alice and Markell. *Now*."

CHAPTER 10

ALICE

Alice thought the knock on her door might be Eva returning, warning her before she entered in case Alice was at her toilette. But it was Markell. At least she wouldn't have to go in search of him.

"I'm glad you're here," she said. "I have something to ask you."

"I have something to ask you too. But you first."

She stepped aside and he brushed past her. He was fully dressed and even wore a sword strapped to his hip. It didn't bode well. She closed the door and leaned against it. This wasn't going to be easy, but she had to ask. His answer would help make up her mind and shape her next move.

"Don't consider it," he said darkly before she spoke. "I can see that you are, Alice, and I want you to put the thought from your mind. You are *not* marrying Quellery."

How had he guessed? "Wonderland will continue to suffer under the Queen of Hearts if we don't accept help from Quellery's army, and the only way to do that is if I marry him."

He sliced his hand through the air. "No! I won't let you."

He clutched the back of a chair and lowered his head. "I can't let you."

The pain in his voice gave her hope. She dared touch his shoulder. The muscles tensed then relaxed. He straightened and looked at her with that direct, honest gaze of his. She wanted to stare into those eyes forever, get lost in them. The thought of being with him struck her like a blow, shaking her to her core. Falling in love wasn't supposed to happen this quickly.

"When you were speaking with Lord Quellery about me last night," she said, "I overheard you call me all manner of things."

His brow lifted and for a moment, he looked like the young man she'd first met in London, without this heavy weight of leadership and his father's death on his shoulders. "I think I told him you were clever and kind. Why?"

"Did you mean it?"

He frowned. "Of course."

She breathed deeply. "When people describe me, those are not the first words they use."

"England might be a different realm than Wonderland, but I can't imagine anyone in any realm thinking you stupid or cruel."

She smiled. "That's not what I meant. I mean my looks are usually the first thing people note."

"I see."

Did he? "So why didn't you?"

He shrugged. "I'm not sure. Is it a problem?"

"Not at all. I like that you consider kindness and cleverness more important than beauty, and that you think I possess both."

"Beauty?" He tapped a finger against his lower lip and circled her, making a great show of inspecting her. "Hmmm. I suppose you are reasonably pretty."

"Reasonably?" she echoed, playing along. "You're too

kind, sir."

"But I'm sorry to disappoint you, since you are a princess, but this is Wonderland. We have different standards of beauty to the English." He bowed ever so deeply. "Please forgive my impertinence and please don't chop off my head when you become queen. It would only disappoint the ladies."

She laughed. "Is that so?"

"Enough about me, let's talk about you. You're a little too short to be considered beautiful."

"Short? I'm the tallest woman I know."

"And you have big feet."

She looked down at her feet. "I do not!" When she looked up, he was trying very hard not to laugh.

She thumped him lightly on the arm. He caught her hand and did not let go.

"What is this about, Alice?" he asked gently, all seriousness again.

"I...I wanted to know if you really do consider cleverness and kindness more important than beauty."

"I do." He inched closer, her hand still trapped in his. "And you possess both, in spades."

She swallowed.

"It's why I..." He shook his head, looked away.

She cupped his jaw and gently forced him to look at her again. "Why you what?"

His gaze locked with hers. "Why I admire you so much."

She had to know. Had to hear him say it. "Admire me as a future queen? Or as a woman?"

"Both," he murmured.

She grazed her thumb over his cheek. "What about as someone more...intimate?"

She felt rather than saw him tense. "Alice...I don't want to influence your decision to stay or go, and I don't want to start something we can't stop."

Nor did she. She admired him for his clear thinking, his

careful consideration and thoughtfulness. But it was hellish on her nerves and her heart. It pained her to see the sadness in his eyes when all she wanted to do was hold him. She closed her eyes.

"Damnation," he muttered. "Forget what I just said."

He was kissing her before she had the chance to open her eyes. He dragged her close, crushing her body against his, her mouth too. The kiss was hungry and fierce, thunder and lightning. It brimmed with wild, abandoned emotion that Alice couldn't contain. It poured out of her into that kiss and he captured it with ease and served it back to her ten-fold. This man might be a careful tactician, but there was nothing safe about the kiss, nothing planned, just heart, soul and passion.

Markell pulled away all too soon. He stepped back, raked both hands through his hair and struggled to catch his breath. Alice clutched the back of the chair, feeling like the earth had tilted beneath her. "We have to stop," he said. "If we go on…" His gaze shifted to the bed. He wiped the back of his hand across his mouth.

She nodded, not trusting her voice yet, but she understood. Their first time would not be in a cold chamber in Quellery Castle.

"Your question," he said. "Did I answer it?"

She smiled. "Yes."

He smiled too. "Good."

"Now it's your turn," she said.

"My question is, have you decided what you want?" he asked.

"Aside from you?"

He grinned, elevating his looks from handsome to magnificent. "What else?"

"Well, I don't want to marry Quellery."

He grunted. "That was never an option."

"As to the rest…I want to be where you are, Markell. And

you want to be here."

He took both her hands. "What I want is for you to be safe."

That meant going back to England, but she didn't think that's where he really wanted to live. He was passionate about overthrowing the Queen of Hearts, and Alice wanted to be by his side, helping him. If his home was in Wonderland, then her home would be too. But how to oust the queen without an army?

"All is not yet over," she told him. "There must be something we can do. What of the other renegades?"

"That's what I came here to tell you. I sent Lord Blaine off with a message for the other cells. Between us, we knew the names of four other leaders, and they in turn will know more. He'll find those leaders and assess whether their cells are in a position to combine and fight."

"Will there be enough?"

"Perhaps."

"How long will it take?"

"Months."

She groaned. *She* could live like this for months, but it wasn't fair on her friends. This wasn't their cause to fight.

A fist pounded on the door. Alice opened it to see Lord Quellery standing there, panting a little from exertion. "Good morning, Your Highness," he said. "Did you sleep well?"

"Well enough considering the difficult circumstances," she said stiffly.

Quellery's gaze shifted and his face darkened. "Ironside," he growled. "I should have known you'd be here."

"The princess knows about your proposal," Markell said.

Quellery's jowls trembled as he fought, and failed, to control his dislike of Markell. "And what has she decided?"

"Kindly address your question to me, and not my advisor," Alice said.

Quellery stiffened. "Apologies."

Alice forced herself to soften and smile. They needed this man on-side. "I want to thank you for your proposal of marriage, sir. I'm humbled and honored that you would consider ending your bachelorhood to wed me. I'm in no doubt that you would make a fine consort, with your experience and resources, but I'm afraid I have to decline."

He showed no surprise. His cool gaze merely shifted back to Markell.

"You see," Alice tried, "where I come from, one doesn't marry for fortune or status. One marries for companionship and love." Queen Victoria and her ilk would have laughing fits if they heard her. Not even Alice's middle class parents wanted her to choose her own husband. It was why she was so determined to do so now that she was free to follow her heart.

"You're Wonderland's rightful queen," Lord Quellery said. "You need a strong, respected and experienced husband beside you to help you navigate the treacherous waters you'll face when you ascend to the throne."

"I completely agree. I feel very fortunate that my heart has chosen a man who is all of that and more."

Quellery's jowls shook violently. "May I speak with you alone, Highness? I should like to put forward my numerous positive attributes for your consideration."

"I'm afraid you cannot sway me, my lord. The heart wants what it wants. I am sorry, but there's nothing to be done on that score. I do hope you understand and won't think ill of me."

"I could never think ill of *you*." It was a barb directed straight at Markell. Markell didn't so much as blink.

Alice hoped that Quellery's jealousy of Markell wouldn't override his good sense. "I am so relieved to hear it," she said. "Now, let's discuss our next moves. I hear your army is highly trained and very skillful. They'll be invaluable to us. Will you come in and discuss strategy?"

"Of course, of course. Allow me to fetch my general and a map."

Alice felt a weight lift from her shoulders. Crisis averted. "Thank you, my lord. Your loyalty will be repaid when I am queen."

He smiled and bowed out.

She shut the door and turned to Markell. "He took it graciously enough."

Markell's eyes blazed bright green. "I don't think I can teach you anything about diplomacy. You're already an expert. Tell me, Your Highness, this man chosen by your heart…do I know him?"

She circled her arms around his waist, and he rested his hands on her hips. It felt so good to be with him like this, so natural and unforced. She'd never felt so comfortable with a man before. He seemed comfortable with her too, not self-conscious as Seth could be. "You might," she teased. "He's everything I told Quellery, yet so much more too."

"Perhaps you should list his qualities for me so I can judge if he's worthy of you."

"Do you mean worthy of a future queen?"

"No." He nuzzled her throat, his lips skimming along the throbbing vein in delicious agony. "I mean worthy of Alice, the woman I've fallen in love with."

Her breath hitched. Her blood pounded in her ears so loudly that she didn't hear the knock on the door until Markell pulled away with a regretful sigh.

He opened the door to a man dressed in dark green. The black crow's wing on his sleeve marked him as one of Quellery's men. This must be the general, come for their meeting. He cradled a large wooden box.

He handed the box to Markell. "Lord Quellery would like you to have a gift."

"Thank you, "Alice said.

She lifted the lid and screamed.

Inside, the vacant eyes of Lord Blaine stared back at her. Blood from his severed head pooled at the corners of the box. She turned away and covered her mouth and nose, trying to block out the stench of death.

She heard the whine of metal as swords were drawn. Markell pulled her back from the door, barking orders she hardly heard. The box had already been tossed aside and the head…oh God, the head had rolled out.

Alice threw up in the bedpan.

The clash and clang of metal against metal forced her to focus. Markell! He'd been pushed back into the room by two men dressed in green livery. He held them at bay, but only just.

Another four armed soldiers surged into the room. Alice rummaged through her pack for the knife she'd stashed there the day before. "Seth!" she shouted. "Gus!" She hoped they could hear her. She hoped they hadn't been set upon by Quellery's men too.

"Alice, the window!" Markell barked. "Jump into the moat!"

The moat! It was so far down and she couldn't swim. Nor could she leave him.

Two of the new soldiers engaged in the fight against Markell while the other two came for her, advancing cautiously as if she were a frightened bird that would fly through the window at any moment.

Markell backed up. Blood dripped from a cut on his sword hand and sweat dampened his forehead. He could not continue to fight all these soldiers alone.

Alice peered out the window and her stomach rolled. But it wasn't the moat that sickened her, it was the sight of an army on its banks. Quellery's army, dressed in the same dark green as their attackers.

They were trapped.

Seth and Gus rushed into the room, brandishing swords.

They quickly felled a man each and engaged the ones fighting Markell, freeing him to grab Alice's hand. He spotted the army on the bank and swore.

"I can't swim," she said.

"We can't go that way anyway," he said.

"Eva!" Seth shouted as he pulled his sword from an opponent's stomach. "David! *Now*!"

Eva appeared at the door and beckoned to Alice. Markell hustled her past the fight and into Eva's arms then rejoined Seth and Gus. One of the renegades joined him and another three stood with Eva and David. Alice took Eva's hand and they followed David along the corridor. The sounds of the fight receded, yet her stomach heaved again. She had nothing left to throw up.

Moments later, Seth, Gus, Markell and the fourth renegade joined them.

"Where are we going?" Markell demanded.

"There's a secret passage this way," Eva said. "When we heard Alice scream, Gus and Seth went to help you while David and I looked for a way out. I found a maid who told us about the hidden stairs."

David pulled on an unlit wall torch. A soft click sounded but nothing happened. Seth and Markell pushed past him and put their shoulders to the wall. The stones parted, revealing a passageway. David hesitated so Gus grabbed the torch and went in first. He lit the rushes using a box of matches fished out of his inside jacket pocket and led the way along the dark corridor.

It reminded Alice of their escape from the queen's castle. That had been successful. She only hoped this one would be too. "Where does it go?" she asked.

"The maid said it leads to the forest," Eva said.

"What if the army is in the forest?"

No one answered her. Markell's hand found hers in the

semi-darkness and squeezed. He was alive, thank God. They both were. They *would* get through this.

They traveled the length of the tunnel quickly. As with their escape from the queen's palace, light filtered in through the cracks around the exit. Gus and Seth pushed the door open just enough to peer through and check the vicinity.

The door was wrenched wide open. There should not have been anyone there, waiting for them.

"Back!" Gus shouted even as he was dragged through the doorway.

"Gus!" Seth tried to grab him but he too was hauled out. He managed a lethal strike on his attacker before a blade sliced his sword arm.

Eva cried out as she too was taken. Markell dragged Alice back along the tunnel but the way was blocked by advancing soldiers.

They were trapped. The maid was loyal to Quellery, the man who paid her, not to a miserable band of rebels. Alice's heart dropped like a stone.

"Come out, Miss Alice, or your friends will be executed." Lord Quellery's sneering voice made her want to throw up again.

Markell adjusted his grip on his sword and assessed the situation. But Alice knew it was hopeless. Too many soldiers blocked the way they'd come, and one by one, soldiers pressed through the door ahead.

"Come, Markell," Alice said quietly. "We have to surrender."

"We can't," he said, voice like broken glass. "They'll take you to the queen, and she'll have you executed."

"At least I'll have a chance to defend myself, and hopefully some of the renegade cells have made their way to the castle since hearing of my return. If we die here…" There was no point in finishing the sentence.

Markell touched the back of her neck and pressed his forehead to hers. "I love you, Alice. Never forget that."

Her throat clogged with tears and she had trouble breathing, let alone speaking, but she had to say it. Had to tell him. "I love you too."

Soldiers wrenched them apart and shoved them into the daylight. Quellery stood before them, flanked by several men. Gus, Seth, Eva, David and the other renegades knelt on the grassy bank of the moat, their hands tied behind their backs. They were alive, at least. That was something.

"Don't hurt them," she pleaded. "Let them go home. They can do nothing to you from there."

Quellery didn't bother answering her. His eyes disappeared among the folds of fat as he squinted at Markell.

"You traitor!" Markell shouted.

"I believe *you* are the traitor, Ironside, not me."

"You lied to us! You betrayed us, betrayed the rightful queen of Wonderland."

"You're a naive fool if you think it matters who sits on the throne. What matters is harnessing that power. If you'd only agreed to my proposal, Alice, I would have made Wonderland the most important kingdom in all the realms. But you're as stupid as he is. You think love is more important than power and wealth. Love fades, girl. It withers and dies just like every other pretty flower."

"I've changed my mind," Alice blurted out. "I'll marry you, my lord. Please, let everyone go and I will do as you ask."

Quellery snorted. "It's too late. I've already sent word to the queen."

"You're spineless, Quellery," Seth snarled. "This isn't right and you know it!"

Quellery flicked a hand toward Seth as if brushing off a fly. "Take them away."

"Where are you taking us?" Alice cried.

"The queen still wants you to face trial. The people will stand for nothing else."

The people could still rise up and start a revolution.

But it would be almost impossible for them to win against not only Wonderland's army, but Quellery's private one too. Not to mention the blood that would be shed.

Alice appealed to Markell but he merely stood with his head bowed, a broken man. Her heart ached for him, for them all. Yet while they lived, there was hope. Always hope.

Markell must have sensed her gaze. He looked up and began to struggle against the soldiers that held him, but he could do nothing with his hands bound. "You murdered Blaine," he snapped at Quellery.

"Sanctimonious fool," Quellery sneered.

Markell gave an almighty roar and wrenched free of the two soldiers holding him. He surged toward Quellery, rage and hatred twisting his handsome features into something unrecognizable.

A group of soldiers stepped in front of their master and blocked Markell. One drew his knife.

"No!" Alice cried, pulling free of her captor. She ran at Markell and the soldiers, screaming for them to stop.

One man went to grab her but she dodged him, only to lose her footing on the damp grass and fall over the edge into the moat. Water enveloped her, filled her ears, her nose, her mouth. She spat it out and kicked, searching for the bottom. But it was too deep. She flailed her arms, trying to reach the surface, but…where was it? Up or down? She couldn't make out the sky through the water, only darkness and a heavy weight squeezing her from all sides, smothering her.

No hands reached for her. No one dove in to rescue her.

The weight grew heavier. It crushed her chest and throat, squeezing until she thought her ribs would crack. Every piece of her craved air but Alice kept her lips shut.

But with every labored thud of her heart, the darkness grew deeper, her limbs heavier.

Then everything went black.

CHAPTER 11

SETH

Seth fought to breathe, to stay focused and watch as Alice's lifeless body was pulled from the moat. Two soldiers had finally dived into the water and rescued her, despite not being ordered to do so.

Quellery watched from the bank, his nostrils flared, his hands at his back. He did not chastise the two soldiers but Seth wouldn't want to be in their shoes later. Quellery hadn't wanted her to live. Seth felt sick.

Alice lay on the ground, a wet bundle of awkwardly placed limbs and mass of hair. Her chest didn't move.

"She's not breathing!" Markell cried. "You murderer, Quellery!"

"She fell in," Quellery said with a shrug. "It was nothing to do with me. You all saw."

Eva ran to the body, almost tripping into the moat herself in her haste. Soldiers trailed after her, but none stopped her. She wasn't deemed a threat.

She crouched and bent Alice's head to the side, brushing damp hair off her face. Water drained from Alice's mouth then Eva centered her head again and tilted it back. She pinched Alice's nose and breathed into her mouth.

"What's she doing?" asked Lady Oxana. Seth hadn't noticed her arrival.

Nobody answered, but Seth knew. Lincoln had taught him the technique of mouth-to-mouth resuscitation as part of their training. Seth had never used it, and had even doubted it would work, but he had faith in Eva's abilities. She was the closest thing to a doctor they had, and if she thought it would work, then it was worth trying. Seth only hoped Quellery wouldn't force the soldiers to stop her.

"She's not breathing," Markell said again as he strained against the men holding him. He looked like a man whose world had fallen apart.

Eva placed her hands over Alice's chest and pushed down hard several times. This hadn't been part of Seth's training in resuscitating drowning victims. What was she doing?

"This is absurd," Quellery spat. "She's dead. Take the prisoners away."

Eva, once again breathing into Alice's mouth, put up her hand to keep the soldiers at bay. They hovered nearby, fascinated yet unsure.

"Stay away from her," Markell growled at them. "Or the queen will be told how her prisoner could have been saved but wasn't. She wouldn't like it if her revenge ended here and not in the courtroom as she planned."

Quellery's neck jiggled with his indignation. He did not give orders again, however, and he too stood by and watched Eva.

Suddenly Alice drew in a breath and coughed up water.

"Alice!" Markell struggled but the soldiers held him. "Alice, are you all right?"

Alice did not get up. She lay on her back and stared at the sky, but her chest rose and fell with her breaths. She lived. Seth had never seen anything like it. She'd stopped breathing for more than a minute. She should be dead. Eva had done that. She'd performed a miracle.

Seth couldn't stop his tears.

Eva spoke quietly to Alice as some of the soldiers crowded closer. Even Quellery and Lady Oxana moved in.

Lady Oxana patted her heart. "That is a relief. Imagine if the queen found out you didn't give orders to—"

"Quiet, Oxana," Quellery growled. "Go inside. You there, help the princess."

"Gently," Eva said. "Her heart has suffered a trauma and will be fragile."

One of the soldiers who wore a brass pin on his chest ordered his men to help Alice to the supply cart.

"Alice?" Markell asked as the two men walked slowly away with her between them.

She smiled weakly at him. "I'm all right. Just tired."

"You'll feel that way for a day or two," Eva told her. "You must rest now."

"She can rest on the journey," Quellery said.

Markell closed his eyes and swallowed hard. Seth wanted to clap him on the back and give him a strong brandy. He huffed out a laugh, surprised at his reaction when he thought he'd lost Alice. While it upset him, he wasn't as devastated as Markell looked. Seth had never truly loved her then, although he didn't really know why. She was a wonderful girl.

The soldiers formed into two rows behind the cart, their prisoners in the middle of the columns. It was an identical procession as the one that had taken them to the queen's castle, except that Markell was now a prisoner too, and their captors wore green livery not crimson.

They walked until late in the day when they stopped by the river and made camp. The soldiers put up tents and lit fires, silently and methodically going about their business. The prisoners were taken into the forest to relieve themselves then tied back to back in pairs to stop them running off. It was damned uncomfortable. The only saving grace was being bound to Eva. Seth wasn't sure if she liked it as much, however. She didn't speak to him. She must still be upset by Alice's near drowning.

"You were marvelous," he told her. "You saved Alice's life even though it meant putting your own in danger."

"She's my friend," she said simply.

"You were extremely brave. I know about mouth-to-mouth, but why were you pressing her heart like that?"

"It's called cardiac massage. It's a new technique developed by a German doctor. He spoke at a lecture I recently attended about re-starting an arrested heart by compressing the chest. It was theory only, though. He'd never performed it in real life."

"Looks like it works excellently."

Eva blew out a shaky breath. She must have doubted it would work too, and the shock of what she'd done—of what she'd averted—was beginning to sink in. Seth wished he could hug her but the damned bonds kept them close yet apart at the same time. He'd have to try a different way to cheer her up. He wished he knew how to do that when he was feeling somewhat shaky himself.

"You'll have to write an article for one of those medical journals when you get back," Seth said. "You'll be the toast of the profession. There'll be no trying to fool everyone into thinking you're training for nursing when they hear what you did."

"I'm a student, Seth. No one will believe me. And what should I tell them? That I used the technique on an exiled princess, but you can't question her because she lives in another realm?"

"You're right. You'll just have to settle for telling Lincoln, Charlie and the others when you get back." He moved and winced as the wound on his arm rubbed against the fabric of his sleeve. It wasn't deep, and he'd forgotten it was there until now.

"You're hurt," Eva said, trying, and failing, to twist so she could inspect his injury. "The wound should be cleaned and dressed." She called over one of the soldiers.

"Worried about your husband?" Seth teased.

"You can stop the ruse now. She's not here." Neither Lady Oxana nor Lord Quellery had joined them, and Seth hoped that was the last they'd see of the pair.

"Pity," he said with a theatrical sigh. "I enjoyed kissing you."

She went quite still and he wished he could see her face. She always looked so pretty when she blushed, and he wanted to tell her so, but the soldier stood over them, scowling. Nothing put a dampener on romantic notions than being tied up and at the mercy of an armed man.

"My friend is injured," Eva said to the soldier. "I'd like to inspect his wound."

"I cannot release you," he said.

"Please. It might fester and—"

"No."

"Damn you!"

The soldier took a step toward her and bared his teeth in a growl.

"Don't touch her!" Seth snapped. "It doesn't matter, Eva. The wound isn't deep."

"It should still be seen to," Eva muttered as the soldier walked off.

"Why me?" Seth asked her.

"What do you mean?"

"Why do you want to check my wound?"

"Professional concern."

"Others are also injured. Markell has a cut on his hand, and Gus's face is more messed up than usual."

"I haven't got anything for bruising," she said. "Only cuts. And I didn't know Markell was injured. He didn't complain about it."

"Nor did I."

She snorted softly.

"I didn't."

"You breathed in sharply just now when you moved your arm."

"It wasn't a sharp breath of pain, I was simply enjoying the fresh air out here in the forest. I like the smell of trees, don't you?"

"The gentleman doth protest too much, methinks."

He grinned, despite himself. "I do love a woman who can misquote Shakespeare to me."

Silence as thick as a London fog enveloped them.

"Can we talk about that kiss we shared earlier?" he asked.

"No."

"It was a nice kiss," he went on, wanting to ward off the silence. "But certainly not my best effort. In the interests of proving to you that I am a great kisser, I'd like to try again."

She went utterly still at his back. Perhaps he shouldn't tease her. He couldn't help it though. He liked the way she looked at him. Liked that she worried about his injuries. Liked that the kiss had rattled her enough that she was too nervous to bring it up again.

He liked a lot of things about her.

"Lady Oxana isn't here," she said again. "There's no need for more kisses between us."

"I beg to differ. What if she shows up all of a sudden and tries to lure me again? My virtue is at stake, Eva. Would you have that on your conscience when you could have saved me with a little kiss?"

"You're incorrigible," she said, a lilt of humor in her voice.

He smiled and tipped his head back so that it rested against hers. She didn't move away. He liked that about her too. He closed his eyes and stretched out his legs.

When they got back home, he was going to pursue these fledgling feelings for Eva to see where they led. *If* they got back home. Right now, he couldn't see a way out of his bonds, let alone a way to escape Quellery's army before they reached the queen's castle. His good mood turned sour.

"Have you noticed how like your mother she is?" Eva asked.

He opened his eyes. "Who?"

"Alice."

He looked at Alice, tied up with Markell. They were making the most of being near one another and talking quietly. Alice rested her head against Markell's back and smiled sadly at something he said. The smallest fingers on their hands linked together, declaring their feelings for each other to the world.

"Her bearing is quite regal," Eva went on. "Like your mother's. I've always thought that of them both, even though I didn't know Alice was a princess when I first met her."

"And my mother only *wishes* she were a princess," Seth added.

Eva laughed softly and Seth felt pleased that her melancholy had lifted. He would do anything not to sadden or worry her again.

"I suppose they're both very good at demanding attention," he said. "And telling others what to do."

That certainly explained a lot. Perhaps part of Seth had recognized that Alice was similar to his mother, and rebelled at developing any sort of romantic relationship with her.

"It's no wonder I never fell in love with her," he said.

Behind him, Eva shifted as if she were trying to see him better. "You're not?"

"No."

"Are you sure?"

"Very. I can look at her with Markell now and not feel an ounce of jealousy. When I first saw that she had feelings for him, I wasn't upset. I was actually pleased for her. She's a great girl and deserves a great man at her side."

"You're a great man."

He smiled. "Thank you. But I'm not Markell. I don't advise queens and princesses, nor would I want to. I prefer slaying supernatural villains and mad scientists. They're more straight forward."

"Oh," she said, sounding distant.

"They make a fine couple." He stifled a yawn. "Don't you think?"

"Yes," she whispered. "I've thought so for some time."

"Well now you know that I think so too."

She tipped her head back against his shoulder blade. He felt her body relax with her sigh. He closed his eyes and sighed too.

* * *

THE PRISONERS somehow managed to get some sleep. Seth awoke feeling stiff in the neck and shoulders. The damned bonds tying their hands together had made it an uncomfortable night.

They set off again after dawn, walking on a track that followed the meandering river. According to the soldier guarding them, they should arrive at the castle by mid-afternoon. At least walking meant they were no longer tied up to one another.

"It's nice to be able to look at your face again when I talk to you," he told Eva.

"Yours too," she said.

"Why? You find me handsome?"

She hesitated. "Everyone finds you handsome."

"I asked if *you* do." He was teasing her, but he found he wanted to know the answer.

"It's a very fine face and..." She waved her hand. "Well proportioned."

"There's nothing like a well-proportioned face to set hearts fluttering."

She pressed her lips together but failed to hide her smile altogether.

"You're blushing, Eva."

"It's hot, that's all."

Why wouldn't she admit she liked flirting with him? Her blushes would indicate she liked him very much. Was she afraid of something? He'd been open with her about his past, excepting one part of it, yet she hadn't been embarrassed or shocked, so it couldn't be that. So why didn't she encourage his flirtations?

A soldier shoved Seth in the back to hurry him along. Now wasn't the time to ask intimate questions of Eva. He only hoped he got the chance one day. The closer they got to the queen's castle, the heavier the weight pressing down on him became. He focused all his attention on how to escape, putting thoughts of Eva behind him as much as he could. Now wasn't the time for distraction.

Lady Oxana and Lord Quellery joined the procession after traveling by barge along the river. They requisitioned horses from the general's senior officers and Lord Quellery led the way at the front of the column of soldiers. Lady Oxana fell back to speak with Seth.

"I could have saved you from this," she said smugly. "If only you'd agreed to break your marital vows for one night. Pity. It'll be a shame to impale your pretty head on a spike."

So she still believed he was married to Eva. He had no reason to tell her the truth and Eva, walking beside him, didn't correct her either. She stared straight ahead and appeared not to be listening, but Seth noticed the rigidity across her shoulders, the pulse throbbing in her throat.

"I take my marriage vows very seriously," he said.

"It's not too late. I can have a word with the queen when we reach the castle. We're friends. She'll allow you to live if I promise to keep you house bound." She leaned down and brushed her fingers along the nape of his neck.

Every part of Seth recoiled. The thought of lying with her made him sick. In the past, he'd slept with women he disliked for money but it had never turned his stomach like this. Some of those women hadn't been nice, but they'd never held any real power over him. He'd been able to walk away without payment if he wanted to. He couldn't walk away from Oxana —she could free him, and if he could be freed then he could free the others. It was the wielding of that power in this exchange that made him hate her.

He forced himself to set aside his disgust. Today, he wasn't selling himself for money to put a roof over his head or pay off his father's debts. Today, his price was higher. "I'll do it on the condition—"

Eva rounded on him. "You will *not*, Seth. Do not even consider it." She looked as fierce as a warrior, as vicious as a wild animal protecting its herd. She turned ice-cold eyes onto Lady Oxana. "My husband is not for sale."

"Not even when I can save his life?"

"We'll find another way."

"I doubt it." Lady Oxana wheeled her horse away. "You there," she said to an officer. "Flog this woman."

"You touch her and I'll break every bone in your body," Seth growled. He directed his threat at both the soldier and the viper. The muscles in Lady Oxana's jaw bunched but she said nothing and rode off. The soldier pretended not to hear and fell back into step with his comrades.

Eva and Seth didn't speak for the rest of the way, but Seth didn't mind. He enjoyed just being near her. There was something so compellingly fascinating about her. Something quiet yet profound. These feelings for her had crept up on him ever so slowly that he couldn't even say he was fully aware of them until now, yet in a way, they had always been there, lurking.

She must feel them too, because not only had she defended him to Lady Oxana, she'd *claimed* him.

Seth just had to convince her to take a chance on him. Then they had to get out of here so they could be together. He liked to think the former was easier than the latter, but going by her stoic silence, he wasn't entirely sure.

CHAPTER 12

EVA

The dungeon was even more crowded than the last time they'd been locked up. Eva recognized the donkey who'd wished them well. He stood silently at the bars of his cell, his shoulders slumped as he watched the guards lead Alice and the others past. They'd been his last hope too.

"What happened?" the rabbit, Sir Uther, asked.

"We were captured," Gus spat. "It's all your fault. We wouldn't be here if it weren't for you."

"That's not true, Gus," Alice chided.

The rabbit's nose twitched. "I'm sorry, Princess. I'm very sorry."

They were pushed into a cell at the end and the door locked behind them. The guards retreated into the inky darkness.

"Did my father survive?" Markell asked Sir Uther in the cell opposite.

The rabbit shook his head and his ears drooped. "I'm sorry."

Markell turned to Alice and she held him in her arms.

Gus and Seth searched for a way out. They shook each of the bars, testing their foundations. They clawed at the grimy stones and thumped their boots on the floor, searching for a hollow space. Eva sat in the corner. She didn't care that it was hard, slippery and smelled like urine, she just wanted to get off her aching feet.

"How do we get out?" David asked, joining her on the floor.

She shrugged.

"Tell me. I need to know."

"I don't have the answer, David. I don't even know if we all get out in the end."

He pulled his knees to his chest and rubbed them, over and over. "If you get out, then I must too." He said it so decisively that she wondered if he had a little second sight too, until he said, "Don't you agree?"

"I'm sure we'll both survive this." She looked to where Seth and Gus spoke quietly near the bars. "We all will." Perhaps if she spoke with conviction, it would come true.

David followed her gaze. "You defended him strongly to Lady Oxana. That was very brave of you."

"It was nothing." She meant it. Defending Seth had come naturally. She'd seen the revulsion in his eyes when he looked at Lady Oxana, and she would never allow him to sell himself to her. Not even in exchange for their lives. Eva just couldn't let him do it.

She knew why; she just didn't want to admit it to her brother. He wouldn't approve and the last thing she wanted was an argument.

"I see the way you look at him, Eva," he said, trying to broach the subject.

"It's none of your affair, David."

He sighed. "It seems you no longer care what I think. Do you hate me that much?"

She frowned at him. "I don't hate you. But I don't appreciate you telling me what to do. I'm a grown woman. I can make my own decisions. Some of them might even be good ones."

"I'm quite sure all of them will be good ones. Speaking of which, well done on saving Alice earlier. She owes you her life."

Was he being sarcastic? "It was instinct and training," she muttered.

"You'll make an excellent doctor. You already do, but I know you need the piece of paper to back up your incredible instincts."

She blinked at him. He hadn't been this nice to her since they were children and he wanted to swap bedrooms with her because she had the bigger one. Either he'd turned a corner or he wanted something from her. Perhaps he still thought she could tell him if he survived this.

He tipped his head back against the wall and stared up at the ceiling. "Will you take some advice from your older brother?"

"That depends on what it is."

His smile was sad. "Don't tell anyone in your workplace that your mother is Romany and has visions."

"I'm not ashamed of her, or of our Romany heritage."

"Nor am I."

He wasn't making sense. "David, is there something you want to tell me?"

A dozen white-clad guards approached their cell. One unlocked the door while another beckoned Alice and Markell.

"You have been summoned by Her Majesty the Queen of Hearts to stand trial for high treason," he announced.

"No!" Seth and Gus both cried.

"We stay together," Seth said. "Either we all go or we all stay here."

Two guards drew their swords. "Come with us, Miss Alice, Sir Markell. This is not a request."

Gus rushed forward, fist raised, but Seth held him back at the same time that Markell blocked his way.

"This isn't your fight," Markell said.

"What will happen to my friends?" Alice asked. "Will you send them home?"

"That's up to the queen," the guard said. He ordered his men to bring them out. One grabbed Alice by the wrist only to let go when Markell bared his teeth in a snarl.

Alice exited of her own accord and Markell followed. The guard was about to shut the door but he hesitated. He studied Seth and Gus before indicating Gus should leave the cell too.

"I'm separating you," he said, slamming the door closed and locking it.

"Why?" Seth asked.

"You've both got shifty eyes and warriors' builds. I don't trust you. You need to be separated."

"You can't!" David said, standing alongside Seth. "This is outrageous! We've done nothing wrong here! I demand better treatment."

The guard unlocked the door again, pulled David out, and re-locked it. He shoved both prisoners into the cell opposite with Sir Uther. Gus glared at the rabbit. Sir Uther shrank back into the shadows.

Eva rushed at the bars. "Alice!" She didn't know what else to say. 'Good luck' didn't seem like enough, and she didn't want to say goodbye. She couldn't bear this to be the last time she ever saw her.

Alice cast a grim smile over her shoulder. Her gaze touched on each of them, lingering longest on Seth. She opened her mouth to speak but closed it again and turned forward. Perhaps no words seemed appropriate.

Eva sat again and rested her forehead on her drawn-up knees. She wished desperately for a vision to know what happened to them, but none came. Her talent was utterly useless if she couldn't control it. She wished she had her mother's power. Then again, perhaps not. Charlie's would be more useful in a situation like this.

Seth sat beside her. He didn't speak but his presence was a comfort. She felt a little stronger, a little more hopeful and less weepy. He would survive, as would she. It was the others she worried about. Alice was most likely being led to her death, and with Gus and David now in a different cell, she could foresee how the separation would allow her and Seth to escape but not them. It was only a matter of time to see how it all played out.

"Close your eyes and rest," Seth said gently. "I have a feeling you're going to need it."

"Do you have a plan?" she asked, hope rising.

"Do you count overpowering the next guard to unlock that door a plan?"

She smiled and nudged his arm. He hissed a little. She'd forgotten about the wound. "Let me see."

He glanced toward David and Gus's cell. They both sat against the back wall, legs outstretched, eyes closed. Seth undid the buttons on his shirt and slipped it off his shoulder. Dried blood crusted the cut and stained the shirt.

Eva fidgeted with the hem of her dress, searching for a loose thread. She found one and started unpicking.

"What are you doing?" Seth asked.

"I brought some carbolic acid with me." She widened the hole in the hem and plucked out the vial wrapped in a piece of gauze.

"You brought it with you?" Seth repeated dully. "In your dress?"

She unwrapped the gauze to reveal a small glass phial filled with liquid.

"Eva," he said carefully, "why did you hide medicine in your dress?"

"In case of cuts like this." She didn't look at him. She didn't want to see the shock in his eyes, the distrust.

"You *knew*. You *knew* you'd end up here. You knew you'd have a use for carbolic acid too, so you sewed it into your dress to make sure it crossed through the portal with you. My God." He barked a brittle laugh. "I can't believe it. You had a vision of yourself in Wonderland and came prepared. I feel like such a fool for not realizing."

"You're not a fool." She dripped some of the carbolic acid onto the gauze and dabbed it on the cut.

"Why didn't you tell me?" he pressed. "Why didn't you tell anyone else?"

"What does it matter? It changes nothing. I didn't know who else came with me or what transpired here. Besides, it wasn't my vision, it was my mother's. She warned me and helped me sew these into my hem. She then made sure I wore this dress the day we visited Lichfield and traveled through the portal."

She felt his gaze on her as she dabbed the antiseptic into his wound. She couldn't bring herself to look at him. What if she saw disappointment, distrust, or worse, dislike?

"Perhaps I should have told you sooner," she said, "but I didn't see the point."

"The point is that you kept something from me, Eva. Don't do that again, please."

"Why?" she asked carefully.

"Because I want us to have an open and honest relationship with one another."

"As far as I'm aware, we don't have a relationship."

"Don't we?"

She fumbled and dropped the gauze. She reached for it but he caught her hand. His other touched her chin, forcing her to look at him.

"You're holding something back," he said, searching her face. "What is it?"

She jerked away. She couldn't tell him what she knew of their future together. How could she admit that she'd known they would marry ever since meeting him? What if it forced him down a path he didn't want? He was a man who'd had many lovers but never proposed to a woman. Why would he want that to change? What if telling him about her vision led him to make the worst mistake of his life?

She concentrated on tying the gauze around his arm and not meeting his gaze.

"Very well then." He folded his arms over his chest. His very bare, very masculine chest. She refused to look him in the eye, but she could look at his bandaged bicep and chest. There was no law against it. "Since you're too afraid to tell me your inner most secret, it seems I'll have to tell you mine. I'll entrust you with my darkest secret so you can entrust yours to me."

"I know you're trustworthy, Seth," she said, finally meeting his gaze. It was a mistake. His warm eyes captured her and held her prisoner.

"I want to tell you anyway." He cleared his throat, shifted his weight. She waited for him to be ready. "You'll recall that I sold myself for money to pay my debts."

"Your father's debts. I recall."

"Well, sometimes the highest bidder was a man."

She fought hard to school her features. He'd taken an enormous leap of faith to tell her and she wouldn't betray her surprise. In truth, she was more surprised at her own naivety than his confession. He was, after all, extraordinarily beautiful, and wealthy men outnumbered women in the world, so why not at the auctions too? She'd heard all sorts of stories through her medical studies, both from patients and doctors, so she knew what acts some men performed behind closed doors.

"Don't tell anyone else," she told him. "You could be thrown in jail."

He cocked his head to the side. "That's all you have to say?"

"I'm not shocked, if that's what you mean." She did have several questions, but she wasn't quite sure if he was ready to answer them.

"Are you...disgusted?"

"No. I do know men sometimes share a bed with other men, and women with other women too. I may have had a sheltered upbringing, but I am an adult with keen observational skills."

He let out a measured breath. "Then you will have observed that I prefer women."

She smiled. "Oh yes, I have definitely observed that."

"My experiences with men were simply a means to an end."

She closed her hand over his. "Thank you for telling me."

He looked up from their linked fingers. "Is there anything else you'd like to know? I can answer your questions. I'm not ashamed, Eva. Not with you."

She was glad he felt he could confide in her, and relieved that he wasn't ashamed to reveal his secret to her. "Then I do have a question. How did it begin? The auctions, I mean. What made you think to do it?"

He turned his hand palm-up so that he was clasping hers. "It was actually a man who gave me the idea. A Frenchman, Monsieur Fernesse. I first met him when he was living in London. He was a friend of my mother's and took a keen interest in me. I knew he wanted to be with me, but I was eighteen at the time and found myself too busy with women to pay him much attention."

"I'm sure you were very busy."

"I took full advantage of all female interest, without a care for how my fickle heart affected them. I'm sorry to say I took the virtue of a number of debutantes before learning my lesson the hard way. One of the fathers confronted me and ordered me to marry his daughter. He withdrew her hand when he learned how poor we really were. After that, I chose more carefully. No more debutantes, only merry widows with no interest in walking down the aisle. The widows were better in another way too—I didn't have to woo them with gifts. In fact, they gave *me* gifts.

"Monsieur Fernesse had been at the edges of my awareness for some time at that point, but he swanned into my life in a bigger way when my reputation grew in certain circles. He told me I should make those widows pay for my services, not with gifts but money. I was skeptical. I didn't think they would. So he set up a private viewing with some of his wealthier clients—he's a decorator—and gauged interest."

"Let me guess," Eva said. "Interest was strong?"

"Enough for me to agree to an auction then and there. It quickly became apparent to us both that it wasn't just women who wanted to bid for me. A few husbands asked him if they could bid on behalf of their wives."

"Really?"

He chuckled. "So I have shocked you."

"I'm shocked that men were prepared to share their wives with another man."

"Some wanted nothing to do with the post-auction prize, some wanted to watch, and others wanted to join in. Monsieur Fernesse refused the latter, telling them I wouldn't cross that line. After a particularly nasty creditor sent his thugs to my door, I told Monsieur Fernesse I'd be willing, for double the final bid. Monsieur Fernesse insisted I be…initiated first. He took me under his wing and showed me what to expect. Once I set my masculine pride aside, I found I didn't dislike it as much as I thought I would. It wasn't…natural for me, but he was a kind lover. He made sure ground rules were set at the auctions too. He was good to me."

"Do you think he was using the initiation as an excuse to be with you?"

"I'm sure of it. Don't worry, Eva." His mouth quirked in a devilish grin. "I dined finely for several weeks as he courted me. I led him to believe we had more than a mentor-mentee relationship when I knew nothing more would ever develop between us. Looking back, I wasn't fair to him."

"You won't get me feeling sorry for him, Seth. He took advantage of you."

"You can't take advantage of someone who knows full well what's going on and can walk away without getting hurt. I didn't have to agree, not to him, not to any of it. He never threatened to expose me to polite society or to my mother. He never held anything over me."

Not like Lady Oxana, Eva could have said but did not. She didn't want to remind him of that witch.

"As I settled into my money-making scheme, I found I no longer had any need for Monsieur Fernesse. I took over the organization of the auctions and slowly untangled myself from him. I told him I could never love men the way he did, and he returned to Paris soon afterward."

"Was he in love with you?"

"Perhaps. I didn't know what love was, so I wouldn't have recognized the signs." His fingers tightened around hers. "So there it is. My innermost secret. You have the power to send me to prison and ruin my reputation if you want to."

"I will never abuse that power, Seth."

"I know. I wouldn't have told you if I had doubts. Now it's your turn. Tell me your secret. It can't be more shameful than mine, surely."

She thought about changing the subject or lying and telling him she had no secrets. But that would be cruel. He'd given her the gift of his trust. She would cherish it and return it with her own gift.

"My secret is quite different to yours," she began. "It involves you, as it happens, and me."

"Then I already like this secret."

"You may not, when you learn what it is." She hesitated,

steadying her nerves, and he squeezed her hand in encouragement. "Do you recall when we first met?"

"You were very quiet and gave me odd looks."

"That's because I'd seen you in my visions."

He pulled away to look at her better. "Really? I'm honored."

"I didn't know your name, nor was I prepared for our meeting. It came as quite a shock to learn that the man in my visions was not only a friend to my new half-brother but also a nobleman. It came as an even bigger shock to see how you looked at Alice."

"With infatuation, no doubt."

She nodded.

"I meant what I said earlier," he said gently. "I am not in love with her. I never was."

"I know that now, but I didn't then."

"Why did it matter that you thought I was in love with Alice?"

"Because in my vision, we were married."

His fingers flexed around hers. Wanting to release her? Or wanting to hold tighter? She watched him closely for a reaction, for signs that her admission disturbed him. She saw nothing, just blankness.

"A real marriage?" he asked, slowly. "Or the false one we made up to trick Lady Oxana?"

"A real marriage. I knew in my soul that we wed. My mother had a similar vision."

"I see."

"Visions don't always come true," she told him. "Perhaps it will never come to pass."

"Have you ever known one not to?"

She gave her head a small shake.

"Well then. It seems a foregone conclusion." He sighed. Sighing after hearing such news was not a good sign.

"It doesn't have to be," she said lamely.

He studied her. "Do you mind marrying me?" It sounded like a proposal. Almost.

"I resented it," she said, wanting to continue their newly set precedence of honesty. "I didn't want to marry anyone. A husband would stifle me, force me to give up my dreams and plans of becoming a doctor. And you were a nobleman. A nobleman would expect his lady to behave conventionally."

"A conventional nobleman might." He stroked her jaw. How could calloused hands be so gentle? "But I am not conventional, Eva." His voice purred and his eyes were no longer blank. They shone with an emotion she couldn't decipher.

She swallowed. Waited.

But he said nothing more, merely stared at her with unwavering intensity that shattered her nerves.

"Eva!" David called, breaking through the fog that clouded her head. "What did you put on Seth's wound earlier?"

She let Seth go, or perhaps he let her go first. She found she couldn't look at him anymore. They knew one another's deepest secrets as well as their future together. The problem was, she didn't know how to proceed. He seemed just as awkward and unsure. He moved away and buttoned up his shirt again, all business.

"I have some carbolic acid," Eva said, reaching for her hem. "It's an antiseptic. Do you need it?"

"Gus does."

Gus held up his wrist. "Got a small cut. Nothing bad but David thinks you can do something. Do you always carry antiseptic in your dress?"

"It's a long story," Seth told him.

Eva felt along the hem, counting the number of vials of carbolic acid. She'd sewn in two and she wasn't sure how many more her mother added before sewing it up. She counted four lumps. No, five, except the middle one didn't feel the same as the others. It was longer and flatter. She pushed the lumps along the hem and plucked them out through the opening. One was definitely different to the other four. She unwrapped it but still had no clue what she was looking at. Two long metal pieces the length of her smallest finger lay on the gauze. Why would her mother hide them with the vials?

"Bloody hell," Seth murmured, picking them up. His face took on a new light, as if he'd been lit from within. "Where did you get these?"

"My mother must have placed them there. Do you know what they are?"

"I certainly do. Is your mother a master burglar, by any chance?"

"No."

"Then someone advised her to give you these. My guess is Lincoln. Eva, it seems your mother and half-brother have been colluding behind your back."

"What are those sticks for?"

"Picking locks." He took the sticks and stood. "Lincoln taught me how to use them." He squatted by the door and tried to reach his hand through the bars but it was too big.

"Let me try." Eva's hand fit and she was able to grab the padlock and draw it closer to the bars so he could insert the sticks into it.

Gus, David and Sir Uther grasped the bars of the cell opposite, their gazes glued to Seth's nimble fingers. None spoke. Eva dared not breathe.

"Damn it," Seth muttered. "I wish I'd practiced more."

Finally the lock clicked open. He grinned at her in triumph. She grinned back and swung the door open. The rabbit hopped on the spot as Seth picked the lock to their cell.

"Fitzroy's saving us and he ain't even in the same realm," Gus said. "The man ain't human."

David picked up the heavy padlock, weighing it in his

palm. "Or he placed those sticks in the dress because his new wife forced him to."

Gus smacked David's shoulder. "Idiot."

"Charlie didn't know we'd need the tools to save ourselves," Eva said. "One look at her worried face as we left would have told you that."

David's lips flattened.

"Lincoln doesn't deserve your hatred," she said. "It's not his fault we share a mother but not a father."

"I don't hate him."

"You don't like him."

"He's so…different."

"You just got to get to know him," Gus said, watching Seth move on to the neighboring cell that harbored a goat. "He ain't so bad."

"Don't waste time freeing us," the donkey said from a cell further down. "You've got to save the princess first. There won't be much time. Trials are notoriously swift."

"And fatal," Sir Uther said on a groan.

"How can we save them?" David asked. "The queen has guards and two armies."

None of the animals answered, but Eva had an idea. "If we can find the magic book and speak the spell that turns an object into a portal, we can slip through it before we're captured." It wasn't a foolproof plan, nor a particularly clever one, but no one could come up with anything better.

"Take the princess with you," the donkey said. "It's the only way to keep her alive."

"And us?" the rabbit whined. "Who will keep us alive when they realize we played a part in this madness?"

"Perhaps you can all come," David said, without much conviction.

"We can't abandon our country," the donkey said. "But thank you. Now, you'll need to get near the princess without anyone noticing."

Seth glanced along the dimly lit corridor. "That won't be a problem. Everyone, back in your cells."

"No," Sir Uther said. "I'm not going in there again." He crossed his arms. "No way."

Gus grabbed the rabbit's ears and pulled him back to the cell. David followed. Seth and Eva returned to theirs.

"My apologies, David," Seth said. "But I'm going to shout at your sister."

"Be my guest," David said.

Seth turned to Eva and shouted about how much he couldn't stand the sight of her. "You're a horrible, cruel woman!" He indicated she should say something back.

"And I hate you!" she screamed.

He looked pleased. "I hate you more! You're a vicious snake, too beautiful for your own good."

She tried not to laugh. "And you've got the face of an angel! Come here and let me mess it up a little for you."

"Guards!" David shouted, joining in. "Guards, come and separate these two before they drive us all mad."

The other prisoners chimed in, shouting at the top of their lungs to be relieved of the ear-splitting duo in the end cell.

Finally a guard emerged like a ghost from the darkness. "What's all the noise down here?"

"It's them," Sir Uther pointed at Eva and Seth.

Eva shouted something at Seth, she hardly even knew what. Seth shouted back at her.

The guard sighed. "You," he said to David, "and you," he said to Eva, "swap cells." He went to unlock the padlock with his key.

Seth shoved the door back. It smashed into the guard's face, bloodying his nose, sending him careening. Before he had a chance to alert his companions, Seth punched him. Gus was already out of his cell and managed to catch the unconscious guard and lower him to the floor so his sword didn't make a sound on the stones.

Seth quickly undressed while David and Eva removed the guard's clothes. She thought her brother might tell her to look away for modesty's sake, but he seemed not to care that she was touching a near naked man.

Sir Uther picked up the key and unlocked the nearest cell as they worked.

"Where will Alice's trial be held?" Seth asked as he pulled on the guard's tunic.

"The audience chamber," Sir Uther said.

"And the spell book?"

Sir Uther shrugged. "The queen's private chambers?"

"I think I know," the donkey said, tapping a hoof against the bars as he waited for the rabbit to unlock his cell. "There are four guards posted at her wardrobe door. The crown jewels aren't kept there, so what is she guarding?"

"Clothes?" Gus offered.

"The spell book," Sir Uther said, opening the donkey's cell door. "You owe me an apology, you moronic oaf. My ears are sensitive."

"So's my pride," Gus said. "I ain't 'pologizing until you 'pologize for calling me an oaf."

Dressed in the guard's white uniform and carrying his sword, Seth headed along the corridor, Gus at his heels. David took Eva's hand but they kept their distance as Seth approached the two guards lounging by the exit. The first guard didn't realize what was happening until Seth smashed his fist into his jaw.

The second guard reached for his sword but Gus struck him before he could draw it. Eva helped David and Gus change into the white uniforms while Seth scouted ahead. Her heart hammered in her throat until she saw him hurry back, safe.

"The coast is clear," he said. To the various animals and humans now clogging the dungeon's corridor, he added,

"There aren't enough of you to fight off the armies and guards."

"She'll have several in the audience chamber with her," the donkey agreed. "And many more spaced through the castle, and outside it. It'll be easy for her to summon them."

"We'll stay out of sight until your signal," said the goat dressed in a cape.

"Eva, stay here," Seth ordered. "Your dress is too conspicuous. David, use that sword if necessary."

"I'm coming with you," David said.

Gus clapped him on the shoulder. "Good man."

"Sir Uther will go with you too," the donkey said.

"Why me?" the rabbit wailed.

"Because you know the way to the queen's chambers and you've got padded paws for feet." The donkey lifted his front hoof. It would make too much noise on the stone floor.

Seth's gaze connected with Eva's. She nodded. He nodded back with a grim smile then disappeared through the exit and out of the dungeon. Gus, David and Sir Uther followed.

Eva folded her arms, rubbing them, but the chill in her bones remained. The two most important men in her life were stepping into unknown dangers, and she hadn't told either of them she loved them.

CHAPTER 13

ALICE

Alice had never felt fear like this before. It clawed at her like a beast, took hold of her entire body and squeezed until she could hardly breathe. She'd faced dangers before with Charlie, but this time the fear was more intense because she was afraid for someone she loved. She was afraid for Markell.

He knelt on the floor, head bowed. She could just make out his swollen eye, almost entirely closed now, and the bruise on his cheek. He'd struggled with the guards on the way up from the dungeon to the audience chamber until Alice begged him to stop. She'd been afraid they would execute him on the spot, without trial.

Now, she almost wished they had. His trial was over and Lord Indrid was announcing the punishment. It involved torture and the removal of limbs. If he survived that, he would be hanged in front of Alice.

She didn't beg. There was no point. The queen didn't possess the capacity for mercy. She'd smiled when Lord Indrid read out Markell's punishments. Then, when he'd finished, she'd turned gleaming eyes onto Alice.

"Miss Alice is charged with high treason," Lord Indrid announced. "She left the realm unlawfully—"

"She was a mere child!" a brave soul called out from the back of the room.

The queen stamped her fist on the arm of her throne. "Who said that? Find him and send him to the dungeon until he learns respect."

A guard moved through the crowd and the courtiers murmured among themselves.

A soldier dressed in army crimson took the opportunity to offer Markell a sip of wine. He held the cup to Markell's lips since Markell's hands were tied at his back. He was one of ten soldiers in the audience chamber. Another twenty guards were interspersed around the room too. All were armed.

"You there!" the queen snapped. "Do not show kindness to the prisoner."

The soldier stepped back and apologized profusely. "Forgive me, Your Majesty. I fought for his father and it pains me to see him—"

"Enough!" She leaned forward. "General Ironside betrayed me. He broke his oath of fealty and would have gleefully led you all to your deaths if he hadn't died first. Is that a man who deserves your loyalty?"

"I'm not loyal to him, Majesty. I merely felt some sympathy for—"

"Get out! Sentimental fools don't belong in my army. Indrid, see that he is expelled without pay."

"No pay?" the soldier cried. "But I have children to feed."

"Then you should have been more careful who you give wine to."

Alice watched him leave, shaking his head. He threw the cup at one of the guards. The wine made a satisfying stain on the white uniform.

Alice's heart lifted. If there was one thing she knew, it was that kindness meant something. Kindness in the face of danger was powerful.

She looked around the room with fresh eyes. Where before she saw only enemies, now she saw potential allies. Where before she thought they were eager to watch her trial, now she thought they seemed afraid. Afraid to rise up against the mad queen who liked to turn her enemies into animals before executing them.

The soldier who'd been seeking the dissenting voice amidst the crowd had stopped looking when he saw the queen's interest wander. He melted into the background.

"We call the first witness, Lord Quellery!" Lord Indrid announced.

Lord Quellery broke away from the crowd and advanced to the queen. His size wouldn't allow him to get down on one knee so he merely bowed. The queen didn't look too pleased but allowed it. "Your Majesty, I offer you my fealty," he said, stating the oath that the witnesses in Markell's trial had also spoken. "I offer you my loyalty and my…guidance."

"And your lands for my use," the queen reminded him. "Come along, Quellery, you know how it goes."

"My lands for your use," Quellery mumbled into his chins.

"Tell the queen and court what transpired seventeen summers ago," Lord Indrid said.

Seventeen years? That was when Alice had been sent to England through the portal.

"The father of the prisoner came to me," Lord Quellery bellowed loud enough so that even the people standing at the back could hear. "He begged me to take her and hide her. I refused, knowing that she was a rival to your good self, Your Majesty."

"We thank you for your loyalty," the queen said. "It's because of you that I was able to remove my corrupt and inept brother from power. It was a pity he'd already sent his daughter into safety."

"Traitor!" Markell spat.

"Silence!" The queen stamped her foot on the floor like a child demanding to get her own way. "Continue, Quellery. Get to the good part."

"When Markell Ironside brought the prisoner to Quellery Castle, I was overjoyed to once again be able to help Your Majesty remove another thorn from the kingdom's side. I pretended to be a sympathizer to gain his trust then sent a man here immediately to alert you."

"Nonsense," Alice scoffed. "He wanted to marry me," she told the queen. "If I had agreed, he was going to give us his army to overthrow you."

Lord Quellery spat rebuttals and saliva at the queen.

The queen put her hand up for silence. "Don't try to fool me, girl," she said. "You might be pretty, but you're a liability for a man like Quellery. I also suspect you're quite mad. Who would want to marry you?"

"I do," Markell said clearly. "I do."

Alice's eyes filled with tears even as her heart swelled. If everything ended today, she at least had this moment to cherish, his declaration to cling to.

"The knave will hold his tongue!" the queen shouted. "Or expect it to be cut out."

Alice quickly shook her head at Markell in warning. Thank God he remained silent.

"Proceed, Quellery," the queen said. "Tell us more of the usurper's treasonous plots."

Quellery pushed out his considerable chest. "They wanted to buy my army and use it to overthrow you, my queen. I bided my time as long as I could, to allow my man to reach you, then captured the rebels and brought them here."

"And did Miss Alice orchestrate these plots?"

"Under the guidance of Ironside." He looked to Markell. "He's the real villain here, Your Majesty. *He* planned to marry her once she was on the throne. Personal power and gain are *his* motivation, not mine."

The crowd of noblemen and women murmured among themselves, but more than one soldier shook his head sadly. They knew Markell best and knew he wasn't motivated by greed.

"If that is so," Markell broke in, "then I wouldn't want to marry her now, would I, since she has nothing but her character to offer?" He turned to Alice and despite everything, his voice gentled. "If she would have me, I would marry her here in this room, at this moment."

She sensed the change in the audience. It began with the shifting of feet and whispers that slowly escalated until she could hear the words.

"...love..." said a woman.

"...from a good family..." said another.

"...conviction and loyalty."

"Quellery's a turncoat," a man said, loud enough for all to hear.

Lord Quellery protested with a vehement quake of his jowls. Lady Oxana stood in the middle of the front row, as still as a pillar, only her pale throat moving with her swallows. She'd sensed the change in the air too, and she was afraid.

"Princess Alice is not the villain the queen paints her to be." Markell's voice rose clear over all others. "She is clever and strong, kind and just. If she weren't, I wouldn't be declaring my love for her now. I wouldn't be prepared to tether my life to hers."

"Quiet!" the queen shouted. "Stop talking, Traitor!"

Despite her temper flaring, the audience's murmurs continued.

Alice knew what Markell was doing, and she knew what she must do next. He urged her with a nod.

"I accept your proposal of marriage, Markell," Alice

announced. A distant part of her considered the absurd theatricality of it, but she set that aside. Now wasn't the time for self-conscience. "I may have only known him a few days but he has proven himself loyal to me, kind and courageous. He has guided me in all things, and I was looking forward to learning so much more about my country and its people, about my parents." Her voice cracked and the tears threatened to spill. "When I first met Sir Markell, I feared him. He explained who I was, my situation, my *birthright,* and when I got to know him—"

"Stop her!" the queen demanded.

"My friends were afraid to lose me and fought Sir Markell and General Ironside. Wonderland's finest men proved how brave they were, how loyal to their country and people. I wasn't brought up as a princess. I didn't know anything about Wonderland until recently, and I feared what faced me here. But Sir Markell made the transition easy, with his patience and guidance. I am yet to meet many Wonderlanders, but if they are all like him, then I know I will be in safe hands. I know I will love them because I love him."

"Stop her, stop her, *stop her*!" the queen screamed, banging her fist on her throne arm and her foot on the floor. "Lord Indrid, *do* something."

Indrid signaled the nearest soldier. He hesitated.

Alice saw her opportunity and took it. "*You* were not chosen by the people." She jutted her chin at the queen. "So you should not be allowed to make decisions that affect them."

The queen stiffened. "Your father wasn't chosen either. Nor your grandfather. Nor you, for that matter. I am the queen. *That* gives me the right to make decisions."

"I disagree. In England, the monarch's power is curtailed. She doesn't rule absolutely."

"What a foolish kingdom then." The queen snorted a laugh.

Alice tuned her out and listened to the murmurs, watched the faces of those in the room, not just the nobles, but the soldiers. The usually stoic men began exchanging glances. Two of them bent their heads together in quiet conversation, their gazes falling on Markell.

Alice had spent much of their time at Quellery Castle explaining the English monarchy and government to Markell and Lord Blaine. They'd been interested and even discussed ways of implementing a similar system in Wonderland. They'd suggested change should be introduced slowly and subtly, but there was no time for slow and subtle now.

"Officials elected by the people make laws after debate in parliament," Alice went on. "When I am queen, I will steer Wonderland toward a constitutional monarchy, and a system where power is not held by one person who hasn't been elected by the people."

"*When* you become queen!" the queen sneered. "Ha! Do you not see your shackles? Are you blind to your situation? It seems I need to spell it out to you. I find you guilty of high treason. As my niece, you are entitled to a swifter, more dignified punishment." To the audience, she said, "I am merciful. The traitor known as Miss Alice will be executed with a sharp sword. Off with her head!" She laughed and leaned forward. "But first, you will watch your lover die painfully." She signaled one of the guards. "Take Markell Ironside to the courtyard and begin his punishment. Court dismissed."

"No!" Alice's cry rose above the other voices. She appealed to the two soldiers who'd been talking to one another. "Don't allow this to happen. You have the power to stop this." She looked at each of the ten soldiers, holding their gazes one by one. "You respected General Ironside. I know you did."

"The traitor," the queen spat.

"He was loyal to Wonderland, a good man."

"He tried to kill me! His queen! The general broke his oath. He deserved his end."

"General Ironside realized his country was suffering under your rule." Alice's voice did not sound like her own. It was all steel and cold fury. She hated the woman who sat on the throne. Hated her for what she'd done to her parents, hated her for taking away her childhood, hated her for the pain she'd inflicted on Markell by killing his father. Alice couldn't hold back her anger anymore. She'd had enough. She would say her piece or die doing so. "The general died for Wonderland. He was loyal to its people. He should be applauded for helping us escape you. When I am queen, I will see that he is honored properly for his sacrifice."

"When, when, when! There you go again, assuming." The queen laughed, but it was nervous laughter that quickly died when she saw the soldiers draw their swords. "Guards! Guards!"

Two guards rushed to her, blocking anyone from getting close. Another threw open the doors and the audience of nobles poured out, sensing trouble. The other guards eyed the soldiers, more loyal to the Ironside name than the queen had expected. The soldiers were armed this time, thank God, but they were outnumbered, two to one. The queen also had Quellery's army, somewhere outside. Both armies were oblivious to the proceedings in the audience chamber. Once they became aware, it would be a different story. Lives would be lost. Panic would ensue. It would be carnage. They had to stop this now.

Markell sensed it too. He was on his feet, still shackled, but no longer looking defeated. He looked alive. So alive, and handsome and in command. "Men! It's time! Are you with me?"

The soldiers raised their swords as one. "Aye!"

"Take the queen prisoner!"

The soldiers engaged the guards in a deafening clash of swords. One of the soldiers slashed his blade through the ropes shackling Markell's hands but a guard attacked.

Everything in Alice screamed in fear.

Markell dove to the side and rolled out of the way of the guard's descending blade then he kicked the guard's shin. He lost his balance and the soldier drove his weapon through the guard's torso. He wasted no time in slicing through the rope tying Markell's feet together.

Markell jumped up and grabbed the fallen guard's sword. He fended off two more, holding them at bay, his sword flashing in the sunlight streaming through the windows. He was magnificent, an excellent swordsman. But he could not reach Alice in time.

She saw the guard coming for her but couldn't flee with her feet and hands tied. She dared not shout for help lest she distract Markell. He had to keep his wits about him to fight off two attackers. The guard slammed into her, punching the breath out of her. He picked her up and slung her over his shoulder and carried her off toward the back of the audience chamber where the secret tunnel led out of the castle. The queen was ahead of them, ushered by another guard. Once inside, with the guards closing ranks around the entrance, it would be impossible to follow.

Alice glanced toward Markell. As if sensing her, he looked away from the fight and so missed the attacking thrust. The blade struck him and he stumbled back. Blood oozed from the wound in his side.

CHAPTER 14

SETH

The rabbit was more conspicuous than Seth would have liked. Gus and David marched Sir Uther between them with Seth leading. That way, it looked like they were transporting a prisoner. Dressed in stark white uniforms, they easily passed the handful of guards standing on duty in corridors and at doors. The castle's rooms joined together, each door leading straight into another chamber, all furnished with thick-legged chairs, embroidered tapestries, and no curtains to speak of, only shutters. Each room became more intimate—formal drawing room, followed by a music room, small sitting room, even smaller antechamber and finally the queen's bedchamber, with two guards standing by the door.

Gus and Seth marched up to them and punched them hard before they had a chance to realize they were not fellow guards. Seth caught one before his fall made a noise, but the other body thudded as it crumpled on the floor.

"Why didn't you catch him?" David whispered.

"Didn't think he deserved a soft landing," Gus said.

Seth put his hand on the door handle, but Sir Uther placed

a paw over it to stay him. "They'll see you from where they stand," he said.

Seth nodded thanks for the warning and cracked open the door just enough to peer through. The bedchamber was as large as Lichfield's drawing room and contained several hazards in the form of solid furniture, and four guards at the wardrobe door on the far side. He closed the door.

"There are two on the left and two on the right, all armed," he said. "Swords are sheathed on left hips."

"That means they're right handed," Gus told David.

"I know that," David said. "I've read books on military battles."

"Then you'll be an expert."

David cut him a withering glare.

"Gus, you take the right two, I'll take the left," Seth said.

David nibbled his lip. "I should help."

Sir Uther held up his paws. "I'm not armed."

"And you're a coward," Gus added. "With sensitive ears."

"You can stand back," Seth said to David. The man had no training and no inclination to fight. He'd frozen when they were set upon by guards in the forest. Besides, Seth didn't want to see Eva's face if her brother got hurt. "Don't interrupt. Gus and I can manage two each."

Gus met his gaze. They both knew they could dispatch two average swordsmen but Seth doubted the guards were average. Their biggest weapon was the element of surprise. It would give them precious seconds in which to strike first before the guards realized they were being duped.

"Sir Uther, stay out of sight," he said.

The rabbit's nose twitched and he quickly melted into the shadows.

"You should too," Seth said to David.

David clasped his sword hilt with both hands and, for a moment, Seth thought he'd volunteer to join them in the fight. But he simply nodded and joined the rabbit.

Seth clasped Gus's shoulder. Gus nodded. There was no point in exchanging more words. They'd been in situations like this before, dozens of times. Words became meaningless after a while. Action was required now—and intense focus.

He opened the door and strode in. The four guards tensed then recognized the uniforms and relaxed. All except one.

"I don't know you," he said.

"We're new," Seth said, striding across the bedchamber, Gus at his side. "We haven't met yet."

One of the other guards unsheathed his sword. "We would have been introduced."

"We're introducing ourselves now."

"It's the prisoners!" said another. "I recognize—"

Seth drew his sword and thrust, but the guard who'd drawn his blade blocked it. Gus drove his sword through the guard's thigh.

One down.

Two against three were better odds but the guards were skillful. They were big men, and each bone shattering blow reverberated along Seth's arm. He danced into the fray and out, dodging those powerful strikes, parrying only when absolutely necessary to save his injured arm. He hadn't thought the cut deep but every blow felt like a hot iron had been shoved into the wound.

He fought two while Gus had one. Gus was the more capable knife man, but Seth was the better swordsman. Gus's technique was more slash and hack while Seth used his feet as much as his sword. He probably had his pugilism background to thank for that, as well as fencing when he was younger.

But these men were good. They carried swords with them all the time and trained with them every day. There was rarely a use for swordplay back home. Seth wished he'd practiced more with Lincoln.

Gus grunted but Seth dared not look to see if his friend

had been struck. He couldn't afford to take his eyes off his two opponents. Sweat beaded on his forehead and trickled down his back. His shoulder burned from the pounding strikes and his earlier wound felt like it was on fire.

Yet he struck hard and fast, using everything in his arsenal. He had to win. He had to get the spell book and take Eva home. There was something real between them, something precious and worth exploring. He couldn't leave her to the mercy of the queen. He couldn't let her die here.

The back of his legs struck the bed and he roared in frustration as he slashed one of the guards across the cheek. Blood oozed from the gash and the guard paused. Seth tried to take advantage of it and strike but the second guard parried it.

Both men came at him from the front and the bed behind him blocked that route.

He slipped to the right, dove and rolled. Both guards were upon him and he could not get up. He thrust up into one guard's stomach but couldn't free his blade. The man toppled, taking Seth's embedded sword with him.

The second guard grasped his sword in both hands, raised it, and with a piercing battle cry, plunged.

Seth rolled out of the way and jumped to his feet. The exercise cost him precious moments in which the guard had time to change his grip and thrust. But the strike missed and the guard fell to his knees clutching his throat, trying to stop the blood from pouring out.

David stood over him, sword in hand, and watched his first ever victim die.

Seth had no time to sympathize over first kills. Gus was trapped in a corner, hacking and slicing with powerful but wild strokes. The guard managed to dodge them but it wouldn't take long for Gus to tire using that technique. Seth swung and felled the guard.

Gus wiped his brow with the back of his hand. They

exchanged grim looks. It was all the thanks Seth needed. "Let's find this book," Gus said.

Seth followed him into the wardrobe. It was as large as the bedchamber with two sofas, a long table, a dressing table, chairs and several chests set around the room. With no windows, they had to strike one of Gus's matches to light both torches positioned inside the door.

The three of them searched and were soon joined by Sir Uther. Nobody spoke as they rifled through the clothing in the chests.

"It's not here," the rabbit said as they emptied the last chest. "By the gods, where is it?"

Seth surveyed the room. If he possessed a precious object, he wouldn't hide it somewhere obvious. If he had a spell book, he'd probably place it in a library but there were no books in the queen's bedchamber or wardrobe. So where else? He paced the room, partly in thought, partly to seek out any hidden nooks.

One of the floor's paving stones rocked. It was loose, the mortar surrounding it cracked. He fell to his knees and pressed his fingers to the edges. It tilted.

Gus helped him with the heavy slab then Seth plunged his hand into the dark hole. HIs fingers closed around a small book.

He handed it to Sir Uther. "Is this it?"

The rabbit flipped pages with his paws. He stopped midway and showed the page to Seth. "When this spell is spoken into an object, it turns that object into a portal. I recommend a watch. It worked well for us in the past."

Seth took the book and tucked it under his arm. He wasn't letting it out of sight.

"You all right?" he asked David as they headed back the way they'd come.

David nodded. A spray of blood covered his forehead. Seth decided not to tell him. The less David thought about what he'd done, the less likely he was to crumble. And Seth needed him to be alert and capable. This wasn't over yet.

Somewhere in the distance, the sound of voices filtered out to them but he couldn't make out the words.

"The audience chamber," the rabbit said heavily.

Gus swore. "We have to get to Alice."

"I'm going to Eva," was all Seth said.

Gus must have heard the bleakness in Seth's voice because he didn't argue.

"You go." Seth handed the book to Sir Uther. "Open a portal and get Alice and Markell out."

The rabbit clutched the book to his chest. "I'm staying with you. I can't go in there alone without protection."

They found Eva where they left her, thank God, surrounded by the other human-like creatures. They all stood around her, seated on the floor, and looked up when Seth and the others arrived.

"What's wrong?" he asked. Eva sat, propped against the wall, her eyes closed and face ashen. *God, no.* Panic smashed into his chest. He fell to his knees beside her and cupped her too-pale cheeks. "Eva!"

She cracked open her eyes. "Seth." She drew in a breath. "Help me up. We have to go."

"You had a vision, didn't you?" David asked, taking her hand as Seth picked her up.

She nodded. "A powerful one."

"Your visions weaken you?" Seth asked.

"Only when they're very strong. This one was strong." She sucked in a breath as if trying to calm herself. "We have to get into the tunnel that leads from the audience chamber."

"Why?" Sir Uther asked.

"It's the best way in. We must be armed and prepared."

Seth went to set her down again. "You'll be safer here."

"No. I'm coming. I can walk. All of us should go."

He clasped her hand and together they followed the

donkey and goat out of the dungeon, through the bowels of the castle to an exit that led to the courtyard. Several royal soldiers dressed in crimson stood, waiting for orders. They watched the procession of three guards dressed in white marching the animals and one woman between them.

"From the trial," Seth told them.

They crossed the courtyard unhindered to the back of the castle where stables and other outbuildings huddled together in a disorganized collection. The donkey stopped at a large wooden gate that must be for the use of the servants and delivery vehicles.

"There'll be guards on the other side," he whispered.

"How many?" Seth asked.

"Two."

Gus tapped Seth on the shoulder. He pointed to a ladder that led to the top of the wall. "The drop won't be too far. What do you say?"

"I say it's our best option."

It wasn't too high but they'd need to land properly to avoid injury. Luckily Seth had jumped from many windows, sometimes with a villain pursuing him, or a jealous husband or father.

He winked at Eva and was rewarded with a flush to her cheeks. Good. She'd been too pale. He led Gus up the ladder, only to pause when he reached the top.

Hell. Quellery's army waited at the base of the hill on which the castle stood. Like the royal army, they weren't aware of what was happening inside the castle. They simply waited for Quellery's orders.

Gus tapped Seth's foot.

Seth continued up but when he reached the top of the wall, he crouched on it. He didn't stand. He didn't want the army dressed in green to see him.

Gus joined him and air hissed between his teeth. Neither spoke as he held up one finger, two, three. They jumped together, taking out one man each. The guards died in silence, their necks broken.

Seth unlocked the gate and put a finger to his lips. He pointed down the hill. "Quellery's army."

The goat swore. "The tunnel entrance is down there."

"We're just three guards taking prisoners away, as ordered," Seth reminded them.

They marched downhill, the animals in front. Gus and Seth both now held two swords each, and used them to urge their so-called prisoners forward.

"Seth, the general knows us." Gus nodded at the leader, breaking away from the pack.

"Stay calm," Seth whispered. When they were still a few feet away, he hailed the general. "We're taking these prisoners to the dungeons." He indicated the tunnel door nearby.

The general didn't nod. He didn't say anything. He and his men simply stared at the creatures walking on two feet, and not at the faces of the guards. Thank God for the ordinary man's obsession with curiosities. It would seem Wonderlanders were no different to everyone else.

They entered the tunnel. The only footsteps Seth heard were their own. "Hand on the shoulder of the person in front of you," he said as the darkness swallowed them.

"Or paw," Gus added. "Or hoof."

"Do you know what we can expect to find?" Seth asked, giving Eva's shoulder a gentle squeeze.

"We won't be troubled until we reach the end," she said.

"And then?"

"And then you'll need your swords. That's all I know, Seth. I'm sorry."

"You gave us a way in. It's more than enough."

She touched his hand, stroking her thumb along his. Then she let go.

The closer they got to the audience chamber, the louder the voices and ominous clash of steel became.

Seth gave Eva one of his swords. "Stay here. David?"

"I'll guard them." David's voice trembled but Seth could just make out his outline, sword ready to swing at anything coming through the door. Seth moved past him and opened the door, but Gus rushed out first, brandishing both swords, and almost bowled over a guard. Gus dispensed with him while Seth took the other. The queen screamed.

Behind her, another guard dislodged a bound Alice from his shoulder and shoved her into Seth. Seth caught her but lost his balance. He would have fallen and been vulnerable to attack if Gus hadn't been at his back to steady him. Seth set Alice aside and parried the guard's blade an inch from his nose.

That had been close. Too close. "I like my nose where it is, thank you," he said, thrusting at the guard. He feinted left, right, then attacked straight down the middle.

The guard dropped his weapon and clutched the wound as he bled out.

Gus must have cut through Alice's bonds because she was free. She picked up the fallen guard's sword and hurried toward the fighting. The white-clad guards fought the crimson soldiers. Somehow the royal army had switched sides. It was the best sight Seth had seen all day. The guards outnumbered the soldiers, however, but that would change when the rest of the royal army joined them. As long as Quellery's army didn't arrive too.

"Wait!" Seth caught Alice's arm before she put herself in harm's way.

"Markell!" she cried, trying to pull away. "He's injured."

Seth followed her gaze to where a bloodied Markell lay on the floor, rolling out of the way of a guard's blade as it viciously struck down, time and again. Another guard, seeing the value of the prize on the floor, joined his comrade, trapping Markell between them.

Alice screamed.

Seth sprinted but he knew he could not fell both men with a single strike of his sword. By the time he recovered from the first thrust, the second guard would have plunged his blade through Markell. He had to take them both at once.

He dove, tackling the nearest guard and using their combined momentum to knock over the second. The three of them went down in a tangle of limbs and swords, but at least Seth was on top.

Gus grabbed him and pulled him out of harm's way. Before either of the guards had a chance to get up, Gus dispatched them with powerful, deadly slashes of his blade.

Alice ran to Markell and helped him to stand. The man was bleeding from a wound in his side but he was alive.

"It's over!" he shouted. "Guards, put down your weapons! The royal army is against you. The people are against you! Surrender now and—"

"No!" the queen shouted from the tunnel entrance. She held the spell book in hand. Beside her, Lady Oxana and Lord Quellery stepped back as their green-clad army surged out of the tunnel. At the head of the column, Eva and David emerged with their hands on their heads, the animals behind them with swords pressed into their backs.

"Eva!" Seth rushed forward, but Lady Oxana grabbed Eva by her hair and held a knife to her throat.

She smiled a sickly, twisted smile at Seth. "Do you want to save your wife?" she asked. "Come here and try. Let's see if you're capable."

He wouldn't be fast enough. His gazed locked with Eva's. His eyes burned but he did not look away, did not blink. He needed that link between them and he suspected she needed it too. *Be strong, my love.* He didn't know if her seer's powers could detect his thoughts but he spoke the words over and over in his mind, just in case. She offered him a weak smile, so perhaps she understood.

The few remaining guards and the green army rounded

up the crimson soldiers. As they did so, more crimson soldiers rushed through the main double doors. They stopped dead and tried to make sense of the scene.

"Your army is against you!" Alice told the queen. "Give up and you will be treated mercifully."

"Quellery's army is well trained," the queen said. "And we have your friends. Put down your weapons or this girl dies first."

Seth's blood chilled. It couldn't end here. Eva had told him they survived this and married.

What if she was wrong?

"There's one way to turn this in our favor," Markell muttered.

"Kill Quellery," Gus said.

He was right. Quellery's soldiers wouldn't fight for a dead man. They were mercenaries, and if the person who paid them was removed, they wouldn't care to fight anymore.

"I was thinking of the queen," Markell said.

"Oxana first," Seth said. He wouldn't put it past her to kill Eva out of vindictive spite, even if all else was lost.

But he was too far away to do anything. Markell, Gus and the crimson army were also too far away. No one could reach the person Seth loved most in the world to rescue her before that knife opened the vein in her neck.

Eva mouthed, *I love you too.*

She'd heard his thoughts! He'd communicated with her without speaking a word. His eyes burned again and moistened too. He didn't care. It took a moment for the sheer wonder of her abilities to subside and his thoughts to kick in again.

Drop, he said in his head. *Drop to the floor like a stone. She isn't holding you; you can get free.*

Eva made no sign that she'd heard. Seconds ticked by. The queen ordered the green army to advance but they wouldn't take orders from her. They waited for Quellery.

Quellery hesitated. Seth could see the moment when he realized he could take the realm for himself. The green army was his. The crimson army could be defeated. The queen and Alice could both be ousted.

Quellery's eyes lit up. His shoulders straightened. He turned to the queen and plunged a knife he must have tucked up his sleeve into her chest.

At that moment, Eva dropped to the floor, rolled out of the way, and kicked Lady Oxana's foot out from beneath her all in one perfectly timed, fluid move. Seth should never have doubted her. She was, after all, Lincoln's sister.

"Attack!" Markell shouted.

"Attack!" Lord Quellery said, snatching the spell book from the dead queen's hands. He flipped through the pages.

Markell swore. "Don't let him speak any spells! There are ones in there that can destroy us all!"

Eva scrambled toward Quellery, but Lady Oxana dove and caught her foot. Eva kicked out and managed to hit Oxana in the face. But Oxana brought her knife down.

Seth lost sight of them as the two armies clashed around him. He fought his way through, blindly slashing. He was dimly aware of Gus at his side, making some headway, cutting a path toward Eva.

"Leave my sister alone!" David's voice rang out over the sounds of fighting.

Seth pushed on. He was covered in blood, some of it his own. He didn't care. He needed to get to Eva.

Finally the way cleared ahead and he saw Eva and David clutching one another. Lady Oxana lay dead at their feet, her throat slashed. David's knife dripped blood. Seth breathed again.

"Seth!" Gus shouted.

Seth turned to see Quellery, shielded by a wall of his soldiers, as he read from the book. They had to stop him before he finished the spell. He didn't need to tell Gus that.

They didn't need to speak to one another at all. They simply engaged the five men and fought with everything they had left.

Seth felled one but he was outnumbered. They both were. Quellery's voice droned on and on and on.

Gus went down, falling to one knee. His two opponents now had the advantage of height. Seth had to get to him. He could not let his friend, the man he thought of as a brother, die here any more than he could let Eva die here.

Seth roared with anger, frustration and pain. It poured out of him. It lit a fire within him. He felled another soldier but out of the corner of his eye, he saw a blade slice through the air, aimed at Gus's head.

"No!" Seth shouted.

The blade was blocked. Markell lunged into Seth's vision, his face a picture of determination. Gus quickly recovered his stance and the two of them dispatched the remaining soldiers while Seth dispatched the last of his opponents.

Then Markell buried his blade in Quellery's stomach.

Quellery's eyes bulged and he looked down at the blade as Markell pulled it out. Blood poured from the wound. He tried to stop it with his hand but it was no use. He let go of the book and used his other hand too, but still the blood did not stop.

He plummeted to his knees and, with a gurgling wheeze, toppled forward. The floor seemed to shake with the impact.

"Enough!" Markell called out to both sets of soldiers. "Quellery is dead! The queen is dead! Fight no more."

Some stopped but others kept going, their blood lust in control.

"You are all Wonderlanders!" Alice shouted. "This is senseless. Do not fight one another. It's over. Anyone who continues will not be paid."

The rest of the soldiers, both crimson and green, stopped and lowered their weapons. One of Quellery's soldiers confirmed he was indeed dead. It was the signal for the entire mercenary army to lay down their weapons.

Seth dropped his sword. Eva was running toward him, tears streaming down her cheeks, her skirts held out of the way of her feet. He scooped her up, lifting her off the floor, and buried his face in her neck.

He held her and she held him just as tightly, their rapidly beating hearts saying more than either of them could manage. When he'd recovered enough from the shock and his fear had subsided, he pulled away and set her down on her feet. Then he kissed her. Thoroughly, completely, willingly offering her every piece of himself. It was more than he'd ever given anyone, and he didn't care. His heart was safe with Eva. He knew it to his core.

She clutched the back of his head and kissed him as if she'd been starved for too long. It was everything he wanted, and more than he deserved, but he'd take it and cherish it forever.

He was dimly aware of someone clearing their throat. It turned to coughing and finally a fist smacked his shoulder.

"Save that for later," Gus said in Seth's ear. "Her brother's getting annoyed."

David scowled at them, his arms crossed, but he didn't look too angry. Seth took Eva's hand then approached David. He was about to shake his hand but decided to hug him instead. It felt right.

"You saved her," Seth murmured in David's ear. "You saved her life."

"*You* saved everyone's life." David pulled away and awkwardly patted Seth's arms. "I suppose you want to marry her now."

"If she'll have me."

"I don't think there's any doubt on that score."

Eva smiled and tucked herself into Seth's side, circling her arms around his waist. He kissed the top of her head.

"How did you get out of the dungeon?" Markell asked.

"Lincoln helped us," Gus said.

"He's here?" Alice asked, looking around.

Seth fished out the lock picks from his pocket. "He sent these with Eva."

Alice's brows rose. "His second sight told him to give them to her?"

"Probably Leisl's, but it was certainly his idea to send these here with her vials of carbolic acid."

"Speaking of which." Eva reached into the deep pocket of her dress and handed the remaining wrapped vials to Alice. "Take these and use them on Markell's wounds after they're cleaned. I don't have enough for everyone." She looked around at the dead and injured and swallowed hard. "I'm sorry."

Seth rubbed her back. It must be difficult to see so much carnage and not be able to help.

"Alice might come back with us," Gus said, blinking fast. "She and Markell can go to hospital, get his wounds seen to, and live quietly in London."

Alice kissed his cheek. "It's a nice thought, but it's not for us. Our home is here, together." She handed the spell book to Markell. He grasped it but she did not let go. His chest heaving with his deep breath, then he pulled her into his arms and kissed her in front of everyone.

Some of the crimson soldiers cheered then a rousing shout of "Long live Queen Alice!" rang out. An eruption of agreement followed. A few noblemen, standing by the door, repeated the cry.

"I think you'll be safe for a while," Seth told her. "But it's not going to be easy."

"Change never is," she said. "I want to implement a constitutional monarchy."

Sir Uther, the rabbit, stepped forward and cleared his throat. "Excuse me, your majesty." He bowed. "May I have the spell book? My friends and I wish to say goodbye to your friends as ourselves, not in these foolish guises."

"You don't look too foolish," Gus said. "Well, *you* do, with them long ears and twitchy nose, but the others are fine looking beasts."

The rabbit rolled his eyes. "Just wait, sir. When I am my normal shape again, you'll cower in fear. I happen to be a very large man."

Gus made a theatrical show of trembling.

Alice handed the book to the rabbit and he flipped through the pages until he found the one he wanted. His clear voice rang out through the audience chamber as he spoke the strange words.

One by one, each of the animals transformed into their human shape again. Most were men but two were women. They peered down at themselves, patted themselves, touched their hair, their faces, to make sure they were whole and human.

Gus looked up at the giant man standing before him, holding the book. The bearded, blond Sir Uther smiled at Gus, his two big front teeth protruding over his bottom lip. Gus swallowed. Sir Uther's smile widened.

"Time to go," Gus said. "Goodbye all." He hugged Alice and shook Markell's hand, then held out his hand to Sir Uther. The former rabbit shook it, chuckling.

Alice stepped toward Seth but hesitated.

He bent to kiss her cheek, then folded her into his arms. "Goodbye and good luck," he said. "Be happy."

"I am. And so are you, I see."

"Very." He let her go and addressed Markell. "I would tell you to take care of her, but I know you will."

Eva hugged Alice, all the while giving final instructions on treating the wounds. But Wonderland's medics had already arrived and moved between the bodies with efficiency.

"Send them home," Alice said to Sir Uther, her eyes shining with tears. "It's time."

Someone had handed Sir Uther a watch and he held it as he read words from the book. At first it didn't look as though anything had happened, but when he spoke a second spell, the watch flared to life.

Markell and Alice held hands, and Alice bit her trembling lip, a hand raised in farewell.

Seth entwined his fingers with Eva's as he felt the pull of the portal's magic.

Then everything went black.

CHAPTER 15

LINCOLN

Lincoln had to admit he'd missed Seth and Gus. Seeing their grinning but battered faces as they strolled into the entrance hall at Lichfield Towers, he realized he would have felt their loss keenly if they hadn't come home. Not that he'd tell them. Charlie was aware of his feelings and that's all that mattered. The night after they left through the portal, she'd told him he was worried. The following night, she'd told him he was going to be devastated if they died. She'd been right on both counts, although he hadn't been fully aware at the time. It was only now, when his heart leapt at the sight of them, that he could admit his wife knew him better than he knew himself.

His wife. He smiled to himself. He'd never get used to calling her that, although he was already very used to the benefits that came with marriage.

He received Seth's hug gladly and returned Gus's clap on the shoulder. Eva hugged him too and kissed his cheek. But it was David's handshake that took him by surprise. It was firm and friendly. He sported blood on his jacket and across his face. He'd killed.

Charlie led them into the drawing room and asked Doyle to bring in brandies and cakes. "Sit, sit. You must be tired."

"We can't sit on your lovely sofas," Eva said. "We're filthy. I don't want to think about what I sat in while in the dungeon."

Charlie waved a hand. "Never mind the upholstery. Monsieur Fernesse will send something just as nice to replace it if it's beyond repair."

Eva and Seth exchanged glances. So he'd told her. Well, well. What else had the two of them shared? Lincoln could guess, but would wait for the announcement and act surprised when it came.

"Thank you," David said to Lincoln. "If it hadn't been for your foresight...we would never have got out of the dungeon."

"He had my mother sew lock picks into my dress," Eva told Charlie.

"I know," Charlie said, as if she had never been sick with worry for their friends. "He told me *after* you left." She gave Lincoln a hard smile. "It would have been nice to have been informed before."

Eva touched Charlie's knee. "We can't speak too much about the future we see in our visions. It could create all manner of havoc."

Charlie crossed her arms and glared at Lincoln. So she still hadn't forgiven him for not immediately telling her about his conversation with Leisl.

"I didn't know what the lock picks were for," Lincoln said again.

"My husband's formidable intelligence, coupled with his seer's sight, still wasn't enough for him to guess why his mother wanted him to give her a pair of lock picks. Added to which, he didn't even ask her!" She turned her shoulder to him.

He blinked at her severe profile and wondered how he

was going to convince her to forgive him. He was going to have to ask Seth later. He always knew the right things to say to women.

Seth looked like he might be busy later, though, going by the way he stared at Eva.

They managed to hold off on announcing their news until Doyle returned with refreshments. He brought Cook, Lady Vickers and Leisl with him. The two women had been keeping one another company these last few days, sharing their joint worry over their children. Although Leisl had known Eva would survive, she hadn't seen David's fate.

Seth swept his mother up into an exuberant hug while Eva and David embraced Leisl. Gus eyed a grinning, teary-eyed Cook as if he'd never seen a better sight. Cook offered him a plate of biscuits and Gus took one.

"Take more," Cook urged him. "Take many. Seth?"

Seth clapped Cook's shoulder. "Thank you," he said cheerfully. "Now, listen up. I have two things I want to tell you, Mother, right here in front of everyone."

Lincoln sighed. This was going to get emotional. He wished he could retreat to his office but Charlie was still looking frosty, and he hoped one of Seth's announcements might put her in a better mood. Lincoln had no idea what the other one would be, and he found he was curious.

"Firstly, Mother, Cook, I want you both to know that I accept your relationship. As odd as it is, you're both good people, deserving of love." He spread out his arms. "So you have my permission to marry."

The room fell silent. Then Cook and Lady Vickers burst out laughing. "Oh, that," she said. "We just pretended to fall in love to irk you."

"Irk me? Why?"

"To teach you a lesson. You can't tell me who I can and can't be with, Seth, just as I can't tell you."

"But…but *you* tried to force *me* to marry women you thought would make good wives. You let it known that you didn't think Alice was a good match for me."

"She wasn't." She nibbled the edge of a biscuit. "You would have grown to hate one another." She smiled gently at Seth then at Eva. Lincoln suspected he knew what Lady Vickers and Leisl had been discussing these last few days. Somehow Leisl had changed Lady Vickers's mind about Seth marrying for money.

Seth gave Cook a withering glare. "You agreed to play along?"

Cook's grin widened. "I be needing some amusement."

"I hate you."

Cook handed him the plate of biscuits again. Seth took one and smirked.

"You said two announcements," Charlie said. "What's the other one?"

Seth took Eva's hand and kissed the back of it. "Eva and I are going to marry."

Leisl clapped her hands in delight. Charlie sprang up from the chair and embraced them both. "Congratulations! I had no idea you two held tender feelings for one another."

"It's surprising what being stuck in another realm together can do." Seth winked at Eva.

Eva smiled back. "We learned a lot about each other. A lot of wonderful things."

"But I thought you didn't particularly like him, let alone love him," Charlie said.

"Well…" Eva lifted one shoulder. "The truth is, I already knew we'd marry. I had a vision."

"You did!" Charlie threw her hands in the air. "Why am I the last to know everything?" She shot another glare at Lincoln. "Did you know?"

"No. No!" He said it twice, just to make sure.

"Only my mother knew," Eva said. "I tried to avoid Seth when we were here in London, but it was impossible in Wonderland. I didn't want it to come true, you see."

"Why ever not?" Charlie asked.

"Because he's pompous and vain," Gus offered.

Eva laughed. "Because I didn't think a nobleman would want…" She looked at her mother. "…would want a doctor for a wife. I thought he'd force me to give up my career."

Leisl sipped her brandy. The room fell silent.

"She will be an excellent doctor," David said quietly. "She saved Alice's life." He waited but Leisl simply sipped again. "Mother, don't do this. It's her dream. If Seth won't stand in her way then you have no right to either."

"What objection do you have to her becoming a doctor?" Lincoln asked.

"Nursing is safe, noble profession for English gentlewomen," Leisl said. "Doctoring is not for good girls. It is unseemly."

"I am not a gentle Englishwoman, Mother," Eva burst out. "I possess all the independence and fire that comes with being half-Romany. I don't care what you or anyone else thinks. I'm smarter than most of the men in my class, and I can make a difference in the medical field. I'm going to graduate with or without your blessing, so you might as well give in."

Leisl sipped again. Lady Vickers reached for her fan on the table beside her. "It's going to take time to get used to the idea," she said, flapping the fan as if she were trying to use it to fly away. "A doctor in the family. Well, imagine that."

Seth glared so hard at his mother that she slowed her flapping. They would get used to the idea eventually, Lincoln suspected. Once Charlie spoke to each of them, they'd be more accepting. She was good at reasoning with people. Very good.

He glanced at her, a little worried that she'd still be glaring back at him. But she wasn't. Indeed, she looked happy and content. Good. Now that the others were back, he could move ahead with their plans.

"Does anyone have anything else to share with me?" Charlie asked, tongue firmly in cheek. "Any more news that I'm the last to hear about?"

"Alice and Markell are together," David said. "They'll probably marry and turn Wonderland into a constitutional monarchy instead of the absolute monarchy it has been."

Charlie stared at him. "It was a busy few days."

"And I lost my job at the bank." He spoke to Leisl, and for the first time since Lincoln had met her, she looked shocked. "My employer dismissed me, but I was too ashamed to tell you."

"Why?" she said, maternal anger hardening her voice.

David stretched out his fingers and thrust out his chin. "I told—"

"He told them he wants more money," Eva said. She smiled at David. "You're better off not working there. I'm sure your next employer will value you more."

Lincoln got the distinct impression it was a lie, but Leisl didn't seem to notice.

She touched David's knee. "She is right. You are very good at your job. You will get better work, more respect and money. Now, Eva, David, let us go home. You need bath. You stink."

"They ain't the only ones." Cook wrinkled his nose as he collected empty glasses. "I could smell Gus before he reached this realm."

"You missed me," Gus said.

"More than apple cake."

"That much?"

"But not more than bacon."

They said their farewells to the Cornells, although it took

some time before Seth was willing to let Eva go. He seemed to think she wouldn't be safe if he couldn't see her. Lincoln knew that feeling all too well.

"Get used to it," Lincoln told him as they re-entered the house. "It never goes away."

"You're an expert on marriage already?" Seth said with a wry smile.

"Far from it." Lincoln waited until Charlie was out of earshot then leaned closer to Seth. "I need your advice. She's angry with me for not telling her about you going to Wonderland. I told her I didn't know, that Leisl only informed me that she needed something that opens padlocks and was small enough to be sewn into Eva's dress."

Seth draped his arm around Lincoln's shoulders. Lincoln wondered how much he'd had to drink, then remembered he was in the first flush of love. Lincoln recalled those first few days very clearly. A fog had descended over him, resulting in strange behavior, not to mention stupid decisions.

"I've learned the secret to keeping a woman's love, my friend, and I'm going to divulge it to you for free," Seth said.

"You and your mother live in my house."

"For the price of rent, then. The secret to keeping Charlie's love is trust. She must know she can trust you, and you must trust her. To do that, you need to share everything, even the bad things."

"Like the secrets you told Eva."

Seth's arm retreated. "Are you sure you're not the devil?"

Lincoln thought it best to remain quiet. "What if those secrets will worry her?" he asked. "Or harm her?"

"Then you have to be there to hold her hand or rescue her. Whatever is required. Now, I have to run or Gus will get to the bath first."

"Thank you, Seth."

"Don't thank me, just increase my wages." He sprinted up

the stairs, passing Gus telling Charlie about the Queen of Hearts.

Gus spent the entire hour that Seth was in the bath telling Lincoln, Charlie, Cook and Lady Vickers what happened to them in Wonderland.

Later, when the household had retired, Lincoln stood behind Charlie as she sat at her dressing table. He picked up her brush and watched it glide through her honey brown tresses.

"I've already brushed it out," she said, giving him a peculiar look.

He said nothing. He was trying to think how to begin. Trust, Seth had said. "I should have told you about the lock picks," he said. "I should have told you everything Leisl told me when she asked for them. I'm sorry."

She said nothing and that forced him to meet her gaze in the mirror's reflection. Damn. She was always doing that. He should be prepared for the trick by now. "Why didn't you?" she asked.

"Because I didn't know how it would turn out for them. I didn't even know if they would have an opportunity to use the lock picks. Leisl didn't tell me, and even if she had, her visions may not come to pass. I didn't want you to worry."

She turned and plucked the brush from his hand and kissed his knuckles.

His heart settled into its usual rhythm again as he released a breath. "You thought I'd interfere, didn't you?" she asked. "You thought I'd try to stop them going."

"No." He sighed. *Trust*. "Yes. A little. But mostly I didn't want to worry you."

"Thank you for your honesty, Lincoln. But please don't keep things from me again. This marriage won't work if we're not honest with one another."

That now familiar panic pinched his chest hard. He nodded. "I promise."

"I'm sorry too. It wasn't fair of me to say that. Our marriage is solid. It always will be. You don't have to worry about that."

He nodded again. There was nothing more to say, which was lucky because he didn't feel like talking. He just wanted to look at her, all lovely in her nightgown. She'd look even lovelier out of it, but he could wait a little longer.

She stood and put her arms around him. She pulled out the ribbon holding his hair back and dug her hands through it. "Now, what else aren't you telling me?"

He lifted his brows. "What makes you think I've got something to tell?"

"I can read you like a book, Lincoln."

Very true. "I've made inquiries about honeymooning on the Côte d'Azur in France. Now that the others are back—"

She kissed him, taking his words and his breath away. She clung to him, her feet off the ground, and he carried her to the bed. Her nimble fingers quickly helped him shed his shirt and then she rolled him onto his back and sat up on his lap, admiring him. He watched, feeling dazed and lucky as she removed her nightgown.

Tomorrow, he was going to raise Seth's wages.

Tonight, he was going to enjoy his wife.

THE END

Have you read:

THE MEDIUM

The 1st novel in the EMILY CHAMBERS SPIRIT MEDIUM TRILOGY

by C.J. Archer

Read on for an excerpt.

Sign up to C.J.'s newsletter via her website to be notified when she releases new books. All subscribers get exclusive

access to a Ministry of Curiosities / Freak House
cross-over story.

THE MEDIUM: AN EXCERPT

About The Medium

Seventeen year-old spirit medium Emily Chambers has a problem. Actually, she has several. As if seeing dead people isn't a big enough social disadvantage, she also has to contend with an escaped demon and a handsome ghost with a secret past. And then there's the question of her parentage. Being born an entire year after her father's death (yes, a year) and without the pale skin of other respectable English ladies, Emily is as much a mystery as the dead boy assigned to her.

Jacob Beaufort's spirit has been unable to crossover since his death. It might have something to do with the fact he was murdered. Or it might not. All he knows is, he has been assigned by the Otherworld's administrators to a girl named Emily. A girl who can see and touch him. A girl who released a shape-shifting demon into the mortal realm. Together they must send the demon back before it wreaks havoc on London. It should be a simple assignment, but they soon learn there's nothing simple when a live girl and a dead boy fall in love.

CHAPTER 1

London, Spring 1880

Whoever said dead men don't tell lies had never met Barnaby Wiggam's ghost. The fat, bulbous-nosed spirit fading in and out beside me like a faulty gas lamp clearly thought he was dealing with a fool. I may only be seventeen but I'm not naïve. I know when someone is lying—being dead didn't alter the tell-tale signs. Mr. Wiggam didn't quite meet my eyes, or those of his widow and her guests—none of whom could see him anyway—and he fidgeted with his crisp white silk necktie as if it strangled him. It hadn't—he'd died of an apoplexy.

"Go on, young lady." He thrust his triple chins at me, making them wobble. "Tell her. I have no hidden fortune."

I swallowed and glanced at the little circle of women holding hands around the card table in Mrs. Wiggam's drawing room, their wide gazes locked on the Ouija board in the center as if Barnaby Wiggam stood there and not beside me. I too stood, behind my sister and opposite the Widow Wiggam who looked just as well-fed as her dead husband in her black crepe dress and mourning cap. However, where his face was covered with a network of angry red veins, hers was so white it glowed like a moon in the dimly lit room.

"Are you sure?" I asked him. If he knew I suspected him of lying, he didn't show it. Or perhaps he simply didn't care.

"Sure?" Mrs. Wiggam suddenly let go of her neighbor's hands. My sister, Celia, clicked her tongue and Mrs. Wiggam quickly took up the lady's hand again. It's not as if anyone needed to hold hands at all during our séances but my sister insisted upon it, along with having candles rather than lamps, a tambourine and an Ouija board even though she rarely used either. She liked things to be done in a way that added to the atmosphere and the enjoyment of the customers, as she put it.

I'm not convinced anyone actually *enjoyed* our séances, but they were effective nevertheless and she was right—people expect certain theatrics from spirit mediums, so if we must put on a performance then so be it.

Celia had taken it one step further this time by wearing a large brass star-shaped amulet on a strap around her neck. The recent purchase was as unnecessary as the hand-holding but she thought it gave us authenticity amidst a city filled with fake mediums. I had to admit it looked wonderfully gothic.

"Sure about what?" Mrs. Wiggam asked again, leaning forward. Her large bosom rested on the damask tablecloth and rose and fell with her labored breathing. "What does he want you to say, Miss Chambers?"

I glanced at Mr. Wiggam's ghost. He crossed his arms and raised his fluffy white eyebrows as if daring me to repeat his lie. "He, er, he said..." Oh lord, if I repeated the lie then I would be contributing to his fate. He could not cross over to the Otherworld until he was at peace, and he would not be at peace until he let go of his anger towards his wife. Lying to her wasn't helping.

On the other hand, it was his choice.

"Emily," Celia said with the false sing-song voice she employed for our séances. "Emily, do tell us what Mr. Wiggam is communicating to you. Give his poor dear widow," she paused and smiled beatifically at Mrs. Wiggam, "some solace in her time of mourning."

"Mourning!" Barnaby Wiggam barked out a laugh that caused the edges of his fuzzy self to briefly sharpen into focus. For a moment he appeared almost human again. To me at least. "Tell that...that WOMAN who sits there pretending to be my demure wife that there is no fortune."

"He says there's no fortune," I repeated.

A series of gasps echoed around the small drawing room

and more than one of the elegant ladies clicked her tongue. Mrs. Wiggam let go of both her neighbors' hands again. "Nonsense!" Her gaze flitted around the room. "Tell that lying, cheating, *scoundrel* of a husband that I know he amassed a fortune before his death." She placed her fists on the table and rose slowly to her considerable height, well above my own. She even dwarfed her ghostly husband. "Where is he? I want to tell him to his face." She reminded me of a great brown bear at the circus Mama had taken me to see as a little girl. The creature had expressed its displeasure at being chained to a bollard by taking a swipe at its handler with an enormous paw. I'd felt sorry for it. I wasn't yet sure if I felt the same emotion towards Mrs. Wiggam.

I must have glanced sideways at her husband because she turned on the spirit beside me even though she couldn't see it. He took a step back and fiddled with his necktie again.

"I *know* there's money somewhere." Her bosom heaved and her lips drew back, revealing crooked teeth. "I *deserve* that money for putting up with you, you wretched little man. Rest assured Barnaby *dearest*, I'll find every last penny of it."

A small, strangled sound escaped Mr. Wiggam's throat and his apparition shimmered. Fool. He was dead—she couldn't do anything to him now. Her four friends shrank from her too.

My sister did not. "Mrs. Wiggam, if you'll please return to your seat," Celia said in her conciliatory church-mouse voice. She ruined the effect by shooting a sharp glance at me. Mrs. Wiggam sat. She did not, however, resume handholding. Celia turned a gracious smile on her. "Now, Mrs. Wiggam, it's time to conclude today's session." My sister must have an internal clock ticking inside her. She always seemed to know when our half hour was over. "Everyone please close your eyes and repeat after me." They all duly closed their eyes, except Mrs. Wiggam who'd taken to glaring at me. As if it were my fault her husband was a liar!

"Return oh spirit from whence you came," Celia chanted.

"Return oh spirit from whence you came," the four guests repeated.

"Go in peace—."

"No!" Mrs. Wiggam slapped her palms down on the table. Everyone jumped, including me, and the tambourine rattled. "I do *not* want him to go in peace. I do *not* want him to go anywhere!" She crossed her arms beneath her bosom and gave me a satisfied sneer.

I'm not your husband! I wanted to shout at her. Why did everyone think I was the embodiment of their loved one? Or in this case, their despised one. I once had a gentleman kiss me when I summoned his deceased fiancée. It had been my first kiss, and hadn't been entirely unpleasant.

"Let him go," Celia said, voice pitching unusually high. She shook her head vigorously, dislodging a brown curl from beneath her hat. "He can't remain here. It's his time to go, to cross over."

"I don't want to cross over," Mr. Wiggam said.

"What?" I blurted out.

"Did he say something?" Celia asked me. I repeated what he'd said. "Good lord," she muttered so quietly I was probably the only one who heard her. Especially since Mrs. Wiggam had started laughing hysterically.

"He wants to stay?" The widow's grin turned smug. "Very well. It'll be just like old times—living with a corpse."

One of the guests snorted a laugh but I couldn't determine which of the ladies had done it. They all covered their mouths with their gloved hands, attempting to hide their snickers. They failed.

"Tell the old crone I'm glad I died," Barnaby Wiggam said, straightening. "Being dead without her is a far better state than being alive with her."

"No, no this won't do," Celia said, thankfully saving me from repeating the spirit's words. She stood up and placed a hand on Mrs. Wiggam's arm. "Your husband *must* return. We summoned him at your behest to answer your question and now he needs to cross over into the Otherworld."

Actually, he probably wouldn't be crossing over. Not while there was so much lingering anger between himself and his wife. He needed to release the anger before he could go anywhere. Until then he was tied to this world and the Waiting Area. That's why some places remain haunted—their ghosts aren't willing to give up the negative emotion keeping them here. Although Celia knew that as well as I, she couldn't be aware of the extent of Barnaby Wiggam's sour mood. She certainly couldn't have known he deliberately lied to his wife about his fortune.

I sighed. As always, I would have to explain it to her later. *After* we returned the ghost to the Waiting Area. "You have to go back," I urged him. "You shouldn't be here. Tell your widow you're sorry, or that you forgive her or whatever and you can cross over and be at peace." At least that's what I assumed happened. Since I wasn't able to summon anyone from the Otherworld—only the Waiting Area—I couldn't know for sure what occurred in their final destination. For all I knew the Otherworld was like a political meeting. Endless and dull.

From what the spirits had told me, all ghosts ended up in the Waiting Area until they'd been assigned to a section in the Otherworld. Which section depended on how they'd behaved in life. However, none knew the fate awaiting them in their respective sections. It caused many of the ghosts I'd summoned an anxious wait.

"I'm not sorry." Barnaby Wiggam sat in an old leather armchair by the hearth and rubbed his knee as if it gave him pain although it couldn't possibly hurt now. He seemed so at home there, nestled between the enormous rounded arms and deeply cushioned high back, that I wondered if it had been his favorite chair. "I think I'll stay a little longer. I rather fancy haunting the old witch. It'll be a jolly time."

"Jolly!" I spluttered. I appealed to Celia but she simply shrugged. "But you can't do this!" I said to him. "It's...it's illegal!" Nothing like this had happened to us in a year and a half of conducting séances. All our spirits had duly answered the questions their loved ones posed then returned to the Waiting Area, content and ready to cross over. Then again, we'd never summoned anyone who clearly wasn't a loved one.

What had we done?

Mr. Wiggam picked up a journal from a nearby table and flipped open the pages.

A woman screamed, others gasped, and one fainted into the arms of her friend. Only Celia, Mrs. Wiggam and I remained calm. Celia was used to seeing objects move without being touched, and I of course could see the ghostly form holding the journal. I suspect Mrs. Wiggam was simply made of sterner stuff than her companions.

"The *Ladies Pictorial*! Utter trash." Mr. Wiggam threw the journal back onto the table where it collected a porcelain cat figurine and sent it clattering to the floor. The two ears and the tip of the tail broke off. He laughed. "I never liked that thing."

Mrs. Wiggam simply stepped around the pieces and flung open the heavy velvet drapes. Hazy light bathed the drawing room in sepia tones. London's days were not bright but I suspected the Wiggams' drawing room would always be dreary even if the sun dared show its face. The dark burgundy walls and squat, heavy furniture made the space feel small and crowded, particularly with all of us crammed into it. I took a deep breath but the air was smoky, close, and stuck in my throat.

"Let's have some refreshments, shall we?" Mrs. Wiggam said as if she didn't have a care in the world. She tugged the bell-pull then bent over the woman who'd fainted, now reclining in one of the chairs at the card table. She slapped her friend's cheeks then saw to it she was made comfortable with an extra cushion at her back.

I turned to Celia. She frowned at me. "Close your mouth, Emily, you are not a fish."

I duly shut my mouth. Then opened it again to speak. "What are we to do?" I whispered.

Celia huffed out a breath and looked thoughtful as she fingered the large amulet dangling from a strip of leather around her neck. She'd purchased it last Thursday from the peddler woman who sells bits and pieces door-to-door. Considering Celia was a stickler for maintaining the same format for our drawing room séances, I was surprised when she'd produced a new artifact. It was rather a magnificent piece though, made of heavy brass in the shape of a star with delicate filigree between the six points. Etched into the brass were swirls and strange, twisting patterns. It looked like an ancient tribal token I'd once seen in a museum. I could see why she'd accepted it although the fact it cost her nothing was probably a factor. Celia was not so careless with our meager income that she would squander it on trinkets.

"I wonder..." she said.

"Wonder what? Celia—?"

Celia's soft chanting interrupted me. With both hands touching the amulet, she repeated some words over and over in a strange, lyrical language I didn't recognize. Considering I only knew English and possessed a basic knowledge of French, that wasn't saying a great deal.

She finished her chant and let the amulet go. As she did so a blast of wind swept through the drawing room, rustling hair and skirts, dousing candles and flapping the journal's pages. A shadow coalesced above the table, a shapeless blob that pulsed and throbbed. It was like the mud that oozed on the riverbank at low tide, sucking and slurping, threatening to swallow small creatures and boots. But the shadow—I could think of no other word to describe the dark, floating mass—altered of its own volition.

No longer shapeless, it became a hand reaching out. Two or three of the guests screamed and scuttled to the far side of the drawing room. Beside me, my sister tensed and circled her arm around my shoulders, pulling me back. She said something under her breath but the loud thud of my heart deafened me to her words, but not to her fear. I could feel it all around me as I stared at the shadow, which was quickly changing shape again.

It became a foot then the head of a rat then a dog with snapping jaws and hungry eyes. A hound from hell, snarling and slavering and vicious. It stretched its neck toward me and before I could react, Celia jerked me back.

Too late.

The shadow creature's sharp teeth closed around my shoulder. I squeezed my eyes shut and braced myself. Nothing happened. Oh there was screaming coming from everyone else, including Celia, but I heard no tearing of flesh or clothing. I felt no pain, just a cool dampness against my cheek. I opened my eyes. The creature had turned back into a shapeless cloud. For a brief moment it hovered near the door and then with a whoosh it was gone.

A breathless moment passed. Two. Three.

"What was that?" I whispered in the ensuing hush.

Celia looked around at the white faces staring wide-eyed back at us, hoping we could give them answers. We couldn't.

She indicated the armchair. "Is he still here?" Her voice shook and she still gripped my shoulders.

"Still here," both Mr. Wiggam and I said together.

"Did you see that?" he said, staring at the door. He didn't look nearly as frightened as the others, but then what did a dead man have to fear? He went to the door and peered out into the hall. "I wonder what it was."

"It's gone now," I said. My words seemed to reassure the ladies who stood huddled in the corner of the room.

"The air in this city," Mrs. Wiggam said with a click of her tongue and a dismissive wave of her hand. "It gets worse and worse every year." She ushered the ladies to seats, plumped cushions and pooh-poohed any suggestions of a menacing spirit ruining her social event. "It was a trick of the light, that's all," she said. "The tense atmosphere in here has got to you all, stirred your imaginations."

"Stupid woman," Mr. Wiggam muttered. "She can't possibly believe that cloud was natural."

I didn't care what Mrs. Wiggam thought, as long as her guests accepted her explanation. Clearly some of them did, or perhaps they simply *wanted* to believe it and so willingly forgot what they'd seen only moments before. One or two seemed unconvinced and I hoped they would not gossip about it later. If word got out that we'd released something sinister during one of our séances, our business could flounder. Celia and I could ill afford such a disaster becoming public knowledge.

"Well," Celia said, peering down at the amulet hanging from its leather strip. "I thought it a harmless piece."

"Then why use it?" I hissed.

She gathered up the tambourine and Ouija board, packed them into her carpet bag and snapped the clasp shut. "The peddler who gave it to me said I was to say those words three times if I needed to solve something."

A maid entered carrying a large tray with teapot and cups. Two other maids followed her with more trays laden with cakes and sandwiches. Celia's face relaxed at the sight of the refreshments.

"What were the words?" I pressed her.

She waved a hand as she accepted a teacup with the other. Her hands shook so much the cup clattered in the saucer. "Oh, some gibberish. She didn't tell me what they meant, just that I should repeat them if I needed to fix something. Well I did need to fix something." She leaned closer to me and lowered her voice. "The spirit of Mr. Wiggam wouldn't leave."

I wasn't entirely convinced that the ongoing presence of Mr. Wiggam was what the woman had meant. Nor was I convinced that the words were gibberish. I looked at the door then at Mr. Wiggam. He stood with his back to the fireplace as if warming himself against the low flames—although he couldn't feel the cold—and stared at the door, a puzzled expression causing his wild brows to collide.

"The peddler was a mad old thing," Celia muttered around the rim of her teacup. "Completely mad." She sipped.

"At least it's gone, whatever it was, and no one seems affected by it."

No. No one at all.

***

"Tell me about the peddler woman," I asked Celia when we were almost home. We'd decided to walk from Mrs. Wiggam's Kensington house instead of taking the omnibus. It wasn't far and we would save on the fare as well as gain some exercise. Celia is all for exercising in the fresh air, although London's air couldn't be considered fresh by anyone's standards as Mrs. Wiggam had reassuringly pointed out to her guests. It stank of smoke and horse dung, made eyes sting and left skin feeling gritty. It was cool, however, and certainly invigorating as the chilly spring breeze nipped at our noses and ruffled the ribbons on our hats.

Celia sighed as if the task of recollection was a burden. "She looked like any other old crone. As wrinkled as unpressed linen, I do recall that. Gray hair, which she wore long and uncovered." She sniffed to indicate what she thought of that. "Oh and she had an East End accent. I'd never seen her before, she wasn't the usual Thursday peddler. I don't know her name, and I don't know anything else about her except that she was dressed all in black. Now stop fretting, Emily. We'll let Mr. and Mrs. Wiggam sort out their differences then return him to the Waiting Area tomorrow. There's nothing more we can do."

"How can they sort out their differences when she can't see him or speak to him?" A strong breeze whipped up the street, flattening our skirts and petticoats to our legs. We both slapped a hand to our hats to keep them from blowing away. We lived on Druids Way in Chelsea and it's always windier than everywhere else in London. It must have something to do with the length and orientation of the street as well as the height of the houses lining both sides of it. None of them were less than two levels and all showed signs of neglect. Much of Chelsea was still occupied by the reasonably prosperous, but our street seemed to have slipped into obscurity some years ago. Paint flaked off front doors and the brick facades were no longer their original red-brown but had turned almost black thanks to the soot permanently shrouding our city. All one had to do was turn the corner and see streets swept clean and houses tenderly kept but Druids Way was like a spinster past her marrying days—avoided by the fashionable set.

I hazarded a sideways glance at Celia and felt a pang of guilt for my unkind comparison. At thirty-three she was unlikely to find a husband. She seemed to have given up on the idea some years ago, preferring to dress in gowns that flattered neither her slim figure nor her lovely complexion. I'd tried many times to have her dress more appropriately for an unwed woman but she refused, saying she'd prefer to see *me* in the pretty gowns.

"We'll pay a call on Mrs. Wiggam tomorrow," Celia said, bowing her head into the wind. "Perhaps Mr. Wiggam will have tired of his wife and be willing to cross over by then. Will that satisfy you?"

"I suppose so." What else could we do? I couldn't simply let the matter drop. Not only had we failed to return Mr. Wiggam to the Waiting Area, we'd left him with a person who despised him. There was no handbook for spirit mediums when it came to summoning the dead, but I knew deep down that this situation wasn't acceptable. Celia and I had no right to rip souls out of the Waiting Area and reignite emotional wounds in this world. It had never been a problem in the past, so I'd never given it much thought. Besides which, the ghosts we summoned at our drawing room séances had always willingly returned to the Waiting Area afterwards, and they'd done so feeling content that their loved ones could move on too.

Or so I liked to think. The Wiggams' situation had shaken me. Celia and I were fools to think we could control the deceased, or the living for that matter.

I also had the awful feeling we'd released something else in Mrs. Wiggam's drawing room by using that strange incantation. Something sinister. I only wish I knew what.

"Now, what shall we have for supper?" Celia asked.

I stopped with one foot on the stairs leading up to our front door and suppressed a small squeak of surprise. A man stood on the landing, leaning against the door, his arms crossed over his chest. He looked older than me but not by much, tall, with short dark hair and a face that was a little too square of jaw and sharp of cheek to be fashionable. It wasn't a beautiful face in the classical statue sense but it was certainly handsome.

The odd thing about him wasn't that we'd not noticed him earlier—we'd had our heads bent against the wind after all—but the way he was dressed. He wore black trousers, boots and a white shirt but nothing else. No hat, no necktie, jacket or vest and, scandalously, the top buttons of his shirt were undone so that his bare chest was partially visible.

I couldn't take my eyes off the skin there. It looked smooth and inexplicably warm considering the cool air, and—.

"There you are," he said. I dragged my gaze up to his face and was greeted by a pair of blue eyes that had an endlessness to their depths. As if that wasn't unsettling enough, his curious gaze slowly took in every inch of me, twice. To my utter horror, my face heated. He smiled at that, or I should say he half-smiled, which didn't help soothe my complexion in the least. "Your mouth is open," he said.

I shut it. Swallowed. "Uh, Celia?"

"Yes?" Celia dug through her reticule, searching for the front door key.

"You can't see him, can you?"

She glanced up, her hand still buried in her reticule, the carpet bag at her feet. "See who?"

"That gentleman standing there." I waggled my fingers at him in a wave. He waved back.

She shook her head. "No-o. Are you trying to tell me Mr. Wiggam is here?"

"Not Mr. Wiggam, no."

"But..." She frowned. "Who?"

"Jacob Beaufort," the spirit said without moving from his position. "Pleased to make your acquaintance. I'd shake your sister's hand," he said to me, "but given she can't see me she won't be able to touch me either." *I* could see him, and therefore touch him, but he didn't offer to shake my hand.

Unlike ordinary people, I could touch the ghosts. Celia and the other guests at our séances simply walked through them as if they were mist but I couldn't, which made sense to me. After all, they could haunt a place by tossing objects about, or upturn tables and knock on wood, why wouldn't they have physical form? At least for the person who could see them.

I wondered what he would feel like. He looked remarkably solid. Indeed, he looked very much alive, more so than any ghost I'd ever seen. Usually they faded in and out and had edges like a smudged charcoal sketch, but Jacob Beaufort was as well defined as Celia.

"Er, pleased to meet you too," I said. "I'm Emily Chambers and this is my sister Miss Celia Chambers."

Celia bobbed a curtsy although she wasn't quite facing Mr. Beaufort, then picked up her bag and approached him. Or rather, approached the door. She walked straight through him and inserted the key into the lock.

"I say!" he said and stepped aside.

"She didn't mean any offense," I said quickly.

"Did I do something wrong?" Celia asked as the door swung open.

"You walked through him."

"Oh dear, I am terribly sorry, Mr..."

"Beaufort," I filled in for her.

"As my sister said, I meant no offense, Mr. Beaufort." She spoke to the door. I cleared my throat and pointed at the ghost now standing to one side on the landing. She turned a little and smiled at him. "Why are you haunting our front porch?"

I winced and gave Mr. Beaufort an apologetic shrug. My sister may be all politeness with the living but she'd yet to grasp the art of tactful communication with the deceased.

"Celia," I hissed at her, but she either didn't hear me or chose to ignore me.

"It's all right," Mr. Beaufort said, amused. "May I enter? I won't harm either of you. I simply need to talk to you and I'm sure you'll be more comfortable out of this breeze."

"Of course." How could one refuse such a considerate suggestion? Or such beautiful eyes that twinkled with a hidden smile. I told Celia what he wanted. She hesitated then nodded, as if her permission mattered. If a ghost wanted to come into our house, he could.

He allowed me to enter behind Celia then followed—walking, as ghosts don't float like most people think they do. They get about by walking, just like the living. Oh and sometimes they disappear then reappear in another location, which can be disconcerting.

Bella our maid met us at the door and took our coats and Celia's bag. "Tea, Miss?" she asked.

Celia nodded. "For two thank you." She didn't mention the addition of Mr. Beaufort. Bella was easily frightened and we didn't want to lose another maid. The last three had left our employment after witnessing one of our in-house séances. It was difficult enough to find good help with what little we could afford to pay but it was made even harder thanks to our line of work. Gentlewomen of leisure may find our séances a diversion, but I've found the servants and poor to be far more superstitious.

Bella hung up hats and coats and had retreated down the hall to the stairs. I indicated the first room to our right. "If you wouldn't mind waiting in the drawing room," I said to Mr. Beaufort. "I need to speak to my sister for a moment."

The ghost bowed and did as I requested. "Celia," I said turning on her when he was no longer visible, "please don't ask him any questions about his death or haunting...or any morbid things."

"Why? We have a right to know more about the people we invite into our home, dead or alive."

"But it's so terribly..." Embarrassing. "...impolite."

"Nonsense. Now, why do you think he's here? To hire us perhaps?"

"I suppose so." I couldn't think of any other explanation.

"Good. Hopefully the other party can afford our fees." She tilted her chin up and plastered a calm smile on her face. "Come along," she said, "let's not keep him waiting."

Jacob Beaufort was studying the two framed daguerreotypes on our mantelpiece when we entered the drawing room. A small frown darkened his brow. "A handsome pair. Your parents?"

"Our mother," I said, "and Celia's father."

"Ah," he said as if that satisfied his curiosity. I could only guess what had piqued his interest. Most likely it was my skin tone, so dusky next to Celia's paleness, and the fact I looked nothing at all like either of the people in the pictures he held.

Celia sighed and sat on the sofa, spreading her skirt to cover as much of the threadbare fabric as possible, as was her habit when we had company. "Really, Emily," she muttered under her breath.

The ghost's gaze darted around the room. "Is there no image of *your* father here?"

"My father?" I said for Celia's benefit. "No."

She narrowed her gaze at me and gave a slight shake of her head as if to say *not now.* It was a well-chewed bone of contention between us. She insisted I call our mother's husband, Celia's father, Papa as she did. She in turn always referred to him as "*Our* father" and even Mama when she was alive had called him "Your Papa" when speaking of him to either one of us.

Despite the fact he'd died over a year before I was born.

I knew he couldn't possibly be my real father but I had long ago accepted he was the closest I'd get to one. Mama had refused to discuss the matter of my paternity despite my repeated questions. Not even Celia cared to talk about it, but I wasn't entirely sure she knew who my father was anyway. She had only been sixteen when I was born, and it was unlikely Mama had confided in her. It must have been terribly scandalous at the time, and explained why we never spoke to any of our relations and had few friends.

Although I accepted I may never know, a part of me still

burned to learn the truth. I'd even tried to summon Mama's ghost once after her death to ask, but she'd not appeared.

"Mr. Beaufort," I said, shaking off the melancholy that usually descended upon me when thinking of my father.

"Call me Jacob," he said. "I think we can dispense with formalities considering the circumstances, not to mention my attire."

"Of course." I tried to smile politely but I fear it looked as awkward as I felt. His attire was not something to be dismissed casually. It was what he happened to be wearing when he died. Mr. Wiggam must have died wearing his formal dinner suit but it seemed Mr. Beaufort—Jacob—had been somewhat more casually dressed. It's the reason why I'll never sleep naked.

"What's he saying?" Celia asked, linking her hands on her lap.

"That we're to call him Jacob," I said.

"I see. Jacob, do you think you could hold something so I know where you are? The daguerreotype of our father will do."

I rolled my eyes. There she goes again—*our* father indeed.

"That's better," she said when Jacob obliged by picking up the wooden frame. "Now, please sit." He sat in the armchair which matched the sofa, right down to the faded upholstery. "Who do you wish us to contact?"

"Contact?" Jacob said.

"She means which of your loved ones do you want to communicate with," I said. "We can establish a meeting and you can tell them anything you wish, or ask a question. It'll give you peace," I said when he looked at me askance. "And help you cross over. Into the Otherworld." Good lord, he must be a fresh one. But he didn't look in the least frightened or wary as most newly deceased do.

"For a small fee," Celia added. "To be paid by your loved one of course."

"You have the wrong idea," he said, putting up his free hand. It was broad and long-fingered with scrapes and bruises on the knuckles, which struck me as odd. They looked fresh. He must have got them just before he died. So what was a handsome man with an aristocratic accent doing brawling with his bare knuckles? "I'm not here to contact anyone."

Bella entered at that moment carrying a tray of tea things. I had to lean to one side to see past her rather prominent rear as she bent over to set the tray on the table. I forked my brows at Jacob to prompt him—asking him outright might seem a little odd to Bella, particularly if Celia, the only other person in the room as far as the maid was concerned, failed to answer.

"I'm here because I've been assigned to you," he said.

"What?" I slapped a hand over my mouth.

Bella straightened and followed my line of sight straight to the framed daguerreotype of Celia's father hovering—as she would have seen it—above the armchair. She screamed and collapsed onto the rug in a dead faint.

Celia sighed. "Oh dear. She was such a good maid too."

CHAPTER 2

"I don't think your maid will last long," Jacob said as the drawing room door closed on Celia guiding a trembling Bella down the hall.

I waited until the door was completely shut and Bella's terrified mutterings had faded before I spoke. "I hope she's already prepared supper." It sounded uncaring but I'd been in this situation before and it was very trying. As our only maid, Bella worked long, hard hours. I appreciated that enough to know I didn't want to take on her chores. "Good maids are difficult to find, particularly ones not afraid of the supernatural." Or ones we could afford.

"Have you tried the North London School for Domestic Service in Clerkenwell?" He returned the picture frame to the mantelpiece and remained standing. "They train suitable orphans in all aspects of domestic service and help them find employment by the age of sixteen or so. We've hired many of our servants from there."

"We?"

"Ghosts." I must have had an odd look on my face because he snorted softly which I think was meant to be a laugh. "Joke," he said without even a twitch of his lips. "I meant my family. The one I had before I died."

"Oh." I swallowed. So he came from a family wealthy enough to afford servants, plural. I wanted to ask more about his life but it didn't seem like the right time. It also wasn't the right time to ask about his death, although I'm not sure there ever is an appropriate time to enquire about that. It feels a little like prying into one's private affairs.

Besides, a far more pressing question was why was he standing in my drawing room looking every bit the gentleman of the house as he rested his elbow on the mantelpiece. Perhaps it was the casual attire that made him look like he belonged precisely *there* as if this really was his home. Or perhaps it was the strength of his presence. I think I would have known where he was at all times even with my eyes closed. A remarkable feat for a spirit. "What did you mean by assigned to me? Assigned by whom and for what purpose?"

"Assigned by the Administrators—."

"The Administrators?"

"The officers who control the Waiting Area and the gateway to the Otherworld's sections. They ensure each spirit crosses to their correctly assigned section, as well as keeping the Waiting Area orderly." It all sounded terribly efficient, more so than our own government's departments, notorious for their crippling rules and mountains of paperwork. "Haven't you ever asked the ghosts you've summoned about their experiences there?"

"Of course," I said, reaching for the teapot on the table beside me. "All the time." I poured tea into a cup. "Why wouldn't I?"

"You haven't, have you?"

I stared into the teacup and sighed. "Not really. I'm not sure I want to find out too much. I mean, I know about the Waiting Area and how ghosts need to release all negative emotions associated with this world in order to cross over but...I don't want to know anything more."

"You mean before your time."

I nodded. Hopefully I had many years to wait.

I glanced at Jacob over the rim of my cup and caught him watching me with a steely intensity that made my skin tingle. I blushed and sipped then risked another look. This time his attention seemed to be diverted by the tea service. I would have offered him a cup but there was no point since he didn't require sustenance. Perhaps I should have offered out of politeness anyway. I wasn't entirely sure of the etiquette for when ghosts came calling.

He really was undeniably handsome though. The more I looked at him, the more I liked his features. None were remarkable on their own—except for the vivid blue of his eyes—but together they made his face extraordinary. What a shame he was dead. Even more so because he'd come from a wealthy family—Celia would be particularly disappointed by the waste. The number of eligible gentlemen we knew could be counted on a butcher's hand—five less a few missing digits and fingertips. Perhaps it wasn't a complete loss however. Jacob might have a living relative or friend he wanted us to contact while he was here. Preferably one of Celia's age or a little older.

"So these Administrators," I said, "why have they sent you

here? Is it something to do with Barnaby Wiggam? Because if it is, I should explain that it was his own choice not to return to the Waiting Area. We tried to convince him—."

"It's nothing to do with Wiggam." He drew his attention from the tea tray and gave it all to me. There was heat in his gaze, an undeniable flare of desire that tugged at me, drew me into those blue eyes and held me there. I couldn't look away but I could blush and I did, although hopefully the darkish shade of my skin hid the worst of it. I hated being the center of attention, which made being a legitimate spirit medium a rather difficult occupation at times. As our reputation grew so did the stares and the whispers. But I'd never been the center of this sort of attention. No man had ever looked at me like that.

"Whether Wiggam's ghost wants to stay and haunt his wife or return to the Waiting Area is entirely up to him," he finally said, breaking the spell. "The Administrators allow spirits to make up their own minds. No, Emily, what you've done is something much more serious."

"Oh." My stomach dropped. I lowered the teacup to my lap and wished the sofa would swallow me up. "You're talking about that...that horrid shadow, aren't you?"

He nodded. "That shadow is a shape-shifting demon."

"What!" The cup rattled and I put my hand over it to still it. I stared at him and he simply stared back, waiting for me to ask the questions. I had many questions but all I said was, "I'm sorry" in a whisper.

He didn't say "You should be" or "You're a stupid girl" but simply "I know" in that rumbling voice that seemed to come from the depths of his chest.

"What is it? What does a shape-shifting demon do?"

"When it first emerges into this world it holds no shape. Its first instinct is survival, safety, until it can gather its strength. Once it has, it takes on the form of someone or something else almost perfectly." He paused and his lips formed a grim line. "And then it needs to satisfy its hunger."

From the way he couldn't meet my gaze, I suspected that hunger wouldn't be satisfied by buying fish from the markets. It would eat whatever it could kill. Rats, dogs. People.

I cleared my throat. "It was summoned quite by accident. I didn't mean to do it." Celia had better thank me later for taking the blame. It was entirely her fault that we'd released a demon with that new amulet. Not that I would tell Jacob. She was the only family member I had left and although we didn't always see eye to eye, we were all the other had and I wouldn't toss her into the lion's den, so to speak, even if the lion appeared relatively tame. I needed to find out more about Jacob and what the Administrators would extract for her folly first. I was better equipped than Celia to cope with the supernatural.

"Tell me how it happened," he said, sitting beside me on the sofa, not at the other end but close so that I could touch him if I moved a little to the right. I felt very alert and aware of him, but I could not meet that gaze. "I want to know exactly what was said, how it was said, and what object was used to summon it."

I stood, reluctantly, and fetched the amulet from Celia's bag. When I sat down again, I made sure I was sitting exactly where I had before, not an inch further away. I wanted to sit closer but I didn't dare even though Celia would never know because she couldn't see him.

"A peddler gave it to my sister."

"Gave it? She didn't buy it?"

"Apparently not."

He ran his thumb over the amulet's points.

"The woman said to repeat an incantation three times if we ever needed to solve something."

His hand stilled. "What was it?"

"We couldn't understand the words."

"But you repeated it nevertheless?"

I chewed the inside of my lower lip and shrugged one shoulder.

"Bloody hell, Emily, do you know what you've done?" He stood and paced across the rug to the hearth and back. He completed the short distance in two strides. "Shape-shifting demons are dangerous. They roam at night, searching for food. And I'm not referring to the pies and boiled potatoes variety. I mean living flesh and blood."

I gulped down the bile rising up my throat. "Oh God," I whispered. I pressed a hand to my stomach to settle it, but to no avail. It continued roiling beneath my corset. *What had we done?*

He suddenly stopped pacing and blinked at me. "Sorry," he said softly, "I shouldn't have gone into detail." He crouched in front of me and went to touch my hands, still holding my stomach, but drew back before making contact. "Are you all right? You've gone pale."

"That's quite a feat considering my skin tone," I said, attempting to smile. I reached out to press his arm in reassurance but he stood suddenly. All the softness in his eyes vanished and I bristled in response to the coldness in them. Obviously physical contact was not something he wanted.

I wondered when he'd last touched a live person. Unless he'd stumbled across someone else who could see spirits—and therefore touch him—it would have been before he died.

"If that incantation is what released the demon," I said, "then it's not a very fool proof system your Administrators have to keep them in check." I couldn't help the sarcasm dripping off the words like rain drops off leaves. His sudden changes of mood had me confused and bothered which in turn threw up my own defenses. I couldn't tell if he was friend or foe yet.

"I think we've already demonstrated that," he said.

I shot him a withering look. "They ought to have better mechanisms for controlling their demons."

"It's not just a matter of repeating the incantation. It must be done when the portals between this world and the Waiting Area are opened as they are during your séances." He held up the amulet. "And while touching a cursed object."

"Cursed? Someone has *cursed* that?"

He nodded.

"It really shouldn't have been given away then."

"Very observant of you."

Another withering look would have been excessive but I gave him one anyway.

He shot me a small smile in return which I found most disconcerting. But then the smile vanished and he was all seriousness again. "The amulet acts as a talisman," he said, "linking the wearer to the demon."

He dangled the amulet from its leather strap and dropped it into my palm. "We need to find the person who gave it to your sister. When does the peddler return?"

"Not until Thursday."

He rubbed his hand over his chin. "Damnation." He glanced at me and bowed his head. "Sorry for my language, it was inappropriate." Despite the bow, he didn't seem sorry at all. There wasn't a hint of regret on his face, just that smile again, as if he was amused at shocking me. Not that I was shocked. I'd heard worse at the markets.

"But you must understand," he went on, "that we need to locate this peddler as soon as possible."

"We need to?"

"You are the one who released the demon so it's only fair you bear some of the responsibility for returning it."

I bristled and bit the inside of my lip to stop myself telling him what had really happened. Celia had better appreciate my covering for her.

My sister took that moment to enter the drawing room

and promptly sat on the sofa and poured herself a cup of tea. She seemed completely oblivious to the tension in the room, even though it was so dense I felt like I couldn't breathe.

"Is the ghost gone?" she asked me.

"No."

"Well Bella is. Packed her bags and almost ran out the door. I couldn't get a sensible word out of her." She lifted her teacup to her lips then lowered it without taking a sip. "I'd no idea she was such a flighty girl. The next one should have a sturdier constitution. Have you still got a copy of the last advertisement we used, Em? No need to write it all out again."

"Jacob suggested we try a school in Clerkenwell. The children learn the art of domestic service there."

Celia scoffed into her teacup. "Hardly an art, my dear, if Bella's efforts at cooking were anything to go by. Very well, I shall go in the morning." She nodded at the framed daguerreotype of her father now back on the mantelpiece. "I see you've put the portrait of Father down." Her voice rose a little, the way it always did when she spoke directly to a spirit. As if it was hard of hearing. Not that she spoke to them very often. She usually left that part of the séance to me. It's why I was the one who received the strange looks from the guests. That way Celia managed to avoid the worst of the Freak label. "Do you mind very much picking it up again so I can see where you are?" she asked him.

Jacob crossed his arms over his chest. "Rather demanding, isn't she?"

I took two steps toward him, bringing me within arm's distance. "You may be ethereal but you are still a guest in our home, Mr. Beaufort, and I would suggest you behave as a gentleman would and do as my sister requests." His eyes grew wider with every word. I squared up to him, and although I was much shorter than he, I felt like I had the upper hand in the exchange. "Or have you forgotten how a gentleman should behave?"

He couldn't have stiffened any more if someone had dripped ice cold water down his spine.

"It is only polite after all to allow Celia to know your general location," I went on, "since you have the advantage of being able to see her."

He lowered his arms to his sides and nodded once. "Point taken." He edged around the furniture to the mantelpiece and picked up the other portrait this time, the one of Mama. "Lucky I'm a ghost or those barbs would have really hurt," he said to the daguerreotype.

My irritation flowed out of me at his absurd sense of humor. I controlled my smile as best I could however. It would have undermined my argument.

"I see you two have become further acquainted with each other during my absence," Celia said, eyeing me carefully. She forked one brow and I shook my head. I was in no danger from Jacob. He needed me to find the amulet peddler. And the demon. "Have you discovered what he means by being assigned to you?" she went on.

I explained about the demon we released, emphasizing the *we* and winking at her as I did so. Now that I had let Jacob think I'd been as guilty as Celia, I didn't want him to know I had deliberately misled him. It felt dishonorable somehow.

Apparently Celia didn't agree with me. "No," she said and placed her teacup and saucer carefully on the table. "I cannot let you take the blame, Em. I was the one who bought the amulet and it was I who invoked the demon. It was nothing to do with Emily," she said to Jacob.

He lowered the picture frame and regarded me levelly. "Very noble of you," he muttered. "And now I suppose I owe you an apology."

"Don't trouble yourself," I said more curtly than I intended.

He winced then bowed. "I've behaved despicably, both as a gentleman and as a guest." He spoke quietly and his mouth softened, no longer forming a grim line. "I hope you can forgive me." As apologies went, it seemed genuine. "I would ask the Administrators to assign someone else to you but there is no one else."

"Isn't the Waiting Area filled with thousands of ghosts? That's what several of them had told me and I'd never had any reason to doubt them.

"There is, but few are like me."

"You mean solid, or at least have the appearance of it?"

He nodded. "Without the solidness as you call it, I couldn't follow you wherever you go. Most spirits are limited to a specific location, as you know. I can go anywhere I please."

"Fascinating." I cast my eye over him again. He certainly looked nothing like the other ghosts with their fuzzy centers and fading edges. Indeed he looked healthy, full of life. And so handsome it was all I could do to stop myself from reaching out and caressing the skin at his throat. It would be smooth and butter-soft, I guessed, but cool. I'd only ever touched a ghost once before and she'd been cool despite it being a warm day.

"Really, Emily," Celia scolded.

I snatched my attention away from Jacob but tried my best to ignore my sister, which wasn't easy considering her annoyance vibrated off her. She didn't need to say anything else. We knew each other well enough to know what the other was thinking. In this case it was my fascination with Jacob. I could almost hear her asking me why a ghost and not the very much alive vicar's son from St. Luke's who always tried to touch my hand or some other part of me after Sunday service.

But how could she understand? She couldn't see Jacob. Couldn't get sucked in by those eyes, so like a dangerous whirlpool, or that classically handsome face. I could, and was, even though my brain told me I was a fool. He was dead.

"Why are you so solid?" I asked him.

He waved a hand and shrugged one shoulder. "It's just the way I am."

I had the feeling there was more to it than that but I didn't want to be rude and pry. Not yet anyway.

"So how do you propose to return this demon to the Otherworld?" Celia asked.

"We must discover who wanted the demon released and why," Jacob said. "We can start by understanding the words you spoke during the séance."

I repeated his answer to Celia and she in turn repeated the incantation. "It means nothing to me," he said, "but I'll ask the souls in the Waiting Area. It might be a more familiar language to one of them."

"Wouldn't the Administrators know?" I asked. "Or if not, can't they just summon the demon back again with an incantation of their own?"

"The Administrators don't have the power to reverse a curse issued in this realm. No one in the Waiting Area does. It can only be done by someone in this realm and only when the demon is near."

I swallowed and looked down at the amulet in my hand. "So much trouble over a piece of cheap jewelry."

"Keep the amulet with you. Whoever speaks the reversing incantation must be wearing it."

"I should be the one to wear it and seek out the peddler," Celia said. She held her head high, her chin up, as if defying us to disagree with her. Despite her stance, I knew she was afraid. The supernatural was my territory. She'd never been as comfortable around the ghosts as me, and demons were another matter altogether. The guilt over releasing one must be great indeed for her to make such a bold offer to rectify the situation.

"No," Jacob and I said together.

"You can't see or talk to Jacob," I said. "And we need his guidance in this."

She lowered her head and nodded. "Very well." She raised her gaze to where he stood, holding the frame. "Is it dangerous, this demon?" she asked, voice barely above a whisper.

"Not terribly," I said and tried to look like I wasn't lying. If she thought it was dangerous, she would not agree to my involvement, no matter how important. I glanced at Jacob but he said nothing, just watched me beneath half-lowered lids. "Don't worry, Sis, we'll send it back before anything happens."

Celia breathed out and settled into the sofa. "That's settled then," she muttered. "Now," she said to Jacob, "tell me *exactly* what you mean when you say you are assigned to my sister? Will you be at her side until the demon is found? Are you tied to her in some invisible way?"

Jacob went very still. "Tell your sister not to worry," he said stiffly. "I'll be the perfect gentleman."

I almost told him he'd mistaken her and she wasn't suggesting he'd do anything untoward, but I couldn't be sure if that assessment was correct. Knowing Celia, it was highly possible she meant exactly that.

As if understanding my hesitation, she added, "Can he protect you against this demon—and don't try to tell me it's harmless because I know it's not. It *is* a demon after all. And can he protect you against the person who cursed the amulet?" Her knuckles had gone white, clasped as they were in her lap. I gently touched her arm. It didn't seem to help—she remained as taut as a stretched rope.

Jacob took a long time to answer and I began to doubt he would when he finally said, "I will do my best." He held up the picture frame. "I can wield Earthly weapons as easily as I can hold this, but I'm afraid weapons from this realm have little effect on demons. They can only be killed with blades forged in the Otherworld. Unfortunately the Administrators don't have access to one which is why I prefer to banish it."

I squeezed Celia's arm again. "He said yes," I lied. "Don't worry, Sis, he looks very capable."

She stared straight ahead at the picture frame held by Jacob and gave a small nod. "Very well," she said in a tired voice. "You may accompany my sister to find this demon and return it. But if anything should happen to her," she coughed to cover her cracking voice but I heard it nevertheless, "I'll find someone who can make sure your soul never crosses over."

I stared at her open-mouthed. My sister, making threats to a ghost? Remarkable. I loved her for it.

She released her grip on the sofa and picked up her teacup. "It would seem nothing can be done before Thursday, anyway, when the peddler returns. The day after tomorrow. Until then, Mr. Beaufort." She nodded and sipped her tea. Dismissed.

He looked like he would argue but thought better of it and returned the daguerreotype to the mantelpiece. "Don't worry, I can see myself out." He bowed to us then vanished like a bubble that's been popped. There one moment, gone the next.

I flopped back in the sofa in a most unladylike fashion. "Oh Celia, I think we've bitten off more than we can chew."

She handed me my teacup. "We'll conquer this demon, don't fret, my dear."

I hadn't been referring to the demon.

CHAPTER 3

It took me a long time to fall asleep. It was bad enough knowing there was a demon out there hiding in the many shadowy lanes of London searching out something—or someone—to eat, but it was thoughts of Jacob Beaufort that occupied my mind more. Whenever I closed my eyes I could see his bright blue ones staring back at me with unnerving intensity. Now that I was alone I could think of a thousand questions I should have asked him, each one circling my head like a carousel. Finally, when the longcase clock in the entrance hall downstairs struck three, I'd had enough. I got up and threw my shawl around my shoulders then lit a candle and padded barefoot to my writing desk. I sat and pulled a piece of paper and the inkstand closer and wrote every question down, one after the other. Except one. I re-read my list and tried to tell myself it wasn't important, I didn't need to know the answer to it.

I wasn't very good at lying, even to myself. So I gave up and wrote the question at the bottom:

Did he meet Mama in the Waiting Area?

If he answered yes to that then there were so many other follow-up questions but I put the quill down without writing them. It was enough for now.

I fell asleep quickly after that.

Much later, I awoke to the sound of the brass knocker on our front door banging. It was daytime because light edged the curtains. It wasn't bright but then the days never were in London thanks to either the smog or rain or both.

I heard Celia's voice and listened for another but no one else spoke. Perhaps I'd imagined the knocking and she was simply reciting poetry in the kitchen.

But that was as absurd as it sounded. Celia regarded poetry as a useless form of literature read only by deluded romantics.

Then I heard footsteps running up the stairs. Only one set. "Emily! Emily, are you decent?" Celia shouted. "I think he's here."

"She means me," came Jacob's voice from just outside my bedroom door.

Jacob! Good lord, I was still in my nightgown! What was

he doing here so early? It couldn't be much past eight o'clock. What was he doing here at all when we'd agreed nothing could be done until the following day?

"She'll be out in a few minutes," I heard Celia say in a loud voice. The door opened a crack and she slipped inside. She was dressed but her hair looked like it had been hastily shoved under her cap. "My sister is not yet ready to receive callers," she said as she shut the door.

I heard Jacob's chuckle and I pictured his handsome features softening with his smile. "It's nice to know the rules of propriety still apply to the dead," he called out.

Celia leaned against the door as if barricading it. "He hasn't zapped his way in here, has he?"

"No. Help me dress," I said, climbing out of bed. "How did you know it was him?"

She passed me a clean chemise from the wardrobe, which I put on over my head after I shucked off my nightgown. "When I answered the knock there was no one there so I closed the door. But then I heard a knock on the hallway wall and I realized someone was inside, alerting me to their presence. The only ghost I know who has turned up here without being summoned is that Beaufort boy."

Hardly a boy. I made up my mind to ask him his age. Or his age at the time of his death. It was the first question on my list, still sitting on my desk.

"I told him I'd fetch you," she said, helping me into my corset. "But as I walked up the stairs I felt a coolness sweep past me and I knew he was going on ahead."

"At least he still possesses a sense of honor and hasn't entered." I gasped as she pulled hard on the corset's laces. "Careful, Sis, I might need to breathe at some point."

"Why bother breathing if you look fat?" We both knew she was being ridiculous—I was washboard flat in stomach and, alas, in chest—but she was in an odd temper so I let her comment go. "The green gown, I think."

"Really? What's the occasion?" The green dress was my newest and favorite. The color complemented my complexion and dark brown eyes. The bodice was shaped in the latest cuirass style, which hugged my frame all the way down to my thighs, emphasizing my small waist and the curve of my hip. It would have looked better on a taller girl, as did all dresses, but with heeled boots it looked quite good on me too. Although the satin had been recycled from one of Mama's old gowns, it nevertheless cost a great deal to have made. Celia had insisted on using the last of our savings for it. I suspected it was her weapon of choice in the battle to find me a husband. I supposed I looked quite good in it. Indeed, the dress never failed to turn heads, which was always a pleasant feeling when the heads were turned for the right reasons. Being singled out because I could see ghosts or because I wasn't fashionably pale, however, made me feel like the bearded lady in a sideshow.

So, considering it was a dress Celia made me wear whenever she thought eligible men would see me, it was a little disconcerting that she was making me wear it now when I was only seeing a ghost.

"I think Jacob will take you somewhere today," she said, fastening the hooks and eyes at the back of the dress. "He has a sense of urgency about him. Hopefully he wishes to communicate with his family after all, and if he has a brother or cousin..." She let the sentence drift, full of potential and possibility.

"It's more likely Jacob is concerned about the demon," I said.

She guided me to my dressing table and forced me to sit at the stool. "It can't hurt to be prepared," she said, undoing my braid. "You never know whose path you'll be thrown into."

I couldn't fault her logic although I didn't like to think about eligible gentlemen, or marriage or any of those things. Some girls of my acquaintance may be married by seventeen, but I wasn't sure wedlock was for me. What would happen to Celia? And why would I want to live with a man, by his rules, in his house, when I could live here with my sister and do as I pleased?

Besides, what sort of husband would want a fatherless bastard for a wife? And if my parentage didn't concern him, surely the fact I had conversations with the dead would.

A knock at my bedroom door made me turn around, yanking the hair out of Celia's hands. "Be still," she snapped, "or I'll have to start over."

"I can appreciate that a lady needs time to prepare herself to face the day," Jacob said through the door, "but do you think you could go faster?"

"He wants us to hurry up," I told Celia.

"Hurry!" she scoffed. "A lady cannot rush her morning toilette."

"I won't be long," I called out.

"Good because we need to get going," he said.

"We're definitely going somewhere," I said to my sister's reflection in the dressing table's oval mirror. "And where are we going to?" I shouted to Jacob.

He suddenly appeared in the room at my right shoulder, his back to me. I jumped and Celia tugged my hair. "Be still."

"Sorry," he said, "but I don't like shouting through doors. Can I turn around?"

"Yes," I said and hoped Celia thought I was speaking to her. I didn't want her to know he was in the room. She was already wary of him and for some reason I didn't want to turn that into outright distrust.

"It's like hundreds of little springs," he said in wonder, watching Celia's nimble fingers work my black curls into a manageable style on top of my head.

"Little springs turn into little knots very easily," I said.

Celia paused. "Pardon?"

"I, uh, was just thinking about my hair and how I wish the

curls were softer like yours." My gaze met Jacob's in the mirror's reflection.

He quickly glanced away, down at the dressing table, up at the ceiling, at the wall, anywhere but at me. "Just tell her to put it up as best she can," he said.

"He's growing impatient," I told her.

"He's no gentleman, that one," she said and put two hair-pins between her lips.

I cringed and caught Jacob's sharp glance in Celia's direction. He seemed...alarmed, and then embarrassed by her off-handed comment.

She removed the pins from her mouth and threaded them through my hair. "I wonder if he ever was one," she said, admiring her handiwork." Perhaps he lost all sense of honor when he died."

"Dying tends to cause one to misplace a great many things," Jacob said, voice dark and distant.

"Can you go out and tell him I'll be there in a moment," I asked Celia.

Her hand hovered near the hair above my temple as if she wanted to touch it but didn't want to mess up her work. "Be careful, Em." She kissed my forehead. "You do look lovely. Let's hope it's worth it."

She left and I heard her telling the empty air outside that I'd be there soon. Her footsteps retreated down the stairs and I turned to Jacob.

"You deserved to hear that if you come and go uninvited," I said.

"I'm not concerned about other people's opinions of me." He gave me a crooked smile. "It's a bad habit carried over from when I was alive."

It was the first time he'd referred to his life and what he'd been like. It wasn't what I'd expected to hear. Instead of giving me a clearer picture of him it just threw up more questions. Why hadn't he cared what people thought? "I'm sure people cared what *you* thought of *them*." I don't know why I said it but it seemed appropriate somehow.

He didn't comment but he was no longer smiling, crookedly or otherwise. Indeed, he'd turned all his attention to my hairbrush sitting on the dressing table as if it was the most interesting object in the world. Its tortoiseshell back and handle certainly weren't worthy of such scrutiny.

I knew an avoidance tactic when I saw one.

"How long ago did you die?" I asked him. He might want to avoid all awkward questions but I certainly wasn't going to shy away from them. If I was to spend time alone with him, I needed to know more about him.

"About nine months ago. I was eighteen." He shook his head, dismissing the topic. "Are you ready?"

So much for my investigative scheme. "Where are we going?"

He strode to the door. I pulled on my boots, quickly laced them and followed at a trot. "The house of someone I went to school with," he said, opening the door. "George Culvert. He lives in the Belgravia area with his mother."

"And why are we visiting this Mr. Culvert?"

He turned around and his gaze dropped to my waist and hips. His mouth fell open and a small, strangled sound escaped. "You're going to wear *that*?"

"Something wrong with it?"

"No," he said thickly. "But can you breathe?"

"Sometimes."

He laughed softly. "I like it. It's very...snug."

"So what were you saying about George Culvert?"

His gaze lifted to mine and a shiver rippled down my spine. His eyes blazed like blue flames but then he blinked rapidly and shifted his focus to something behind my left shoulder. He cleared his throat. "He's a demonologist."

"A what?"

"A demonologist. Someone who studies demons, fallen

angels, that sort of thing." He waved a hand casually, as if 'that sort of thing' was like studying for a career in law. "We can't wait until tomorrow to start looking for this demon. We have to start today. Now." He ushered me through the door onto the landing without actually touching me.

"Before it hurts someone?" I asked.

His gaze met mine for a brief second but in that moment I saw genuine worry in his eyes. There was no need for him to answer me. We both knew the demon might have already killed overnight.

"Why didn't it attack us when it was released in Mrs. Wiggam's house?"

"Until it makes contact with the master who set the curse on the amulet and controls it, the demon is weak and relies on instinct. It would have seen it was outnumbered and felt too vulnerable to attack so it fled. Once it felt safe, it would begin to search for nourishment."

I swallowed. "How awful. So tell me more about this Culvert fellow."

"George's father was a demonologist before his death and George has an interest in the field too."

"Demonology," I said. "What an odd thing to study."

"Not really. You'd be surprised at how many people are interested in the paranormal. Although I doubt there's much money in it. Not sure how his father could have sent George to Eton. He must have had another source of income."

"You went to Eton?" The boy's school was the most exclusive in all of England. Money wasn't enough to get accepted into the school, it required wealth *and* privilege. It would seem Jacob's family had both. Another piece to the puzzle that was Jacob Beaufort fell into place.

He shrugged and it would seem the question was dismissed, just like that. As if it were nothing. As if my curiosity could be swept away without consideration. It was most frustrating.

"I'll meet you there," he said. "I need to speak to more spirits in the Waiting Area."

"About the meaning of the words spoken in the incantation?"

He nodded. "The language must be an obscure one as none of the spirits I've asked so far knew its meaning. And anyway, someone might have heard of another demonologist who can aid us. That's how I learned Culvert's name."

"I thought you went to school with him."

"I did but we didn't socialize. Different friends, you understand."

I didn't. Not really. My formal schooling had finished at age thirteen, as it did for most girls, and I'd known every pupil at the small school. After I left, Mama had continued to tutor me and then Celia had tried after Mama's death, but much of my understanding of the world had come from reading books left behind in Celia's father's study. He'd been a lawyer and a great reader apparently. His study was still in tact and the bookshelves covered two entire walls, but most of the books were dry texts with only a few novels squeezed in between. Not a single one touched on the supernatural.

"So what shall I tell this George Culvert when I meet him?" I asked. "I can't very well ask him about shape-shifting demons straight away. He'll think it odd."

He paused then said, "Tell him you have a general interest in demonology and you'd like to look at his books." He shrugged. "We'll make it up as we go."

"Very well." I couldn't see any other way that didn't involve telling George Culvert everything. And that wasn't an option. Not yet. Not until I'd decided if I cared whether he thought I was mad for speaking to ghosts. "Give me Mr. Culvert's address and I'll meet you there after breakfast."

"Fifty-two Wilton Crescent in Belgravia." He gave me one more appraisal—a lingering one—from head to toe then vanished. But not before I saw the same heated flare in his eyes that had been there when he first noticed me in the dress. It would seem the gown hadn't lost any of its power.

Celia had a simple breakfast of toast and boiled eggs waiting for me in the dining room when I arrived.

"I thought we'd eat in the kitchen since we have no maid," I said picking up a plate.

"Just because there's no one here to see us doesn't mean we can let ourselves go. We have standards."

Celia had standards. I had a growling stomach and didn't care where I ate. I buttered a piece of toast and took two eggs from the sideboard and joined her at the table.

"What did he want?" she asked.

I filled her in and her interest piqued at the mention of George Culvert. "I wonder what he's like," she said more to herself than me.

"He went to Eton," I said, rapping the knife on the eggshell. "With Jacob."

I'd thought it impossible for her eyes to light up even more but they did. "Oh! He must be a gentleman then. I'm so glad you're wearing that dress, it's perfect. But you can't go alone. I'll accompany you."

"I'll be all right."

"Emily," she said on a sigh.

"Please, Celia, I'm old enough." Because our lives were so thoroughly interconnected, my sister and I usually went everywhere together. We just had no need to be separate. But of late I found I wanted to go out more and more without her. It would be nice to have people deal with *me* as an individual and a woman rather than as Celia's little sister. The visit to George Culvert was a perfect opportunity to do so and I wasn't going to let it pass me by.

She paused with her fork in the air, a piece of buttered toast only inches from her mouth.

"Jacob will be with me," I added before she could protest.

"That's all the protection I need. Besides, you've got to go to the Clerkenwell school and hire another maid."

She seemed to struggle between the two options. "It's not seemly for a young lady to pay calls on a young gentleman alone. You know that."

"His mother will probably be in at this early hour," I said hopefully. "And besides, I could be there all day studying his books." Celia's eyes went blank at the thought, just as I'd hoped. My sister had never been a great reader. Whereas I'd devoured all of her father's books, even the dull ones, she'd not been in his study for a long time. "Besides, if you don't find another maid today *you'll* have to cook supper. I'm sure I won't be home in time. And of course there's all the cleaning..."

Celia sighed. "You're right."

I ate the toast and one of the eggs and left the other. It was too dry. When we'd finished, Celia collected our plates. "You'd better go or Jacob will be back demanding to know why you haven't left yet."

She didn't need to tell me a second time. I'd avoided both the cooking and the cleaning so far but I wasn't about to test my luck by staying home any longer.

"Wear the hat that matches the dress," she said as I left. "But don't take a parasol. We don't have one in the right shade of green."

Five minutes later, I walked out the door feeling like a perfectly matching green peacock. A few pairs of eyes followed me down Druids Way and I can't deny that it felt good to be noticed for all the right reasons. It made a pleasant change to the suspicious glances usually cast my way by those neighbors and shopkeepers who knew I could speak to ghosts. The stares were something I'd not yet grown used to, even though we'd been in business for over a year. I wondered if there ever would be a day when I'd enjoy the attention.

Oh dear. It sounded like I resented being a medium and wished I didn't have the gift. Sometimes I did, true, but on the other hand I liked being able to reconnect people with their deceased loved ones. I just wished those same people wouldn't treat me with such wariness.

I had to hold onto my hat until I turned off Druids Way and the strong wind eased to a gentle breeze. The sun came out from behind the clouds, briefly, but did little to brighten the day, covered as it was by London's smoky haze. I knew how to get to Wilton Crescent so my thoughts were left to wander. And they didn't wander to the demon or the dangers it posed but to Jacob. The way he'd noticed me in the dress, and how he watched me with such intensity when he thought I wasn't looking.

But there was something troubling him too, something that had nothing to do with the demon. Despite telling me he didn't care what people thought of him, he seemed to bristle at Celia's assessment of his ungentlemanly conduct. And he avoided all questions about his life and what it had been like.

Was he ashamed of it? Or was there something else, something he was hiding?

Whatever it was, his behavior was very confusing, but then he was a ghost so I suppose he could do what he wanted.

I wished he'd accompanied me on the walk. The twenty minutes it took to reach Wilton Crescent would have given me ample opportunity to find out more about him. But then I would have drawn many unwanted stares by seemingly conversing with myself. The mere thought made me cringe and I lowered my head, not wishing to encounter any ghosts that happened to haunt the streets. I'd seen only two over the years who'd met with a road accident and had not progressed to the Waiting Area, having chosen to maintain the negative emotion tying them to this world. I never understood why anyone would choose to linger where they couldn't be seen or heard. Perhaps I would think differently if I were dead.

I turned into Wilton Crescent and strolled along the elegant curved street until I reached number fifty-two. It looked like the other grand houses in the crescent-shaped terrace with its cream stucco façade and colonnaded porch. The main difference I could see was the brass knocker on the door. It was shaped like a large paw.

A footman answered my knock and showed me into a spacious drawing room on the first floor crammed with furniture and knick-knacks. Aside from the usual piano, sofa and chairs, there were tables. Many, many small tables—a console table, a sofa table, at least three occasional tables and a sideboard. Scattered on top of them all were framed daguerreotypes, figurines, vases, busts, decorative jars, boxes and other little objects that seemed to have no use whatsoever except to occupy a surface.

I was admiring an elaborate display of shells arranged into the shape of a flower bouquet when a tall young man entered, smiling in greeting. He was handsome but not in the masculine, classical sense like Jacob but more angelic, prettier although not feminine. Definitely not. Blond hair sprang off his head in soft curls and his pale skin stretched taut over high, sharp cheeks. He wore small, round spectacles through which gray eyes danced. He looked younger than Jacob and if I hadn't known they went to school together and were about the same age, I'd have thought him my own age or younger.

"Miss Chambers?" He glanced around the room, perhaps looking for a chaperone. Eventually his gaze settled back on me, or rather my hips, before sweeping up to my face. His cheeks colored slightly. "The footman said you wished to see me and not my mother?" It was a question not a statement. Mr. Culvert was probably unused to visits from unchaperoned girls.

I cleared my throat then held out my hand for him to

shake. He looked at it like he didn't know what to do with it then took my fingers and gave them a gentle squeeze. "I'm definitely here to see you if you are Mr. George Culvert."

His face lit up. "Indeed I am." He squeezed again. His own hand was smooth, soft. It made me think of the split skin and bruises on Jacob's knuckles and again I wondered why a gentleman had hands more suited to a laborer or a pugilist.

Jacob chose that moment to appear beside me and I jumped in surprise. "Tell him you knew me before my death," he said, crossing his arms over his chest as he studied Mr. Culvert, "and that I told you about his interest in demonology. Pretend you also have an interest too and decided it was time you met. That should suffice."

But before I could say anything, Mr. Culvert said, "Do you have a supernatural matter to discuss with me?"

I choked on air and tried to cover it with a cough.

"Are you all right, Miss Chambers?" he said, frowning. "Tea is on its way but if there's anything else I can get you?" He took my hand again and patted it.

Jacob scowled at him.

I managed to stop coughing long enough to say, "Thank you, I'm fine."

Jacob, still scowling, approached our host and waved a hand in front of his face. Mr. Culvert didn't blink. "He definitely can't see me," Jacob said. "It must have been a guess—an uncannily good one."

"You're right," I said. "I do have a supernatural question. That's very intuitive of you, Mr. Culvert."

"Not really." He smiled sheepishly and dipped his head. "I happen to be aware of your work as a medium. I've wanted to meet you for some time." A faint blush crept across his cheeks. It was rather charming. Until I caught Jacob watching me out of the corner of my eye. No, he wasn't watching, he was *glaring* and his eyes had turned the color of a stormy sea. I tried not to look at him. I needed all my wits about me if I was to lie to George Culvert convincingly.

"So you believe I can really talk to spirits?" I said to Mr. Culvert.

"Yes of course. Why wouldn't I?"

"Many people do not."

"Many people don't know what I know about the supernatural." He indicated I should sit on the blood-red velvet sofa.

The footman re-entered carrying a tea tray stacked with tea things and a plate of butter biscuits, freshly baked going by their delicious smell. It was early for refreshments, early for making calls for that matter, but Mr. Culvert didn't seem to mind. Indeed, he seemed quite eager to chat. He sat in the chair opposite and leaned forward as the footman poured the tea.

I took my teacup and wondered where Mrs. Culvert was in the vast house. When the footman left I hazarded a glance at Jacob. He stood beside the mantelpiece, its height perfect for resting his elbow, and watched the proceedings with a closed expression. I thought he'd be impatient for me to ask questions but he said nothing, simply waited.

I decided to follow our original plan. "I heard about you through a mutual friend of ours," I said to Mr. Culvert. "Jacob Beaufort. I believe you went to Eton with him."

George Culvert's brows shot up into his snowy blond curls. "You knew him?"

I nodded and sipped my tea in an effort to disguise my lie. I had one of those faces that was easy to read so the better I hid it, the better I could lie. "His sudden death must have shocked everyone at the school."

"It must have, but I wouldn't know." He too took a sip of his tea but watched me the entire time over the rim of his cup. "He died after we'd both left Eton. Jacob had gone on to Oxford I believe."

My ghost had failed to mention that fact. Jacob shifted his weight. "It was so long ago," I said lightly. "I find it hard to recall the dates."

Mr. Culvert lowered his cup and locked his gaze with mine. "And he wasn't my friend."

Oh dear. This was going to be more difficult than I imagined. "He, uh, mentioned you though. Frequently."

Jacob groaned. "Tell him we were in the same debating team once."

"You were on the debating team together," I said.

"No, that was my cousin, another Culvert," Mr. Culvert said.

"Oh."

Jacob shrugged. "I thought it was him." He frowned, shook his head. "I just can't seem to recall him. The uncle I spoke to in the Waiting Area was adamant his nephew George went to Eton in my year level. Why can't I remember him?"

"It must have been some other team then," I offered. "Cricket?"

"I didn't play sports unless I had to," Mr. Culvert said. "And Jacob and I were never on the same team. He was always in the firsts—cricket, rugby *et cetera*. I was...not. So you see, I'd be very surprised if he noticed me at all."

Jacob sighed. "He's right. It's a large school and our paths probably never crossed."

"He was like that," Mr. Culvert went on.

"Like what?" I finally had a chance to find out more about my ghost and unfortunately he had to be listening. Perhaps I should have stopped Mr. Culvert before he said something Jacob ought not to hear.

Or perhaps not. I might not get another opportunity to discover more. If Jacob didn't want to listen he could simply vanish and return later.

Jacob, however, did not disappear. He'd gone very rigid and that steely glare was back. "Emily, don't," he said.

He was right. It wasn't fair. I sighed. "Nevermind," I said.

"I don't mind," said Mr. Culvert cheerily. He passed me the plate of biscuits and I took one. "But surely you would know what he was like, being his friend."

"Emily," Jacob warned.

"Uh..." With my mouth full of biscuit I couldn't say anything else without spraying crumbs in my lap and over the floor. The thick Oriental rug was so lovely and I really didn't want to embarrass myself in front of my host...

"He was quite oblivious to those around him, wouldn't you say?" Mr. Culvert said, somewhat oblivious himself to my plight.

Jacob stepped between us and I could practically see steam rising from his ears. "Emily, stop this line of questioning. Now." His fingers curled into fists at his sides. "Please." The plea, uttered so quietly I barely heard it, caught me off guard and I inhaled sharply.

It was the wrong thing to do. A clump of half-chewed biscuit lodged in my throat and a fit of coughs gripped me. Mr. Culvert handed me my teacup, stretching straight through Jacob to do so. I dared a glance at the ghost's face as I sipped. It was dark and threatening but there was something else there, something...vulnerable. I wanted to reach out to him but I dared not. Instead I held on tightly to the cup as I moved a little to the left along the sofa to see around him.

"Yes, oblivious," Mr. Culvert said, not looking at me now. He seemed lost in memories from his Etonian days. "And self-absorbed."

"Self-absorbed?" Jacob spun round. "I was not!"

"He had his circle of friends and anyone who fell outside that circle simply didn't get...seen." Culvert shrugged and I didn't get the feeling he was bitter, just observant. I suspect

George Culvert was very good at observing people. There was something quiet and watchful about him. Whereas Jacob was all contained energy simmering beneath the surface, Culvert seemed gentle to the core. I could imagine him watching people from a corner of a room through his spectacles, determining their strengths and faults, seeing how they interacted with others. Jacob on the other hand, was a man of action.

And the action I suspected he was about to perform could end in someone getting hurt and himself being exposed.

"Tell him I am not self-absorbed," Jacob snapped.

I gulped and tried not to look at him. "That's a shame," I said quickly. "Because you're both nice people. I'm sure you would have got along."

"Not everyone would think that way," Culvert said.

"Oh but you seem very nice to me."

He blushed again and bowed his head. "I was referring to Beaufort. He was well liked by most at school," he said, "adored even. But certainly not everyone put him up on a pedestal. I'm sure some would have preferred to drag him off it."

"I wasn't on any bloody pedestal," Jacob said, drawing himself up to his full height.

I found that hard to believe. I'd spent much of the previous night picturing him on one, made of white marble and carved in the Roman style.

Jacob edged toward Culvert, looking like he wanted to make his presence known in the most dramatic way a ghost can. It was time to steer the conversation away from the subject of Jacob before Culvert found the rug pulled out from under him, quite literally.

"Perhaps it wasn't Jacob who told me about your father's collection of books on demonology, perhaps it was someone else." I hoped I sounded convincing but I suspect I came across like a flighty female. "The fact of the matter is, I have an interest in demons and I'm hoping you'll be kind enough to allow me to make use of your library to further my studies."

Culvert pushed his spectacles up his nose. *"You're* interested in demons?"

"Yes. It's a natural extension from my other activities, don't you think?"

His mouth twisted in thought. "I suppose so. Is there any demon in particular you want to study?"

"Shape-shifting demons."

He paused. "Well that's a coincidence."

"Why?"

"A book on shape-shifting demons was stolen from my library just last week."

THE MEDIUM is now available.

A MESSAGE FROM THE AUTHOR

I hope you enjoyed reading THE WISDOM OF MADNESS as much as I enjoyed writing it. As an independent author, getting the word out about my book is vital to its success, so if you liked this book please consider telling your friends and writing a review at the store where you purchased it. If you would like to be contacted when I release a new book, subscribe to my newsletter at http://cjarcher.com/contact-cj/newsletter/. You will only be contacted when I have a new book out.

GET A FREE SHORT STORY

I wrote a short story featuring Lincoln Fitzroy that is set before THE LAST NECROMANCER. Titled STRANGE HORIZONS, it reveals how he learned where to look for Charlie during a visit to Paris. While the story can be read as a standalone, it contains spoilers from The 1st Freak House Trilogy, so I advise you to read that series first. The best part is, the short story is FREE, but only to my newsletter subscribers. So subscribe now via my website if you haven't already.

ALSO BY C.J. ARCHER

SERIES WITH 2 OR MORE BOOKS

Glass and Steele

The Emily Chambers Spirit Medium Trilogy

The 1st Freak House Trilogy

The 2nd Freak House Trilogy

The 3rd Freak House Trilogy

The Ministry of Curiosities Series

The Assassins Guild Series

Lord Hawkesbury's Players Series

The Witchblade Chronicles

SINGLE TITLES NOT IN A SERIES

Courting His Countess

Surrender

Redemption

The Mercenary's Price

ABOUT THE AUTHOR

C.J. Archer has loved history and books for as long as she can remember and feels fortunate that she found a way to combine the two. She spent her early childhood in the dramatic beauty of outback Queensland, Australia, but now lives in suburban Melbourne with her husband, two children and a mischievous black & white cat named Coco.

Subscribe to C.J.'s newsletter through her website to be notified when she releases a new book, as well as get access to exclusive content and subscriber-only giveaways. Her website also contains up to date details on all her books: http://cjarcher.com She loves to hear from readers. You can contact her through email cj@cjarcher.com or follow her on social media to get the latest updates on her books.

Printed in Great Britain
by Amazon